A Reasonable Arrangement

Annalise Allen

Contents

Chapter One: The Visit Begun - 1812

The road to Hunsford did not improve on acquaintance, but Elizabeth Bennet had learned, in one-and-twenty years, to be grateful for roads that went somewhere. This one went away from Longbourn in March, away from her mother's nerves and her sister Lydia's noise, and the specific friction of a household confined to itself through a long winter. Sir William Lucas and his daughter Maria had made the journey with her, propriety requiring a companion for so long a road, and Sir William being amiable enough to supply one without making the obligation feel like one. They had deposited her at the parsonage gate that afternoon and gone on, their part in the arrangement discharged with characteristic good humor.

Charlotte, now married these four months to her cousin, Mr. William Collins, met her at the gate of the Hunsford parsonage where they lived under the patronage of Lady Catherine de Bourgh. Collins stood to inherit Longbourn upon Mr. Bennet's death, the entail having arranged things so.

The match had been, to Elizabeth, a surprise; to Charlotte, she suspected, a calculation. They had not spoken of it directly.

Charlotte met her with the composed warmth of a friend who has made her choice and intends to be well, and Elizabeth, stepping through the gate, saw at once that she looked it: not merely settled, but composed in some more deliberate way that Elizabeth had not seen on her before.

The parsonage was orderly in a way that Longbourn, with five daughters and one ironic father, had never managed to be. The furniture was placed with a care that suggested thought rather than habit, not the care of a woman decorating, but of one who had studied where she would need to sit and arranged accordingly. The fire in the parlor was built to be warm without being extravagant. There were flowers on the table near the window, not many and not particularly fine, but positioned to catch what light the March afternoon offered, which was less than one might wish but more than nothing.

"You have made it very comfortable," Elizabeth said, and meant it.

"I have had time to consider what I wanted," Charlotte said, setting Elizabeth's traveling bag near the door.

Mr. Collins appeared before she had fully removed her gloves. He expressed, at considerable length, his gratification at her visit, his admiration of Lady Catherine's condescension in permitting it, Lady Catherine de Bourgh being the great lady of Rosings Park and the principal authority of the neighborhood in every sense she could arrange, and his settled conviction that the distance from Longbourn, though not inconsiderable, was nothing to a journey undertaken with proper planning and fair weather. The weather having been, he acknowledged, somewhat variable, but not, in his judgment, prohibitively so. He asked after her mother and sisters with the warmth of a man who had recently become part of the family and wished to make good on the connection. He asked after Mr. Bennet's health in a way that suggested he was preparing complimentary remarks for later use. He made observations about the journey that implied he had not made it himself but had formed strong opinions in the abstract, which was, Elizabeth supposed, the next best thing.

She answered him warmly, because he was Charlotte's husband and would be for the rest of Charlotte's life, and that fact had to be worth something in how one addressed him.

During this exchange, Charlotte had moved without appearing to move to the far end of the parlor, where she stood examining the arrangement of objects on the mantelpiece with the attentiveness of someone who has found, through practice, the exact distance at which a husband's remarks become inaudible. The distance was not large. Perhaps eight feet. Elizabeth noted it and put it away, with the comfortable room and the well-placed flowers and Charlotte's composed look at the gate, in a drawer of her mind she intended to return to.

She did not know what to make of any of it. She had had four months to decide, and found she was no closer.

In the days that followed, the parsonage and its habits became familiar. Charlotte managed the household as she managed everything: without display, and with a thoroughness that left very little to chance. She had arranged the rooms so that the study Collins occupied in the mornings was at a remove from the parlor she preferred. She had arranged the daily schedule so that he was often out during the hours she appeared to value, to the garden, the lane, a visit to Rosings, an errand whose nature was never quite specified but which reliably produced an hour or two of quiet. The house, in his absence, ran with efficient calm. The house, in his presence, ran with slightly louder efficiency, Charlotte directing the cook or reviewing accounts in a way that gave her occupation and Collins the impression of industrious domesticity, two things that were not always easy to reconcile and which she appeared to have reconciled without visible effort.

Whether this constituted happiness, Elizabeth could not determine. It constituted something. Charlotte did not appear to be suffering. She did not appear, either, to be someone for whom the question of suffering had recently been relevant. She was occupied, purposeful, and entirely engaged with the business of managing what she had chosen to manage. She asked Elizabeth about Jane, about the winter, about their mother's nerves and Lydia's latest escapades, with the warm interest of someone who had arranged her own life satisfactorily and remains genuinely curious about other arrangements. Elizabeth answered and watched and could not always tell, when Charlotte laughed at something, whether it was contentment expressing itself or discipline doing the same.

One morning she sat in the kitchen doorway and watched Charlotte direct the cook through the week's provisions; Monday the cold chicken, Tuesday the pork if the butcher proved reliable, a remove of some kind on Thursday, the preserves from the stillroom to be assessed before they planned any remove at all. Charlotte moved through the list with the calm of someone who had identified what mattered and made certain it was attended to, and the cook received her directions with a respect that came from experience of being well-managed rather than from ceremony. The kitchen ran. The garden ran, under Collins's enthusiastic stewardship, according to principles Lady Catherine had communicated and which he reproduced with the devotion of a man writing down scripture. The whole establishment ran reliably and smoothly on the energy of Charlotte's precision.

It was not the life Elizabeth would have chosen. But she had not been offered it on Charlotte's terms, at seven-and-twenty, with the drawing rooms thinning and the alternatives narrowing to a point. She did not think she was in a position to say with any confidence what she would have done.

She did not say this. Charlotte did not require her to, which was its own evidence of something Elizabeth had not yet classified.

On the second day, Mr. Collins walked her through the garden and along the lane and through the general geography of his consequence, which was considerable and required some time to convey. He pointed out the gap in the hedge through which Rosings was visible. There was one tall chimney and a section of east-facing gable in view, promising great things beyond. He indicated the road by which Lady Catherine's carriage most often passed, and the road from which her ladyship could sometimes be heard before she was seen, which constituted, he implied, an anticipatory pleasure available only to those who lived close enough to benefit from it. He showed Elizabeth the kitchen garden and the flower beds and the gate at the far end of the lane, and then he showed her the gate again from the other direction, because it was through this gate that Lady Catherine had once entered the parsonage grounds and declared herself satisfied with the cultivation of the beds; satisfied being a word he repeated with the gravity of someone quoting primary scripture.

"She must be a great comfort to the neighborhood," Elizabeth said. "So much attention distributed so generally."

"A comfort!" Mr. Collins stopped walking and turned to her with an expression of such earnest agreement that the word comfort seemed to have fallen significantly short of the thing. "She is, Miss Bennet, the most condescending of all great ladies. The word does not... it cannot fully... she condescends to interest herself in everything. The condition of the lane.

The welfare of the poorer cottagers. She has opinions about the timing of the harvest in the home farm, which the steward receives, one understands, with great respect. The arrangements of this household are naturally also — that is, Charlotte is very sensible of the privilege. We both are." He looked back toward the parsonage with the warm satisfaction of a man who has surveyed his prosperity and found it good. "I cannot imagine a more fortunate situation for a young clergyman."

Elizabeth said that she could see it must be a very agreeable thing to have so engaged a patron.

Mr. Collins said that engaged was the word, exactly the word, and then found several more things to show her, and she looked at all of them and said what was required, and kept her face in order through the portion of the circuit that passed within sight of the gap in the hedge, through which the chimney of Rosings stood against the sky in a way that was, she thought, admirably suited to the purposes of Mr. Collins's particular happiness.

The visit to Rosings occurred on the third evening. Elizabeth described it to her father that night, at the writing desk in the small room Charlotte had allotted her whose window faced east and away from Rosings, a detail she thought probably intentional.

She told him about the drawing room: large and cold and grand in the way of rooms arranged to produce an impression of grandeur, which is rather different from rooms arranged for the comfort of people who must sit in them. She told him about the fire, situated at the end of the room farthest from the guests, a distance that seemed, on a March evening, to have been decided upon by someone who was not planning to feel cold. She told him about Sir William and Maria, who had accompanied them and whose sense of occasion had been so engaged by the grandeur of the proceedings that their wonder performed the useful function of making Elizabeth feel, by contrast, entirely at her ease.

She told him about Lady Catherine.

Lady Catherine de Bourgh was very large in presence and very decided in opinion, and appeared to feel that these two qualities, taken together, constituted wisdom — a confusion, Elizabeth had observed, common to people who have never been seriously contradicted in a room they own. She had conducted a thorough inventory of Elizabeth during the course of dinner: her age, her education, whether she had had a governess, whether she played and to what standard, whether she drew, whether she sang, whether her sisters were also out and did not their mother find it rather trying to manage so many of them at once without anyone to relieve her.

She delivered observations about Elizabeth's answers before Elizabeth had quite finished giving them. She had opinions about the Bennet household's management, Elizabeth's playing, the scheduling of young ladies' accomplishments, and the general approach to winter travel, none of which she had been invited to share and all of which she appeared to consider well within her jurisdiction, the limits of her authority extending, as far as Elizabeth could determine, to whatever room she happened to be occupying.

Elizabeth had answered every question with a composure she was reasonably pleased with. Lady Catherine appeared to regard the composure as either admirable or insolent and had not yet settled the matter, the ambiguity seeming in itself to constitute a mild impertinence that she intended to investigate further. Elizabeth rather looked forward to the investigation.

She told him that the plate was very fine and very numerous, and that Mr. Collins had catalogued it on the walk home, so that no one need feel uncertain about its provenance or quantity.

She told him she was very glad she had come.

She sealed the letter and set it on the corner of the desk for the morning post. The candle had burned down while she wrote, and she did not immediately get up to replace it but sat in the partial dark for a while with the house quiet around her. Through the east window, the lane was a pale line. She was thinking, with some part of her mind, about Lady Catherine's certainty that her observations were owed to whatever room she entered, the absolute fluency of it, the way she moved through opinion as through owned territory. And with another part, rather more quietly, about Charlotte managing a household in the precise direction she had chosen, eight feet from whatever remarks she had decided not to hear.

She was not thinking about the future with any urgency. The future was Longbourn and Jane and her father's letters and the texture of a life whose shape she knew exactly. It would be there when she returned. It always was.

His reply came four days later. One page, in the hand she would have known without a signature.

He had read her account of Rosings with, he said, very great satisfaction. It confirmed several suspicions he had long entertained about the internal temperature of grand rooms and the principles governing where fires were placed in them. He was assembling questions for Lady Catherine's particular method of wisdom and intended to put them to Elizabeth upon her return, at which point he trusted she would have gathered sufficient evidence to supply authoritative answers.

He was well. Her mother was very sensible that the Lucases should have had the pleasure of the journey when no Bennet daughter of equivalent usefulness had been free to take it. He did not say which daughter would have been equivalent, but the implication was clear enough.

Kitty had a cold and was managing it with the energy she generally brought to things that attracted sympathy. Lydia had visited Meryton three times in four days, which was not a cold but might, he suggested, benefit from the same treatment: confinement, some distance from other people, and the limited stimulation of a quieter room. Mary had discovered an author on the subject of moral improvement whose arguments she was pursuing with an intensity he expected either to have reformed her entirely by spring or confirmed her in everything she already believed, the distinction being, he thought, probably immaterial.

He had enjoyed her letter very much. He generally did.

Elizabeth read it twice: once for the sense of it, and once more slowly, for the pleasure of his company at a distance, which was one of the more reliable pleasures of her life and one she appreciated in direct proportion to the distances she had tested it over. She folded it carefully along its original creases and placed it in the writing case, in the section where she kept his letters, which was where she kept all of them, without having made a conscious decision to do so.

It was, she thought, exactly what she had expected him to say.

Outside the east window, the afternoon was bright and still. Mr. Collins was visible at the far end of the garden with a spade, doing something methodical and absorbed that had the quality of a man executing instructions he had received on good authority and intended to honor. From downstairs came the sounds of Charlotte in the parlor: a page turned, a chair adjusted, the fire worked with a small iron that rang once and then was silent. The house held these sounds the way it held everything — quietly, efficiently, with the particular competence of a place that was arranged to work.

Elizabeth's own life was waiting for her at a distance she could calculate exactly: Longbourn, Jane, her father's next letter, the familiar disorder that was, in the end, her familiar disorder and therefore entirely different from anyone else's. She could return to it whenever she chose. She would, in a fortnight, close the writing case and put it in the coach and go back to all of it, and it would be exactly as she had left it.

She put the writing case on the shelf above the desk and went downstairs.

She was nearly at the parlor door when the maidservant appeared from the hall with the small correspondence tray, and on it a letter. It was not the ordinary morning post, which had come and gone already, but an express by the look of it, the paper thicker, the seal pressed in haste. She took it before the girl had finished offering it. The direction was in Jane's hand. The border of the envelope was black.

Chapter 2: The Express

She had received Jane's letters all her life. She knew the handwriting from a hundred notes and a few years of correspondence sent back and forth during visits of varying length, the careful regularity of it, the even spacing of the lines. She recognized it the moment the tray was offered, and she had taken the letter without looking at the maidservant. The maidservant had withdrawn, and Elizabeth was still standing in the doorway of the parlor with the letter in her hand, because the border of the envelope was black.

Charlotte's pen had stopped moving. Elizabeth was aware of this without turning toward it. She was aware, also, of the fire and the arrangement of the chairs, the room entirely as it had been a moment ago when she had come downstairs expecting nothing more than tea. She crossed to the table, sat down, and broke the seal.

She read the first line and then she read it again, because the grammar of it did not resolve on the first pass into anything she recognized as possible. The second reading produced the same result as the first. The sentence remained what it was.

Her father was dead. A seizure, sudden, two days ago. There had been no illness before it, no period of decline that might have softened the fact by making it something that was coming rather than something that had arrived. He had been at breakfast, Jane wrote. And then he had not.

Elizabeth sat with the letter in her hands and did not move. The fire was the same fire it had been a moment ago. The flowers Charlotte had placed near the window were the same flowers. Outside, the lane ran between the same hedges in the same thin March light. Charlotte's pen continued its movement across the page. None of this was altered. Elizabeth was aware of each of these facts with a sharpness that had nothing to do with caring about them, the mind fixing itself to the surfaces of things when the thing it is actually required to absorb is too large to absorb directly.

Charlotte had looked up. Elizabeth did not know how long ago that had happened. It could have been moments or longer. Whatever her own face had done in the interval, it had been enough, because Charlotte set her pen down without any explanation being offered and came around the end of the table and sat. Not across from Elizabeth, beside her close enough that the presence was felt without being imposed. She did not reach for the letter. She did not ask what had happened. She did not offer the quality of sympathy that requires the recipient to attend to the feelings of the sympathizer, the kind that produces more work than it relieves. She said nothing and was there, and Elizabeth, who had not known until that moment what she required of another person, understood that this was precisely it.

She read the letter a third time. She read the sentence about breakfast. Jane had written it plainly, without softening, because Jane understood that the plain sentence was the honest one and that what Elizabeth would want was the honest account. She read the apothecary's note, transcribed in Jane's careful hand, and the brief account of the house in the hours afterward, and the sentence about their mother, which said that Mrs. Bennet was in great distress and that Mr. Jones had been sent for a second time.

Jane did not editorialize. She had never been a person who editorialized. She reported what had happened in the order in which it had happened, and Elizabeth was grateful for this in a way she could not have explained to anyone who had not, at some point, desperately needed facts rather than comfort.

"My father," she said.

Charlotte said she was very sorry. She said it once and did not add to it. The brevity was the right choice. Elizabeth received it as it was meant.

Mr. Collins returned from the glebe before noon. He came into the parlor still carrying his hat, his outdoor color high, his expression arranged in advance into something that announced itself as solemn attention. The maidservant had told him something, evidently, enough to allow him time, on the walk back from the gate, to prepare. He set his hat on the side table. He looked at Elizabeth. He drew a breath that was its own small performance.

He expressed himself at length. He began with the uncertainty of human life, moved through the dispensation of Providence, touched on the particular affliction of losing a father as opposed to other relations, and arrived at the duty of Christian resignation, which he recommended warmly and in some detail. He spoke of Mr. Bennet with a generosity that owed more to the occasion than to personal acquaintance, attributing to him several qualities of diligence and piety that Elizabeth had not, in two-and-twenty years of observation, noticed him to possess in any great degree — though she understood that this was Collins being kind, in his fashion, which was not nothing.

Then he addressed the entail. He had felt it necessary, he said; he trusted Elizabeth would understand that it was necessary to raise the subject directly, since it was a matter she would be aware of and since he did not wish there to be any sense of obscurity or embarrassment between them on a point that was already, he feared, a source of considerable distress to the family.

He wanted Elizabeth to know and he hoped she would convey this to her mother and sisters that the entail was not a circumstance of his own devising. He had not written the laws of property. He had not arranged the documents that governed the descent of Longbourn. He had inherited the legal situation as he had found it, and he intended, he was quite decided on this, to approach whatever practical arrangements became necessary with every consideration for the feelings and comfort of the bereaved family.

He would not be in haste. He wished them to understand that. He would not act with any want of feeling for their situation. He intended to handle the matter with the utmost - here he paused and selected the word - delicacy. Yes. Delicacy. He hoped they would believe him.

Elizabeth said that she was sure of it. She said that it was very thoughtful of him to address the matter so directly. She said that she was grateful for his condolences and for his kindness, and that she was sure her mother and sisters would feel the same. She said these things with the steadiness of someone who has located a particular resource within herself and is drawing on it carefully, aware that it is not inexhaustible. Then she excused herself and went upstairs.

She climbed the stairs slowly, not because her legs required it but because the landing was a place between rooms and for a moment she did not know which room she was going to or what she would do when she arrived in it. She was aware, on the stairs, of the sounds of the house continuing around her: Collins's voice saying something to Charlotte in the parlor below, the cook moving in the back of the house, the ordinary household noise of a Tuesday morning at the parsonage, unchanged, all of it unchanged, and her father three days dead and the letters on the desk in her room waiting to be read again.

Before she left the room, she caught Charlotte's eye for the space of a second. Charlotte did not say anything. The look said that she had heard every word her husband had spoken, had understood its practical implications rather more clearly than she would ever say aloud to anyone, and that Elizabeth might want to think carefully, and with some urgency, about what her situation actually was. It was efficient. Charlotte had always been efficient.

A letter arrived in the early afternoon on Friday. Elizabeth was at the writing desk in her room, Jane's letter open before her having been reread several times, the east window showing a sky that had flattened to dull white, a day that had given up on being fine without committing to rain. This letter was from her aunt, Mrs. Gardiner of Gracechurch Street, her mother's brother's wife and the most practically intelligent person of Elizabeth's acquaintance. Mrs. Gardiner did not write letters carelessly. Every sentence was written to be read.

She had received Jane's express and was writing with further information now that there was some to share. She wrote with the precision of a woman who had assessed the situation and concluded that what Elizabeth needed first was not sympathy but information, sympathy being better received once the recipient knows clearly what they are being sympathized about. Her father had died on Sunday morning. Mr. Gardiner had gone to Longbourn at once, arriving Monday evening. The following was the state of things as of Wednesday, the day she wrote.

Mr. Collins had sent an express letter to Longbourn. It had arrived, Mrs. Gardiner noted, early Wednesday morning, which said a great deal without requiring her to say it. The letter had expressed condolences. It had also communicated Mr. Collins's intention to take possession in a manner consistent with the legal situation, and had expressed the hope that the family would find themselves in a position to make whatever arrangements were necessary within the month.

Mr. Gardiner was doing what could be done. Mrs. Bennet was not, at present, able to assist in the management of the household's practical affairs and was not expected to become so in the near term. Jane was managing with admirable composure and should not be left to manage alone longer than necessity required. As to the question of funds for Elizabeth's return to Hertfordshire: the household accounts were not, at present, equal to the expense. Mr. Gardiner expected to arrange something within the fortnight, though he could not at this moment commit to a precise date. She trusted Elizabeth was comfortable at Hunsford and that Mr. and Mrs. Collins had been attentive.

Elizabeth read this letter straight through, and then read it again from the sentence about the household accounts. She had not misread it. She set it beside Jane's letter on the desk and looked at both of them and the room was very quiet.

Sir William and Maria were due to pass back through in two weeks on the way to Hertfordshire. She could ask, without difficulty or ceremony, to travel with them. Sir William was entirely agreeable by nature, and Maria would welcome the company. The road was the same road. She could be home before the end of the week, if she asked.

She could be home, that was, if home was a place she could return to. And that was the question the two letters had combined to make genuinely uncertain in a way it had not been before this morning.

She had not thought about the entail with any real seriousness before today. It had always been present at Longbourn in the way that certain large uncomfortable facts are present in a household. It was acknowledged in outline, referenced occasionally in her mother's more agitated speeches, but never examined directly by the people most affected by it because direct examination would require sitting with conclusions that nobody was prepared to sit with. Her father had managed it with irony, which she had taken, without ever articulating the assumption, as a way of managing it at all. Her mother had managed it with anxiety, which was her method for managing everything, and which had the effect of making the anxiety about the entail indistinguishable from the anxiety about the next assembly, or the state of a particular bonnet, or whether a given officer had been sufficiently attentive to Lydia. The result was that Elizabeth, at one-and-twenty, understood the broad view of her family's situation without having worked through what it all meant in practice when the entail was no longer a vague future fact but a document in motion.

She worked through it now. The estate went to Collins. That was the center of it, the point from which everything else proceeded. The house went. The home farm and its income went. The contents of the house were her father's and therefore now, in a sense she did not have time to be precise about, Collins's as well, though in practice she thought he would not press that particular point immediately.

Her mother's own income was something under fifty pounds per annum, derived from her marriage settlement and entirely independent of Longbourn, which was one fact on the right side of the ledger. Her own portion and those of her sisters were approximately one thousand pounds each, left by her uncle Philips and generating perhaps forty or fifty pounds a year in interest at any reasonable rate. She was one of five daughters. The five portions together amounted to perhaps two hundred pounds a year in income, added to her mother's fifty. Two hundred and fifty pounds a year, for six people, assuming they could all live together in a single establishment. Two hundred and fifty pounds a year was not nothing. It was also not, by any honest arithmetic, enough.

She went through the connections. The Gardiners were generous and would do what they could, and she trusted them to mean it, but Mr. Gardiner was a man in trade supporting a household of his own, and Gracechurch Street had its limits. She could not ask the Gardiners to absorb five Bennets for any extended period without that generosity beginning to constitute an imposition on a family that had done nothing to deserve imposing upon.

Her Aunt Philips was in Meryton and had a smaller house than Longbourn and fewer resources. There were cousins on her mother's side: the Longs, who were comfortable, and the Gouldings, who were not exactly comfortable, and there was a connection in Derbyshire that her mother occasionally mentioned, and there were one or two others that she worked through in turn, holding each one against the question, and each one failed it in some respect that could not be rearranged away.

Jane had not found her situation. She was two-and-twenty, steady, and genuinely good and had not, as yet, found it, and the winter had not produced anyone likely to supply it. Netherfield had been emptied of its hope when Bingley left in November without a word that adequately explained his departure.

Without a household to operate from, Jane's prospects for finding her situation were materially reduced, because the society that produced eligible men required the kind of continued presence in that society. That required an address and an income to support it. Lydia and Kitty were younger and further from the question, which meant they were also further from any solution it might supply. Mary's priorities were spiritual and literary and not, as far as Elizabeth could determine, oriented toward the practical problem currently before all five of them.

She could go to Hertfordshire with Sir William on Thursday. She could be on the road within two days, in a respectable carriage, with companions who would ask nothing of her beyond ordinary civility. She could arrive in Hertfordshire at the end of the week.

But the thing she had been planning to return to, Longbourn, the known disorder of it, her father's study with his particular books in their particular disorder, Jane in the room next to hers, the lane between the house and the road that she had walked since she was a child was not, she now understood, what she would find when she got there.

What she would find was a house that had been served notice. A household in the process of being vacated of what made it a household. Sir William's carriage could carry her to Hertfordshire. It could not carry her to the thing she had been calling home when she was thinking, this morning, about going there.

She got up and went to the window. The lane was still there. The gap in the hedge at the far end showed the chimney of Rosings above the trees; the same chimney Collins had pointed out with the satisfaction of a man surveying the outer borders of his good fortune. She looked at it for a moment. Then she returned to the desk.

She picked up Mrs. Gardiner's letter and read the relevant passages one more time, in case she had misread something. She had not. She set it down and picked up Jane's and read the sentence about breakfast - her father at breakfast, and then not - and then she set that down as well.

She took up the pen. She went through the figures one more time, arranged them in order, and examined the result. She had made no error.

The numbers came out the same way they had come out before, and the same way they would come out if she did it again, which she did not intend to do.

She put down the pen.

Chapter 3: The Limits of Collins

The difficulty with Mr. Collins was not malice. Elizabeth had thought, in the first hours after Jane's express, that malice might have been easier, something to push against, a reason to feel the anger that kept circling the grief and not quite landing. But Collins was not malicious. He was impervious, which was an uncommon thing and harder to manage.

He came to find her the morning after she had received Mrs. Gardiner's letter, while Charlotte was in the kitchen and the parsonage was quiet. He wore his expression of condolence like a garment selected with some care; not ill-fitting exactly, but belonging to someone else, and the face of a man who had imagined grief often enough to produce a reasonable facsimile of it.

"My dear Cousin Elizabeth," he said, "I trust you have found some comfort in reflection upon the natural order of providence, which ordains that all earthly arrangements must come to their appointed conclusion."

Elizabeth said she had.

"The entail," he continued, settling into the chair across from her with the air of a man preparing to be helpful, "is of course a very ancient and rational instrument, designed by those wiser than ourselves to ensure the proper succession of property. I am certain that Mr. Bennet himself, in his more composed moments, would have acknowledged the justice of it."

She was watching a spider negotiate the corner of the window frame. The spider was making better progress than this conversation.

"I have taken the liberty," Collins said, "of writing to Longbourn on the matter of the estate's administration, so that your mother and sisters may have early reassurance as to the orderly transition that will follow. I flatter myself that my letter will provide a measure of comfort."

He looked at her with an expression of modest satisfaction.

Elizabeth said that was very good of him. It came out more flatly than she intended, but he received it as warmth.

He had offered, the evening before, to write on her behalf to arrange the particulars of her return journey, to smooth the way, as he put it, for her passage back to her family. The offer had sounded like assistance. Examined overnight, it contained no actual provision: no mention of funds for the posting fees, no arrangement with a neighbor who might share a carriage, no practical mechanism by which Elizabeth Bennet, currently a guest in a house that now belonged to him, was to get herself from Kent to Hertfordshire on less than two pounds and the goodwill of the road.

Charlotte appeared in the doorway. Her glance at Elizabeth was brief and contained considerable information.

She looked at her husband and said, "I believe you were expected at Rosings this morning."

He was. He had entirely forgotten. He gathered himself with the efficiency of a man who keeps his obligations to Lady Catherine organized above all others, expressed again his sincere condolences, and was gone.

Charlotte sat down in the chair he had vacated. She did not speak immediately. Outside, a great deal of wind blew across the gardens . The window rattled once and then settled.

"How long had you planned to stay?" she asked.

The question was asked in Charlotte's usual manner, quietly, as if she were asking about the weather and not about the fact that neither of them could say directly what they were both thinking.

"Three weeks," Elizabeth said. "I had not planned beyond that."

Charlotte nodded. She picked up her mending from the basket beside the chair, not to work it, Elizabeth thought, but to have something in her hands.

"The arrangements here," Charlotte said carefully, "are naturally somewhat dependent on—" She paused and chose her words. "Mr. Collins has his own household now to consider."

Which was not Charlotte's household. Which had never, technically, been Charlotte's household, though Charlotte had arranged every part to suit herself and managed it with the quiet competence of someone who understood perfectly that the bargain she had made was a bargain, and that a bargain honored efficiently was the best that could be said of it. Elizabeth had always respected this about her. She respected it more now.

"I understand," Elizabeth said.

"I am not--" Charlotte began, then stopped.

"I know you are not," Elizabeth said. "Charlotte. I know."

She looked up from the mending she had not touched. Something in her face that had been managed very carefully for the past days shifted, briefly, into the expression of someone who would have said more if more could be usefully said. Then she folded the mending and put it back in the basket.

"I will ask about carriages going north," she said. "Someone passing through will have room, perhaps."

Elizabeth wrote to Jane that afternoon.

"I cannot come yet. Tell me what is happening with the house. Tell me what you need."

She sealed it and gave it to the boy who ran letters to the village. Then she sat at the writing desk and wrote nothing else for a considerable time.

The desk was Charlotte's. It was practical and neat, with a small jar of dried lavender set in the corner that Elizabeth had not noticed until now. She noticed it now. She thought about her father's study, which smelled of pipe tobacco and old paper and a particular variety of must that she had always associated with books that had been loved rather than preserved.

She had not written to tell anyone in Hertfordshire what she had worked out. There was no point in it yet. The arithmetic was straightforward enough: the posting fees for a private carriage would take more than she had with her, and sharing a chaise required coordination that took time, and time was the one thing that was also running out.

Mrs. Bennet could not manage the correspondence with Collins. Elizabeth knew this the way she knew the sound of her mother's voice when it reached the register that meant panic had overtaken sense. Jane could manage the correspondence, but Jane was already managing their mother, and the younger girls, and the household, and whatever her own feelings were on the matter of their circumstances; all of it with the composure that Jane applied to things when composure was needed and nothing else was available.

The letter from Jane arrived the following morning. It had crossed Elizabeth's own in the post.

About Mr. Collins, "He has been civil," she wrote. "Very civil. He expressed his sincere condolences and his intention to take possession at the end of the quarter. I cannot be certain, but Collins's name was mentioned in a letter we saw Mother reading, and she has not been calm since. Mr. Gardiner has been written to. He is in trade, Lizzy, and you know he cannot simply leave his business. He will come again as soon as he is able."

Elizabeth read this twice. Then once more.

"At the end of the quarter" was six weeks. Six weeks from now, her family would require another address. Mr. Gardiner could not be in Hertfordshire before the week was out at the earliest, and even then, his authority was moral rather than legal. He could advise, he could advocate, he could write letters; he could not alter the entail. Collins would take possession of Longbourn. The only question was what happened to the Bennet women when he did.

She folded Jane's letter into the writing case beside her father's last note: the wry, brief, pleased letter from three weeks ago, which now read like a dispatch from a country that no longer existed.

She went for a walk.

The path behind the parsonage ran along the edge of the park and then out into a lane that eventually reached the road to Rosings, but she turned before the road and walked instead toward the field where Collins's glebe land gave way to common ground. The wind was still up. Her half-boots were not ideal for the mud near the stile, and she navigated it with the attention it required.

She thought about the entail.

Not as an injustice. She had thought about it as an injustice many times, had said sharp and accurate things about it in conversation, and none of it had produced any practical result. She thought about it instead as a mechanism: a set of specific actions that Collins was legally entitled to take, arranged in a specific sequence, with specific consequences at each step.

Door closing. Furniture assessed. The question of where Mrs. Bennet was to go, and Lydia, and Kitty, and Mary, and Jane. Jane who would not complain, and who deserved better than to spend the next several years in a situation she had not chosen and could not correct.

And Elizabeth, who was in Kent.

There was nothing shameful in being in Kent. She had come at Charlotte's invitation and with her father's blessing, and she could not have known, two weeks ago, that his blessing would be the last thing he gave her. The situation was not her fault. The situation was also not improved by the assignment of fault.

She walked back to the parsonage. The mud had got into the seam of her left boot somewhere near the stile, and she felt it with every step on the return, a small, cold, specific discomfort that required no interpretation.

Charlotte had left tea on the table in the front parlor. She was not in the room, but the tea was fresh. This was, Elizabeth thought, a very Charlotte thing to have done.

She poured a cup and sat down and considered her options with the same method she had applied to the entail: not as an emotional question but as an arithmetic one. What she had. What each possibility cost. What the numbers came to.

By the time the tea was cold, she had run through the arithmetic twice. It came out the same way both times.

She needed either money or a plan. She was not certain yet which was more likely to arrive first.

The answer, when it came, was neither.

The reply from Jane the following day. Her second letter, written after she had received Elizabeth's, was composed in Jane's particular style of conveying alarming information in the most temperate language available.

"Lizzy, I think you must not hurry back on our account, because there is very little that can be done at present, and I have the Gardiners' letter to expect within the week. Mother is better than she was, though she requires a good deal of managing, which Mary has attempted with more earnestness than success. Collins's letter was rather formal, which I think alarmed her less than a warmer one might have done, because she could not find in it any cruelty to fix upon. We are all quite well. I hope you will not worry."

Elizabeth read, "I hope you will not worry" and set the letter down.

Jane, who had written that sentence while managing their mother and the household and the correspondence with Collins and the uncertainty about their home, was asking Elizabeth not to worry.

She was going to worry. The worry was rational, and the information warranted it.

What she would not do was despair, because despair was not useful and she had not the luxury of it.

She went to the writing desk and took out a fresh sheet of paper and tried to think of who else she might write to, and what they could be reasonably expected to do, and what the practical effect of it would be.

She wrote three letters and tore up two of them. The third she kept, because it said only what was true and asked only what was possible, and there was no point in anything beyond that.

She sealed the letter and left it for the post. Then she sat a moment with her hands flat on the desk, looking at nothing in particular, until Charlotte came to say that dinner was nearly ready.

She went.

Chapter 4: Darcy and Fitzwilliam Arrive

They arrived on a Tuesday, as they always did, Darcy and his cousin, every spring, as regular as the cherry trees along the Rosings drive and considerably less welcome to Elizabeth's nerves.

She had known they were coming. Charlotte had mentioned it with the careful evenness she applied to most news she suspected Elizabeth would rather not hear. Elizabeth had received it the same way: a fact, manageable, to be filed alongside the entail mechanics and Mrs. Bennet's last letter and the ongoing question of what could be arranged before Collins required his house. She had been doing a great deal of filing lately.

She went to the dinner because Charlotte was right that she should, and because refusing would cost something she could not afford to spend.

After dressing in the gray she had brought, the only thing she owned that would still pass for half-mourning in a room where Lady Catherine would be looking, she walked with Charlotte along the road that Collins had shown her three times, each time as if she had not seen it before. The evening was cool, but not unkind. That was the best she could find to say for it.

Collins was already positioned in the drawing room when they arrived, at an angle that suggested he had calculated the sightlines some time before their entrance. He greeted Elizabeth with the warmth he reserved for moments when Rosings was watching, and she returned it in kind, because they had reached an understanding — unspoken, and unnecessary to speak — about what each required from the other's behavior in this house.

Lady Catherine received her with the condescension of a woman whose charity had recently been tested.

"Miss Bennet." The title landed with precision; Lady Catherine had a gift for emphasis. "You are looking well, considering."

"Thank you, ma'am."

"The gray is appropriate. One can always tell good breeding by how a young woman handles mourning. Some make quite an occasion of grief. You seem to have more sense." She surveyed Elizabeth's dress with the eye of someone determining whether a compliment was warranted. "Sit there, where I can see you. Anne, ring for tea."

Anne de Bourgh observed from her chair near the fire, where she had been observing since before Elizabeth arrived and would likely observe until long after she left. Elizabeth observed back. It was one of the few pleasures currently available.

Darcy and Fitzwilliam came in late enough to be noticed and early enough to take the room's temperature. It was Fitzwilliam's timing, Elizabeth suspected; Darcy merely followed. The room reorganized itself around their entrance with the efficiency that rank produced without trying.

Lady Catherine's pleasure in her nephew was genuine. This was one of the most revealing things about her. She simply showed it the way people show things they have never had reason to conceal. She placed Darcy beside

Anne within three minutes of his arrival and began speaking to him about the east garden at Pemberley.

Fitzwilliam found Elizabeth almost immediately.

"Miss Bennet." He bowed; his eyes were already warm. "I am very glad to see you."

"And I you, Colonel. How was the journey?"

"Damp," he said, "and then not, and then damp again. Darcy endured it with more equanimity than I did. He always does. I believe he finds the roads less objectionable than I do."

"Or he simply finds complaint less useful."

"Yes," Fitzwilliam said, as if she had diagnosed something he had long suspected. "That is almost certainly it."

They talked about other things: London, spring's late arrival, whether the Rosings cook had changed something about the pastry because Fitzwilliam was fairly certain he'd noticed a difference. Elizabeth was grateful for the ordinary texture of it. There had not been enough ordinary conversation this month.

She was aware, through most of it, of Darcy across the room. This was not new. She had been aware of Darcy across rooms before: at Netherfield, at the Meryton assembly, at her own doorstep that morning he had arrived at the parsonage uninvited and stood in the parlor making stilted conversation as if he were uncertain why he had come. The awareness was not comfortable. It had never been comfortable. He was a man who occupied space in a way that made other people organize their attention around him whether or not they wished to, and she found this quality in him irritating in the same way she found his general manner irritating: because it was the irritation of acknowledging something real.

Across the room, Lady Catherine was speaking; Darcy was listening with a patience that read, to those who did not know him, as haughtiness. Elizabeth, who had watched him at Netherfield long enough to distinguish between the two, recognized it as endurance. Whether this distinction made her think better or worse of him, she had not decided.

She had not decided a great many things lately. There was not enough time, and there were always more urgent calculations to make.

Dinner was served at a length that suited Lady Catherine, which was long.

Elizabeth sat three chairs from Darcy and occupied herself, through the first course, with eating steadily and listening to Lady Catherine manage the conversation the way a general manages a campaign: with territorial instinct, clear objectives, and no interest in dissent. Collins nodded at intervals. Charlotte listened without appearing to listen. Fitzwilliam contributed just enough to prevent any single subject from becoming a grievance.

Darcy said almost nothing, which was consistent with every meal Elizabeth had witnessed him attend. He answered when addressed and refrained when not. The economy of it was discipline or disinterest; she had spent some time, at Netherfield, deciding which it was, and had concluded disinterest, and was no longer entirely certain the conclusion was sound.

He refilled her glass once. Without ceremony, without comment, without looking at her afterward to see whether she had noticed.

She noticed. She was not sure what it signified beyond the ordinary attentiveness of a man seated close enough to observe an empty glass, which signified very little.

She drank the wine and returned her attention to the soup.

Lady Catherine turned to the matter of the Bennet entail after the fish course.

"These arrangements are always unfortunate," she said, to no one in particular, and therefore to the whole table. "An estate entailed away from the female line is a difficulty I have never understood the necessity for. In your family's case, Miss Bennet, the situation is of course rather acute."

"It is," Elizabeth agreed.

"Your father was not a prudent man, I understand, in matters of economy."

"He was a very kind one."

"Yes, that is often the case," Lady Catherine said, as if kindness and imprudence were confirmed synonyms. "It does not speak to the question, in the end. You have sisters, I believe. Several?"

"Four."

"And their situations are now all somewhat altered; the eldest especially. I am told she had some expectations in that direction, but nothing came of it." She looked at the table in a way that suggested she had more to say on the subject and was exercising restraint by not saying it. "These things happen. One cannot depend on expectations. I have always held that a young woman of no fortune ought to be prudent above all other qualities."

"I shall pass the recommendation along."

"I hope you will." Lady Catherine surveyed her with an expression that had recently softened, fractionally, from its usual set. Not warmer, precisely, but recalibrated. "You are a sensible girl, Miss Bennet, whatever your family's circumstances. I have said so to Mr. Collins, who agrees with me entirely, as he ought."

Collins, who had been nodding since the word sensible, nodded again with added conviction.

Elizabeth thanked her. It was the only available response.

She did not look at Darcy. She was aware, without looking, that he had been still since Lady Catherine began the subject of the entail, and that he had not contributed a single word to it. This was either courtesy, or discomfort, or the complete indifference of a man to whom other people's financial difficulties were a class of problem he had never had occasion to consider.

She could not, from three chairs away, determine which.

After dinner, the party moved to the drawing room. Lady Catherine held court at the center. Anne returned to the fire. Collins positioned himself within range of Darcy. Charlotte took up the embroidery frame she had placed there before dinner, and she was positioned, Elizabeth had noted, at an angle that allowed her to see everything without being consulted about any of it.

Elizabeth sat near the window, which was cool enough to be useful and far enough from the main current of conversation to allow thinking. She had been doing most of her serious thinking near windows lately; there was something about having a fixed view outward that made the internal arithmetic easier.

Fitzwilliam came and sat nearby, and they resumed their conversation from before dinner. While they talked, she was aware, still, of Darcy across the room.

He had moved from Collins, which suggested a limit had been reached. He was speaking with Lady Catherine again, or rather attending to Lady Catherine, which was a different thing. He stood rather than sat. He listened. His expression had the quality she had identified earlier: endurance.

He looked over toward the window, or toward Fitzwilliam, or perhaps simply at that quarter of the room, and Elizabeth was looking at him when he did it, which was inconvenient. She returned her attention to Fitzwilliam with no change of expression. Darcy looked away.

"You are well, Miss Bennet," Fitzwilliam said. Not a question.

"You asked me that once already this evening."

"I know. I am asking with more specificity now." His manner was pleasant but not careless. "This has been a great deal to navigate, on your own, in someone else's house."

Elizabeth was quiet for a moment. Outside, the Rosings drive was dark. The cherry trees were invisible; she knew they were there.

"Charlotte has been very good," she said. "And you are kind to ask."

He did not press further. This was, she thought, the thing she valued most about him: he knew where the floor was, and he stopped at it.

They talked of other things until Lady Catherine called the room's attention to the tea tray, and the evening began its resolution.

Walking back with Charlotte in the dark, the lantern swinging between them, Elizabeth said nothing about any of it.

Charlotte did not ask. This was one of Charlotte's great and underrated qualities.

The parsonage gate required lifting before it opened. Elizabeth had learned this in the first week; even so, each time, felt the small resistance before she remembered. Charlotte pushed it through. Elizabeth walked past her and into the hallway, and stood for a moment in the light, her gloves still on, not thinking about anything.

This was not true. She was thinking about a glass of wine refilled without comment, and about a man who sat very still when the entail was mentioned, and about whether she was mistaking quiet for meaning when possibly it was nothing of the sort.

She had enough to think about. She would not add to it speculatively.

Charlotte carried the lantern inside.

Elizabeth went up to bed. In the room that smelled of someone else's lavender, she did not sleep immediately; not from grief, exactly, but from the persistent habit of calculation that grief had made worse.

Eventually, she slept. In the morning there was another letter from Jane, and the numbers had not changed.

Chapter 5: What Fitzwilliam Lets Slip

She had taken to walking in the morning because the parsonage, for all its arrangements, was Charlotte's arrangement, and Charlotte's arrangement was built around Collins, which meant it was built around Rosings, which meant it was built around the assumption that the great house was the center of every day and its inhabitants the measure of every judgment. Elizabeth could admire the architecture of Charlotte's life without wishing to live inside it for more than an hour at a time.

The park was better. The park had trees and a path and the indifferent noise of birds, and no one in it required her to look composed when she was not entirely certain she was. She had discovered in the last week that grief did not diminish with company; it merely became harder to carry without showing, which was a different problem and, in some respects, a worse one. Alone on the path, she did not have to manage it. She could let it sit wherever it had settled and simply walk.

She was thinking, as she had been thinking for three days, about the arithmetic. Not the emotional arithmetic, which she found she could not yet approach directly, but the practical kind: what existed, what was owed, what timeline Collins's intentions imposed, what Mr. Gardiner could realistically do from London and how quickly he could do it. She had laid these figures out in her mind so many times that they had taken on the quality of a familiar room. She could move through them in the dark, know exactly where each piece of furniture stood, know which ones would not shift no matter how many times she rearranged them.

She was nearly to the lower gate when she heard a step on the path behind her, unhurried, male, and not Collins's, and turned to find Colonel Fitzwilliam approaching with the ease of a man who expects to be a welcome addition to whatever he finds. He had been exactly so at their first meeting, in Meryton, the previous autumn, and she had liked him for it then. She liked him for it now, which was a more difficult thing to manage.

"I was told I might find you here," he said, raising his hat and falling into step beside her with the confidence of a prior acquaintance rather than the formality of a new one. "Mrs. Collins suggested the park, and the park is obligingly small. I hope the intrusion is not unwelcome."

"Not at all," Elizabeth said, and meant it, which was not always the case with the inhabitants of the Rosings sphere. He was amiable company: a man who had learned, through the education of a younger son without fortune, that the way to be received well was to attend to people rather than to require their attendance. She had observed it in Meryton; it was unchanged.

He asked after her family with the genuine warmth of someone who remembered names, which she noticed. Her mother, her sisters, and Jane in particular. He had met Jane, had spoken well of her then, did so again now without any appearance of it being a courtesy. Elizabeth thanked him and answered briefly, aware that the answers were abbreviated by a grief she had no intention of displaying on the path, and that he was perceptive enough to notice the abbreviation without pressing it.

They talked of other things. The park, the spring's lateness. A walk he had taken in Derbyshire that he recommended very much if she ever found herself there. She said she had not been north of Meryton for some years. He expressed the opinion that this was a deficiency easily corrected and described Derbyshire with the affection of a man whose good memories were attached to a place rather than to any allegiance to its landscape.

"You are fond of travel, then," she said.

"I am fond of movement," he said. "Which is not quite the same thing. A soldier develops it as a habit or goes to pieces. Darcy, for instance, is a good traveler, always has some object at the other end of the journey. I merely like the road."

She thought of Darcy as she had seen him at the Rosings dinner the previous evening: the quality of his attention in that room, which had seemed, when she turned to find it directed at her, less like admiration than like study. She noted it and set it aside, uncertain where it belonged.

"And Mr. Darcy is at Pemberley most of the year?"

"When he is not in London, yes. He manages it with--" Fitzwilliam considered, "well, the same way he manages everything. Thoroughly. His tenants are well looked after. His accounts are never in disorder. His steward has been with the family since before Darcy was born and shows no inclination to leave, which tells you something." He paused. "He does not find it easy, being responsible for everyone. But he does it."

This was, Elizabeth thought, rather more than she had expected him to say. She did not examine why she was cataloguing it.

They had reached a low stone bench at the edge of the path where the trees opened enough to show the distant chimneys of Rosings above the treeline. Fitzwilliam gestured at the bench with a question in his expression; Elizabeth shook her head and they continued, the path curving back through a stand of oak that had leafed out only at the tips, the rest of the branches still winter-bare and indifferent.

"Darcy is looking well," Fitzwilliam said, with the tone of someone making conversation rather than advancing an argument. "Better than last autumn, which was a wearing time for all of us."

"Wearing in what way?"

""Oh, various matters." He was choosing his words; she could hear it, not with any great care, just with the instinct of a man who has learned to leave certain doors shut in public. "Georgiana had... but that is quite settled now, and I ought not to go into it. And then Darcy had a piece of business in the autumn he managed rather well, I thought, though he did not see fit to congratulate himself on it. He rarely does."

"Rarely the mark of a poor decision," Elizabeth said.

Fitzwilliam laughed, a real laugh, short and unguarded. "Quite right. Here it was a friend of his, Bingley, a very good sort of fellow but not the most fixed sort of character. Easily led, if you understand me. Very susceptible to feelings, and feelings of the kind that makes a man act before he's thought twice."

Elizabeth understood him. She did not say so. She was also aware with a precision that arrived faster than she would have liked that she knew Bingley's name, knew it well, and that Fitzwilliam had no reason on earth to suppose she did.

"Darcy stepped in," Fitzwilliam continued, with the ease of a man recounting something that cost him nothing because it had cost him nothing, "and extracted Bingley from what would have been a very imprudent attachment. The young woman's family was entirely unsuitable. No connections, very little money, and some members whose behavior in public was--" he made a slight gesture that substituted for the words he was declining to use. "Well, conspicuous. You take my meaning."

He glanced at her, perhaps expecting the small nod of agreement that usually arrived at this point in the story. He did not receive it. Elizabeth was looking at the path ahead with an expression of attention that gave nothing away, and he found himself, for no reason he could have named, adjusting his tone by half a degree.

"Darcy saw the difficulty before Bingley did," he said, with slightly less relish than he had begun, "and handled it decisively, before any actual harm was done. Bingley never quite knows whether to thank him for these things or resent them, but there it is. One does what one must for one's friends."

He finished and waited. She said nothing. Fitzwilliam was a sociable man and had a sociable man's sensitivity to the texture of a conversation, enough to feel that something had changed in the last thirty seconds with no corresponding ability to identify what. He concluded, after a moment's private recalibration, that she was perhaps finding the subject dull; it was, after all, nothing to do with her. He had been talking about people she had never met. He resolved to do better.

She said nothing. She let the silence run long enough that it required filling.

"Bingley is a pleasant fellow," he offered, in a tone that was making a conscious effort toward brightness. "He'll find someone else. These things pass."

"No doubt," said Elizabeth.

The flatness of it registered. He looked at her sidelong, with an expression that was almost, but not quite, a question. She met his glance with one of perfectly civil composure, and he let it go. Whatever he had half-perceived retreated into the unexamined category of things a sociable man notices and a tactful man does not pursue.

He asked about her plans for the rest of the visit. She answered him. They walked back toward the parsonage in a manner that was, on the surface, perfectly pleasant.

She did not tell him. There was nothing to be gained by telling him, and a great deal to be lost: his comfort, their easy acquaintance, and whatever remained of the conversation's surface, which she needed intact to think. She would think better alone.

At the parsonage gate she thanked him for his company and meant it, which was, under the circumstances, a not inconsiderable thing. He had told her something she needed to know. That he had told it in the wrong spirit to the wrong person, without the smallest awareness of either, was not his fault, and she did not hold it against him. She held it somewhere else entirely.

Inside, Charlotte was in the front room arranging flowers with the focused efficiency she brought to every domestic task, which was to say with the air of someone who has decided that competence is its own reward and has stopped requiring any other. She looked up when Elizabeth came in. She did not ask where Elizabeth had been or whom she had met on the path. This was one of Charlotte's better qualities, the one Elizabeth valued most precisely: she knew the difference between a silence that wanted interrupting and one that wanted keeping.

Elizabeth went upstairs.

She sat at the small writing desk in her room. The surface was empty. She had answered Jane's last letter two days ago, and there was nothing else requiring a reply. The letter she had been composing in her head since she passed the stone bench would not be sent. It was a letter that existed only to make the mind proceed in order, to force each piece into its correct position so that none of them could shift or blur.

First: Bingley's attachment had been real. Jane had not imagined it, had not inflated it, had not read warmth into civility and called it love. Whatever she had felt, he had felt. This was not a comfort, exactly, but it was a correction, and corrections mattered.

Second: Darcy had seen it, judged it imprudent, and removed it. Deliberately. On the grounds that included the Bennet's behavior and connections, because what other grounds were there? Fitzwilliam had named them without knowing he was naming them: no connections, very little money, members whose behavior in public was conspicuous. The unsuitable family near the estate. She was one of those members. Her mother was. Lydia was. The whole of Longbourn, weighed from the outside, found wanting, and set aside and then described to her, pleasantly, on a morning walk, as a problem that had been managed.

Third: Jane did not know. Jane had attributed Bingley's departure to Bingley's own uncertainty, to Miss Bingley's influence, to the ordinary inconstancy of a man not quite fixed enough in his own feelings. Jane had been kind about it, which was to say Jane had blamed no one, had distributed the disappointment so evenly across general circumstance that no single person had to bear the weight of having caused it. This was characteristic of Jane. It was also, Elizabeth could see now, a kindness extended to people who had not deserved it.

Fourth: Darcy was yards away across the park at Rosings, where she would see him at dinner on Thursday. He would sit at Lady Catherine's table with that same contained attention and refill her glass when it was empty and say nothing she could object to, and she would know what she now knew, and he would not know that she knew it.

She put her hands flat on the desk. The wood was cool. Outside, a bird was working at something in the eaves making a quick, purposeful sound, entirely indifferent to the room and everything in it.

Downstairs she could hear Collins's voice, the familiar rhythm of a man explaining something at length to someone who has decided to stop replying, and Charlotte's responses, brief and even, the conversational equivalent of opening a valve just enough to prevent pressure from building.

She thought about what Fitzwilliam had said; the ease of it, the complete absence of any sense that the story reflected badly on anyone. He had told it as a success. Darcy had seen the difficulty and stepped in decisively. One does what one must for one's friends. The friend in question being Bingley, who did not know what had been done on his behalf and would perhaps have not wanted it done. The family in question being the Bennets, who had not known they were being assessed and set aside.

Jane had spent the autumn saying cheerful things about Bingley's departure and what it likely meant and what she had perhaps misunderstood about his feelings. Elizabeth had spent the autumn telling her she was certain he would return, that his warmth had been too evident to be mistaken, that these things sometimes required time.

She had been wrong. Not about Bingley's feelings. That much, she now knew, had been real. She had been wrong about what stood between feeling and action, about what a man of Bingley's temperament was actually free to do when someone he trusted had decided for him.

She did not permit herself to think about what Jane's face had looked like the morning after the Netherfield ball, when it had become clear that Bingley was not coming back. It was one of those images that, once admitted, had a way of staying.

She sat for a long time. The bird in the eaves finished whatever it was doing and left. Collins's voice reached its conclusion and was replaced by the quieter sounds of Charlotte moving through the house below, efficient and unhurried, managing everything.

Eventually, Elizabeth picked up her pen. She did not write a letter. She drew a line across the page, a single, clean line. It was a habit her father had taught her, the thing you did when you needed to mark where a set of figures ended and the next set began. Then she put the pen down again.

The numbers, this set, came out the same way they always came out. She had simply added one more column.

Chapter 6: The Proposal

The parlor at Hunsford was quiet. Charlotte had gone to Rosings two hours ago, Collins following with the solemnity of a man who understood that his aunt's dinner invitations were not, strictly speaking, invitations. The fire had been built up before they left, and it was still burning now, though it had passed the point of cheerfulness into something more workmanlike.

Elizabeth sat with a letter she was not reading.

It was her third attempt. The first two she had folded away without finishing because she could hear herself in them, the careful, qualified reassurances, the management of her mother's terror dressed up as practical fact, and she had not had enough sleep to maintain that kind of steadiness. She had not slept properly in a few days. This was not a circumstance she had told anyone, because there was nothing useful to be done about it.

The numbers were unchanged. She had checked them twice last night and once this morning. Mr. Gardiner could not send funds until he had wound up the current quarter's business; he had said so, kindly and precisely, in the letter that arrived yesterday, and Elizabeth did not blame him for it. Mrs. Bennet could not manage the conversation with Collins that was going to have to happen regardless. Jane was managing it, which meant that Jane was carrying the weight of two people's composure while feeling the full force of her own grief, and Elizabeth was fifty miles away being of no practical use to anyone.

There was a knock at the parlor door.

She assumed it was the maid and said, without looking up, "Yes, come in."

It was not the maid.

Mr. Darcy came in with the expression of a man who had prepared himself for a different scene, perhaps an empty room, perhaps Charlotte, and found the room not empty and Charlotte not present. He checked fractionally in the doorway. Elizabeth stood.

"Mr. Darcy." She was aware that her voice was very level. She had been practicing level without intending to.

"Miss Bennet. Forgive the intrusion. I understood that Mrs. Collins and Mr. Collins were at Rosings this evening."

"They are."

He did not, as she expected, produce an immediate reason for his presence. He came further into the room instead, and she watched him take in the letter on the table, the general evidence of the evening, and she did not offer him a seat.

"I had hoped," he said, "to find you. I have something I must say."

Elizabeth's first thought was not what the something might be. Her first thought was the number she had done three times in the last twelve hours and arrived at the same place: No. Not enough. Not close.

"Then say it," she said.

He opened the parlor door wide and stepped just inside. He began his speech with Netherfield. She could see the outline before he reached his point; the careful opening, the concession of surprise at his own feeling, and then the turn, the place where feeling became insufficient on its own and required the support of qualification.

"In vain have I struggled," Darcy said. "It will not do. My feelings will not be repressed. You must allow me to tell you how ardently I admire and love you."

She did not move.

"I am sensible that this address may not be entirely welcome, that your family's situation, your connections, the very inferiority of your circumstances, are objections I have long had to reason away." He paused. He seemed to expect that she would interrupt him. She did not.

He paused as the maid went by the open door.

"I have struggled against my better judgment," he said when she had passed, "against the expectations of those whose opinions I respect, and against my own sense of duty. I tell you this not to insult you, but because honesty seems to me the only foundation on which I have determined it must be said.

Miss Bennet, will you do me the honor of accepting my hand?"

The room was quiet enough that she could hear the fire.She looked at him. He was standing with the expression of a man who had prepared for refusal and was not, she thought, entirely certain he had not received it.

He had come in with a speech and she had heard it, every clause of it. What it contained was real feeling clumsily delivered, which was a different thing from Collins and not, in the circumstances, more comfortable.

What she needed to know was something the speech had not answered.

"Before I reply," she said, "I would ask you something. What would you settle on my mother and sisters? Not in general terms, in specific ones."

He did not prevaricate. She would remember this afterward: that he did not retreat into sentiment, did not produce the expression men sometimes produced when women asked directly about money. He thought, then he began to speak.

"Longbourn first," he said. "Collins has not yet taken possession. I will approach him about a term, two years perhaps, in which your mother and sisters may remain. He will want something for it, and I will provide it. I cannot promise he will agree, but I believe he can be persuaded."

Elizabeth said nothing. She was doing the arithmetic.

"If he will not, or when the term ends, I would provide for a removal. A cottage near Meryton, if your mother wishes to remain among her neighbors. A house in a market town, if she would prefer more society." He paused. "The choice should be hers."

"And my sisters?"

He stopped before Jane. Something crossed his face that was not calculation. "Miss Bennet would receive a settlement in her own right," he said. "Independent of any future marriage. Enough that her choices need not be made under the same constraints as the present ones."

He said it differently than that. The meaning was the same.

The younger girls: a provision for their maintenance until they married or were otherwise established. He revised one figure mid-sentence, paused, and revised it again. She watched him work. Not displaying generosity: working.

A man who had thought about money all his life in one direction was now thinking about it in another and finding the adjustment less difficult than she would have predicted.

He stopped. "This is not what I imagined saying," he said.

"No," Elizabeth agreed. "I expect not."

He knew her situation. Lady Catherine had made certain of that. He was standing there with full knowledge of how narrow her circumstances had become, and he had priced his proposal against them with the precision of someone who understood that she understood what she was being offered. She could not yet see whether that made him more trustworthy or simply more legible. She suspected she would not know for some time.

"Yes," she said.

One word. He received it without the satisfaction she suspected he had been expecting, because her face was doing nothing that warranted satisfaction. She was looking at him with the attention of someone who had made a calculation, arrived at an answer, and was waiting to see whether the answer held.

The fire had burned to ash while they were talking. She had not noticed it happening.

He said something about arrangements, about Lady Catherine, about the settlements being drawn up. She would need to listen to every one of them. She would hold him to each. She would not pretend to warmth she did not feel. That much she already knew.

He dipped his head in a slight nod and left.

The door closed.

She sat down in the chair and looked at the fire. The last of it, a piece of wood gone entirely to black, dropped into ash with a small, decisive sound, and the room was dark on that side.

She did not move to rebuild it.

She sat with the letter she had still not finished, and the numbers she did not need to run again, and the fact of what she had just done, which was reasonable and also, she thought, possibly the most consequential single word sentence she had spoken in her life.

Chapter 7: Terms

Lady Catherine did not receive the news; she absorbed it and returned it, transformed, as an injury.

Darcy told her himself in the drawing room at Rosings, before the morning had properly settled. Elizabeth was not present for this. She learned of it afterward from the way he walked back into the parsonage: not quickly, not with any visible alteration, but with the countenance of stillness that she was beginning to understand meant he had said something he had calculated and did not intend to revisit.

"How did she receive it?" Elizabeth asked.

"As I expected."

That, she thought, was almost certainly not a complete account, but she did not press him; she had already understood, from the morning's arrangements, that Lady Catherine's reaction would make itself known by its own means.

It did so at dinner.

Lady Catherine waited until the removes had been cleared, a gesture toward civilization that cost her some visible effort, and then turned to

Elizabeth with the careful deliberateness of a woman who has decided to address a problem before it becomes a habit.

"You have, I understand, accepted my nephew's proposal."

"I have," Elizabeth said.

Lady Catherine looked at her as one might look at a document bearing a signature that ought not to be there. "I confess I find it difficult to comprehend what considerations could have produced such an outcome. Darcy is not a man who acts without reflection. That he has done so in this instance speaks, I think, to the nature of the circumstances which prompted him."

"Circumstances of my family, you mean."

"Circumstances," Lady Catherine said, with precision, "of every kind."

It was not a sentence one could argue with directly; the whole of its meaning lay in the space between words, and to dispute that space would require naming things that Lady Catherine had taken care not to name. Elizabeth found she had no desire to perform that service for her.

"Lady Catherine," she said, "I am sure you speak from your concern for your nephew, and I will not suggest otherwise. But I think you must find, on reflection, that the decision has been made and that there is very little to be usefully said against it now."

Lady Catherine's expression suggested she found quite a great deal to be usefully said. She said some of it. It concerned the entail, the Bennets of Longbourn in general, Elizabeth's own position in particular, and what she characterized, in terms that remained just inside the boundaries of civility, as the exploitation of a man's better feelings at a moment of weakness. Darcy had been susceptible. Elizabeth had been convenient. These were the facts as Lady Catherine arranged them, and she presented them with the confidence of a woman accustomed to having her arrangements stand.

Elizabeth allowed her to finish.

"I hope," she said then, pleasantly, "that you will come to see it differently in time. I do not intend to be a disappointment to your nephew. I cannot, of course, promise to be what I am not."

Lady Catherine looked at her for a long moment. Elizabeth did not look away.

Darcy, when he entered the room twenty minutes later, read the temperature correctly and did not attempt to correct it. He sat beside Elizabeth, said something quiet and unremarkable to his aunt, and declined, by the simple fact of his posture, to open any line of discussion that had not been invited. Lady Catherine was not appeased. But she did not, after that, continue.

Walking back in the dark with Charlotte, Elizabeth said nothing about any of it. Charlotte did not ask. She held the lantern and kept pace, which was precisely what Elizabeth required of her.

The morning after, Elizabeth and Darcy met in the parlor before the household had fully assembled. It was not arranged; he had come to speak to Collins about the practical matters of the estate papers, and Elizabeth had come down early because she had not slept well, and neither of them had yet developed the habit of retreating when they found themselves alone together.

She sat by the window. He stood near the fireplace. The arrangement was not uncomfortable; it was simply the arrangement of two people who had agreed to something and were still working out what that meant in practice.

"I want to tell you what I expect," Elizabeth said, without preliminaries. She had thought it through the night before, between one hour and the next, and was satisfied with the order of it. "I do not think it is useful to leave this to implication."

Darcy looked at her with an attention that was, she thought, one of his more honest qualities. He was not performing listening. He was listening.

"I will not be managed," she said. "If there are things that concern me, my family, the household, or your decisions where they affect my family, I expect to be told, not protected. I have no objection to protection when it is warranted. I object to being protected from information because someone else has decided I could not bear it."

"Understood."

"I will not pretend to feel what I do not feel. I accepted your proposal because it was the sensible answer to a set of difficult facts, and I intend to honor it completely. But I will not perform gratitude I do not feel, or warmth that has not been established, simply because the performance would be more comfortable for those around me."

"I did not ask you to."

"No," she said. "But it may arise as an expectation. From Lady Catherine, certainly, possibly from others. I want you to know, in advance, that it will not be met."

There was a brief silence. Outside, she could hear Collins beginning his survey of the garden, which he did every morning as though the garden might have changed significantly overnight.

"I have one request to make of you in return," Darcy said.

She looked at him.

"If there is something I have done, or not done, that gives you reason to object, I would prefer to be told directly rather than discover it through its effects. I am not—" He paused with the care of a man who has been wrong before about such a matter. "I am not always quick to notice what I have failed to understand. I would rather be corrected than persist in ignorance."

It was, she thought, a more honest statement than she had expected. It acknowledged a specific failing without making a performance of the acknowledgment.

"That seems reasonable," she said.

"Then we are agreed."

He held out his hand. She looked at it for a moment. The gesture was deliberate, she thought, and not theatrical; it was the form of agreement he knew how to make, and then she took it briefly and let it go.

"We are agreed," she said.

Colonel Fitzwilliam heard the news before luncheon, from Darcy, in a manner that Elizabeth was not present for. She observed its effects at the table: a warmth in his address to her that was genuine without being excessive, and a quality of attention in the way he looked between them she recognized as a man working something out.

He was, she thought, more perceptive than his ease of manner suggested, and more careful than his frankness implied. She found she did not mind that he was looking; she minded rather less than she had expected to mind most things today.

After dinner, when the gentlemen had rejoined them and the evening had settled into its familiar arrangement, Fitzwilliam found a moment to speak to her without the rest of the room.

"I am very glad," he said, which was simple and, from him, sufficient.

"Thank you," Elizabeth said. She meant it in the limited way she was able to mean it; he accepted it in the generous way he was able to accept things.

"He will not make it easy," Fitzwilliam said, without unkindness, "by nature. But he will make it — I think — something better than easy. In time."

Elizabeth considered this. "That is a very careful formulation."

"It is the accurate one." He smiled at her with the easy confidence of someone who has known Darcy long enough to be honest about him. "I have observed him in several situations that called for more than he thought he had. He has not, so far, disappointed."

It was not precisely a reassurance; it was better than that. It was evidence.

Collins's response came at breakfast, in the form of a speech that lasted eleven minutes and managed, by some feat of construction, to imply that the entire arrangement had been facilitated by his own benevolence in providing Elizabeth with the opportunity to be at Hunsford in the first place. He appeared genuinely satisfied by this version of events. She ate her toast.

That afternoon, she wrote two letters.

The first was to Mrs. Gardiner. She wrote it plainly: the facts, the settlement figures as she understood them, the date expected, the arrangements for her mother and sisters that she had discussed with Darcy, and a clear account of his character as she had observed it so far — neither flattering nor the reverse, simply what she had seen. Her aunt was not a woman who required cushioning, and Elizabeth had no interest in providing it.

The second letter was to Jane.

She sat with it for a quarter of an hour and wrote several opening sentences and discarded them. She wrote: Dear Jane, I am engaged to Mr. Darcy. She crossed it out. She wrote: There is a great deal I want to explain. She crossed that out too.

In the end, she wrote three sentences. She sealed the letter before she could decide whether they were the right ones.

They were not the right ones. They were the honest ones, which was the closest she could manage.

She put both letters in her writing case. Outside, Darcy was crossing the garden toward the road to Rosings, attending, she supposed, to whatever remained to be attended to there. He walked, she noticed, as though he expected the ground to be solid underfoot, which struck her, for reasons she could not immediately explain, as a quality she had perhaps undervalued.

She closed the writing case and went to find Charlotte.

Chapter 8: Longbourn, at Last

The house looked the same.

This was the first and most disorienting fact. Elizabeth had braced for alterations; something visible, some evidence in the brickwork or the garden path that corresponded to the collapse she had been managing at a distance for three weeks. There was none. The elms still leaned at their familiar angle; the kitchen garden still smelled of cold earth and last season's thyme; the front step still needed its left corner re-pointed, a repair her father had meant to see to every fall for as long as she could remember.

He was dead, and the step still needed pointing, and the house looked exactly the same.

Elizabeth's trunk was taken inside. She followed it.

Mrs. Bennet was in the drawing room. Her response to Elizabeth's arrival was, characteristically, two things at once and therefore slightly incoherent. She wept a genuine, heaving sort of weeping that was as much exhaustion as grief and then, before Elizabeth had fully set down her gloves, she asked whether it had been a proper proposal or the sort of thing that might still be called off.

"It was proper," Elizabeth said.

"With solicitors? Has he spoken to your uncle?"

"He has written to Mr. Gardiner. The settlement will be negotiated in London next week."

This satisfied something in Mrs. Bennet that the weeping had not. She sat up straighter. She looked at Elizabeth with the sort of attention she reserved for fabric samples and the neighbors' carriages, a rapid, calculating appraisal that was not unkind but was undeniably practical.

"Well," she said at last, with the air of a woman who has performed a great deal of mental arithmetic and arrived at a satisfactory sum, "you have done very well. Very well indeed. I could not have imagined, that is, I always hoped, of course, but —" She stopped, appeared to reconsider, and started again on a slightly different footing. "He is everything I could have wished Lizzy, for you. For all of us."

Elizabeth received this without comment.

Her mother's face moved through several more expressions — relief predominant, the grief periodically reasserting itself, and underneath both, a quality of bright, barely suppressible triumph that she was clearly trying, with incomplete success, to keep out of the room. She was not a malicious woman. She was only a frightened one who had just discovered that she did not need to be frightened, and the sensation of that reprieve was too large to be entirely contained.

Elizabeth understood this. She was also, in this moment, grateful that Jane was coming through the doorway.

Jane looked well. Her color was good; her expression was composed; and she had the slightly deliberate air of a person who has been managing a household and a mother and four sisters through grief and upheaval and has not once permitted herself the luxury of stopping.

She embraced Elizabeth, and Elizabeth held on for a moment longer than she intended.

"Come upstairs," Jane said.

They sat in Jane's room, which was the quietest in the house, with the door shut against the sort of noise their mother generated when she was processing good news.

Elizabeth told Jane the truth of the proposal in the same order she had lived it: the arithmetic, the question she had asked Darcy, his answer, the single word she had given him in return. She did not soften it or arrange it into something more becoming. Jane deserved the truth without ornament.

Jane listened without interrupting, which was her great gift and also, Elizabeth had always thought, one of the more demanding forms of generosity.

When Elizabeth finished, Jane said: "And do you believe he is a good man?"

Elizabeth had expected something closer to relief, or perhaps the careful sort of comfort Jane excelled at. The directness surprised her.

"I believe," she said, after a moment, "that he is trying to be. I have seen enough to think the trying is genuine."

Jane nodded. "That is more than many people manage."

"It is also not the same as certainty."

"No," Jane agreed. "But it is a place to begin."

She did not ask whether Elizabeth was happy. Elizabeth noticed this and was grateful for it. Her sister understood, as she always did, the difference between the question that would comfort the asker and the question that was actually useful.

There was a pause, the comfortable kind. Outside, a starling worked its way along the guttering.

Elizabeth had not told Jane yet about Bingley. She turned the decision over once more in her mind and arrived at the same place she had reached three times before: not yet. She did not have Darcy's full accounting; she had only Fitzwilliam's casual, unguarded version, which was accurate but incomplete. She would not give Jane something to hope for or grieve over until she understood what she actually knew.

"I should go to Papa's study," she said.

Jane's hand, briefly, on her wrist. "Yes."

The door opened without difficulty, which struck her as a small injustice. She had half-expected resistance from old hinges that would need coaxing, or some bodily memory of the man who had opened them daily. It swung back smoothly, and the room beyond was an ordinary room in the afternoon light.

It smelled of him. Pipe tobacco and old paper and a faint, mineral smell she had never identified and would not, now, have the occasion to ask about. She stood in the doorway for a moment before going in.

A book was still open on the desk. Jane had mentioned it, matter-of-factly, in a letter that explained that no one had gone in to touch anything, but knowing it and seeing it were different. It was a Fielding she didn't recognize the title of from this angle; she would have to go closer to read the spine, and she found that she did not want to be closer.

His reading glasses were folded on top of the page.

She sat in his chair. It had always been too large for her; at twelve she had come in and sat in it as an act of mild transgression, reading his books without asking while he pretended not to notice, her feet not quite reaching the floor. They reached the floor now, and it was still too large. She put her hands on the armrests, which were worn smooth along the outer edge where he had rested his thumbs.

She did not cry. She had cried twice since the express arrived at Hunsford, once on the first night, alone in the parsonage parlor with

Charlotte's lamp and her own arithmetic, and once in the carriage coming home, with her face turned to the window so the driver need not feel he had witnessed anything. She was not certain she had any more of it immediately available.

The room held his presence still, not in any single object but in the arrangement of all of them, the accumulated evidence of a man's daily habits. It felt less like loss than like... she reached for the word and did not find an adequate one. Remainder, perhaps. What grief leaves when it takes the man and lets his things stand.

She thought about the letter she had written him from Hunsford, the easy, lightly comic one, the one she had been pleased with and about his reply, four lines, wry and warm and utterly characteristic. She had put it in her writing case. She had not been able to read it again.

After a while she rose and went to the window. The garden below was in its late-winter state: the beds cut back, the kitchen plot bare, the old pear tree that had never produced anything worth eating still occupying its corner with the confidence of a tree that expects to be there indefinitely.

She thought about Darcy at Longbourn. He would come; she had asked him to, for the sake of the practical questions that still required answers. He would stand in this house and she would introduce him to rooms that were not, legally, any longer hers to introduce him to, and her mother would be anxious and Lydia would be loud and Jane would be composed, and none of it would feel the way she had once imagined an engagement might feel.

She had not, she realized, imagined an engagement. She had imagined various versions of staying unmarried, or marrying someone moderately agreeable at some undefined future point, or occasionally, with the amused detachment of a person who does not expect a thing and therefore does not guard against imagining it, marrying someone she actually loved. She had not imagined this: a proposal taken in the firelight of a borrowed parlor, accepted in one syllable, the fire gone cold before she thought to notice.

No matter. The imagination could be revised. People revised their circumstances every day.

She turned back to the room and looked at the desk. At the book, still open to whatever page he had last read; at the glasses folded across it; at the small careful accumulation of a man's daily habits, left exactly as they were because no one had known what to do with them.

She found Lydia at tea.

The others had assembled in the drawing room by now: Kitty with a length of ribbon she was unspooling and respooling for no discernible reason; Mary with a book she was not reading; her mother seated at her usual position near the fire, recovered enough from the earlier weeping to be engaged in something more resembling contentment. Only Lydia was in motion, as Lydia generally was: crossing from the window to the mantelpiece, rearranging objects that did not need rearranging, telling a story she had already told once before to Kitty, who was listening with the resigned attention of a person who has learned that Lydia's stories are shorter when uninterrupted.

The story, as Elizabeth gathered upon her entrance, concerned a sighting in Meryton from the Philipses' doorstep, or the street outside, the precise geography shifting slightly with each retelling, and a Lieutenant Wickham who had bowed to Lydia and said something she found exceedingly clever, and who was, according to every report Lydia had since collected from every available source, the most agreeable officer in the entire regiment. She had used the phrase "most particularly agreeable" at least twice before Elizabeth sat down.

Elizabeth poured her tea.

The name meant nothing to her. An officer, agreeable, encountered in Meryton. This described a significant portion of the militia and told her nothing worth knowing about any individual within it.

The unease she felt watching Lydia was not new and was not specific to Wickham. It was the familiar unease of watching her youngest sister in proximity to anyone who paid her attention; the brightness that came up too quickly, the laugh deployed before the joke had finished, the quality of listening that was really only waiting for confirmation of what Lydia had already decided to feel. An agreeable officer who singled her out was, in Lydia's current state, a pleasanter version of the situation Elizabeth had worried about in a general way for years.

She watched Lydia describe what the first assembly would be like — the officers arranged along one side of the room, Wickham's bow, the set she had already choreographed in her imagination and noticed, with the quiet attention she generally applied to things she could not yet act on, the way her youngest sister's voice lifted.

Lydia was not a stupid girl. She was impulsive and under-supervised and had been told, in a thousand small and large ways, that her value lay in being admired; and she had, in consequence, become very efficient at finding situations in which she could be admired, and very poor at evaluating the character of the people doing the admiring. The mourning period that kept her from assemblies had not diminished the appetite. It had only concentrated it.

"He is so agreeable," Lydia said, for what Elizabeth suspected was the third time. "And very handsome, in that way officers always are when the coat fits properly. Do you not think, Lizzy, that officers are always the most agreeable men in any room?"

"Not invariably," Elizabeth said.

"Well, you would say that," Lydia returned, cheerfully, "because you are to marry one of the brooding sort who does not dance properly and stands in corners. Not that I mean anything against Mr. Darcy," she added, in the tone of someone who did mean something but preferred not to be held to it, "only that he seems very grave, and I cannot imagine him ever laughing at a good story."

"He laughs," Elizabeth said, and was surprised to find that she knew this as a fact rather than a surmise.

Lydia waved a hand. "In any case, we cannot be in mourning forever, and when we are out again, you must come to the first assembly. Once you are married, you will have the best position in the room and everyone will want to speak to you, and I shall be standing right beside you, and Lieutenant Wickham will be there, I am quite sure of it, and, oh, it will be the best kind of evening."

She said this with the total confidence of a person who has not yet been given a reason to imagine the evening going any other way, and she crossed to the mantelpiece again to rearrange two candlesticks that did not need rearranging, and hummed something under her breath.

Elizabeth drank her tea.

She thought, not for the first time and not productively, about what it would take to make Lydia cautious. The answer was always the same: more than Elizabeth currently had available.

Lydia hummed. Outside, a cold wind moved through the elms with a sound like water.

That evening, after supper, Elizabeth went back to her father's study.

She moved the reading glasses to his watch stand, where he had kept them when he remembered to. She found a bookmark, a strip of leather she recognized as the cut-off end of an old bridle, the kind of repurposing that had always amused her, and closed the Fielding to a page she chose at random, so that it would not seem, to whoever eventually came in to sort things, that time itself had stopped on a particular evening in March.

She stood for a moment with her hand on the cover.

Then she left the study and closed the door behind her, and did not go back in.

Chapter 9: What the Letter Contains

The letter arrived the morning after Elizabeth returned to Longbourn.

She knew it was from Darcy before she broke the seal. The hand was precise, the paper heavier than anything that came from Longbourn neighbors, and no one else would have directed it so plainly to her alone. She stood in the entrance hall with her pelisse still buttoned and read the direction twice. Then she carried it upstairs and sat in the chair by the window and looked at it for a moment before she opened it.

The wedding was a fortnight away. She had not been counting, but she knew.

Below the window, Jane was crossing the yard with a basket over one arm — something domestic, purposeful. She moved with the deliberateness she had adopted since their father died, not heaviness exactly, but a careful attention to the ground underfoot, as if she had learned she could not trust it to stay where she had left it. The kitchen garden beyond the gate was coming into early leaf, the beds patchy and newly turned, the light thin in the way of April mornings. She watched her sister until she disappeared around the corner of the house, and then she unfolded the letter and read it.

He covered two things.

The first was the settlement itself. There was a brief, factual account of what he had instructed his solicitor to draw up, not as a preamble to negotiation, but as information she was being given before the formal process began. The figures were specific. He did not explain them as generosity, which would have been insufferable, but he did not present them as convention either, which would have been dishonest. He named them as what they were: his answer, confirmed in writing, to the question she had put to him the evening he proposed; the question about her mother and sisters, which had reframed the entire scene and which he had not seemed to resent being asked.

She had not known whether he would honor what he had said. She had been operating on the balance of probability and the absence of any better option. The settlement he described was not merely honorable. It was precise in the places where precision would matter most: provision for her mother during her lifetime, funds set aside for Kitty, Mary, and Lydia's portions. The Longbourn situation was addressed in terms that Collins could not contest, and Mrs. Bennet could not accidentally dismantle with a single ill-chosen confidence to a neighbor. He did not say what he intended to propose to Collins. He had mentioned, once, a lease arrangement; she had not forgotten, and the omission told her the terms were not yet settled rather than that he wished to conceal them.

He had thought through the weak points. He had found them before she needed to point them out to him.

Elizabeth set the first section down in her lap and looked out the window.

The garden below was half-woken. The plum tree at the corner of the wall had gone into blossom ahead of everything else, the way it always did, frothy and slightly absurd against the bare hedges. Her father had had an opinion about the plum tree; something wry about optimism that outpaced its evidence and she had laughed at the time without registering why. She did not try to reconstruct the joke. It was enough to remember that it had been funny, and that he had said it, and that the tree was doing what it always did whether or not anyone remarked on it.

She picked the letter back up.

The second thing was Bingley.

This section was shorter and harder to read.

He described his interference at Netherfield, the timing of it the previous autumn, the conclusion he had drawn after observing the Bennet family at length and watching Jane through the scrutiny of someone looking for reasons to be concerned. He had believed Jane's feelings were not seriously engaged. He had observed her composure and interpreted it as indifference. This was his first stated reason, and he separated it cleanly from his second, which was that he had also considered the match beneath his friend's station and the Bennet family's connections an active liability to Bingley's standing. He named this second reason with the accuracy of someone who had looked at his own motives without benefit of flattery, and he did not attempt to arrange them in order of palatability.

Elizabeth read this paragraph twice and then set the letter on the windowsill and did not pick it up again for several minutes.

Jane. Jane, who had conducted herself through every public occasion since Bingley's departure with a composure so complete and so careful that Elizabeth had sometimes, to her shame, been relieved by it. Relieved that there was no scene to manage, no evidence that might embarrass them, no feeling that required an audience. Jane, who had received the news of Elizabeth's engagement to Darcy with a warmth that was entirely genuine and had asked no questions about what Elizabeth felt, only what Elizabeth needed. Jane, who was at this moment crossing the yard below attending to what had to be attended to because their father was dead and Collins would have the house by summer and someone had to keep the household upright in the interval, and Jane was the one who did what had to be done without requiring it to be noticed.

Jane did not know any of this.

She did not know that Bingley's departure had been arranged, that her own behavior had been observed and misread by someone she had barely spoken to, that the interpretation placed on her composure had been used as evidence against her. She had spent the better part of a year assuming that Bingley had simply changed his mind, or been persuaded by his sisters, or found the silence and distance sufficient reason to let the thing lapse. She had accepted this the way she accepted most painful things, by finding it comprehensible, by declining to assign blame, by continuing to behave as if goodwill were the most reasonable interpretation of everyone involved.

The most reasonable interpretation had not been correct.

Elizabeth got up and walked to the writing desk and stood at it without sitting down. Somewhere below she could hear Mrs. Bennet and Hill in close conference; the linen question, or the silver question, or one of the dozen other household questions that had acquired new urgency since the engagement, since the house was no longer theirs to arrange at leisure. Her mother was doing the only thing available to her, which was to attend very closely to everything that was not the central fact, and Elizabeth had concluded that this was not stupidity but a form of endurance she did not intend to criticize.

She went back to the letter.

She read the Bingley section again from the beginning, not the facts this time, which she had organized, but the structure of the argument he had made to himself. He had separated the two reasons deliberately.

She kept returning to this. He could have folded them together, presented the question of Jane's feelings as the only operative concern, allowed the class consideration to remain unspoken and therefore unpunishable. He had not done that. He had put the less creditable motive in the same sentence as the more defensible one and declined to arrange them in order of palatability.

She did not know what to do with this, exactly. It did not excuse what had been done. But it was a different kind of document than she had expected to be holding.

He had sent Bingley back. That was also in the letter, briefly, in a subordinate clause that did not linger on itself. A statement that the visit to Longbourn had not been coincidental, that Darcy had spoken to Bingley before they came, that what she had watched from across the sitting room was an amendment in progress. She had known it at the time, in the way she knew most things about Darcy now: by watching closely and filing what she saw without naming it aloud. She had not been ready to name it. The letter was asking her to name it.

He had caused the damage. He was also attempting, without theater and without requiring her to acknowledge the attempt, to repair it.

These two facts sat in the same account, and the account did not balance, and she did not think it was supposed to balance yet.

At the end, one paragraph that was neither apology nor justification, or rather, it contained both without leaning on either. He described what he intended going forward. Not promised: intended, and he was careful about the word, using it twice. He would not interfere with Bingley's decisions again. If Bingley asked for his opinion, he would give it honestly, but the decision would remain Bingley's. He intended to be a different influence than he had been, in this and in other matters, and he understood that intention was not the same as a record, and that a record would take time.

Then, at the close, one sentence.

I do not ask you to trust conclusions you cannot verify, but I hope you will allow that the account I have given you is complete.

Elizabeth folded the letter along its original creases and set it on the desk.

She sat for a while doing nothing. This was not, for her, a usual condition, and she did not settle into it comfortably. Her mind kept moving over the Bingley section; not the content, which she had absorbed, but the question of what it meant that he had written it. He had not been required to write it. The settlements were being drawn. She had accepted him; the legal machinery was in motion; there was nothing she could have done at this stage that would have materially altered the outcome. He had written it anyway, in advance of the formal process, without being asked and without signaling that he expected a particular response.

She thought about her father, not deliberately, but in the way he kept arriving unbidden, in the gap between one thought and the next, in the space of a silence that he would once have filled with something wry and precise and true. She allowed herself the question for a moment and then set it aside, because the answer she arrived at was not one she was prepared to examine at length, and because there was still something she needed to do before the afternoon post went out.

She went for a walk first. She needed the lower field's offering of straight and uninterrupted distance before she could write anything she would not immediately regret.

The morning was cold in the way of early spring and the lane was still soft underfoot from recent rain. She walked past the stile and through the near meadow and stood for a moment looking at the line of elms coming into leaf, and a crow working at something in the far corner of the field, then she walked back. The light had shifted by the time she reached the garden gate. She noticed she was cold, which meant she had been out longer than she thought.

Back at the desk, she sat down and pulled a sheet of paper from the writing case and considered it for a while.

There was a great deal she could say. She could say that the account of Bingley was both more honest and more damning than she had expected, and that honesty and damage were not the same thing as exoneration. She could say that she had noted what he had done about the settlement and what it indicated about his understanding of what had been asked of him. She could say that she was not grateful, exactly, but that she was - she searched for the correct word and found it - attentive. She was paying closer attention than she had been, and it was not comfortable attention, and she was not certain yet what it was for.

She did not write any of this.

She wrote three lines.

I have read it. I will need to speak with you before the settlements are signed. There are things I want you to understand I know.

She read them back. They were not warm and they were not hostile and they established a position without overcommitting to one. They were honest, which was the one quality she had told him she would not compromise, and they were brief enough that the wording could not become a problem if she sat with them too long.

She wrote his name at the top, sealed it, and set it on the tray for the afternoon post.

Jane came in from the yard with mud on her half-boots and set the basket down just inside the door. She looked at the tray, then at Elizabeth with the particular attention she brought to things she would not ask about directly, and asked instead whether Elizabeth wanted tea.

She said yes.

Jane went to see about it. She did not ask what Elizabeth had been writing, or who had written to her, or what her expression meant. She understood the difference between privacy and secrecy, and she did not treat them as the same, which was one of the best things about her, and which Elizabeth noticed now with a sharpness she associated lately with things she had always known and was only now properly valuing.

She put Darcy's letter in the inner pocket of her writing case and listened to Jane's voice carry through from the kitchen, asking Hill something about the kettle — ordinary and unhurried, the sound of a household continuing.

The note to Darcy was still on the tray. She did not retrieve it.

Chapter 10: The Reckoning

Darcy arrived at Longbourn without Bingley.

She had noted that before she had finished reading his note. The note itself was brief. Thursday morning, if convenient; he wished to speak with her before the settlements were signed, and it contained no further explanation. She had spent Wednesday evening resolving not to think about it and had instead thought about little else.

She received him in the small sitting room. The drawing-room was her mother's territory now: every morning caller received there, every compliment on the engagement acknowledged there, Mrs. Bennet at full productive occupation with the pleasures of being right about something at last. The small sitting room was Jane's room, or had been; the distinction between what belonged to whom had grown uncertain since her father's death, and Elizabeth found she preferred rooms where the uncertainty was at least quiet.

Jane was there when Darcy was shown in, seated by the window with her needlework. Elizabeth had said only that she was expecting Mr. Darcy, and Jane had understood what was required without requiring it to be said. She had the tact of a person who knows the difference between being needed and being in the way, and who arranges herself accordingly.

He came in with the posture she had come to catalogue: straight, careful, his face giving away less than he imagined. He said good morning, first to Elizabeth, then to Jane; Jane returned it with a small smile and looked back at her cloth. His eyes went to Elizabeth, and she saw the moment he took in the black: the dress, the ribbon at her throat, the absence of anything that might catch the light. He had seen her in mourning at Hunsford and at Rosings, but he had not, she thought, seen her at Longbourn in it, in her father's house, in the room where her father had never sat. Something shifted in his expression, briefly, and was composed again before she could name it.

She indicated a chair and took her own. He sat.

They had exchanged perhaps four sentences - pleasantries, the weather, the state of the roads from wherever he had come - when Jane folded her needlework with the unhurried deliberateness of someone who has just remembered an errand that will not wait. She set the sewing basket beside the chair, rose, and excused herself with a word or two directed at neither of them in particular. The door, as she went out, she left open by some four inches.

A minute or two passed. Hill came along the passage outside. Her step was recognizable, unhurried. She paused fractionally and moved on. Through the gap in the door, the ordinary sounds of the house continued: a distant voice, the settling of a floorboard, the quiet of a morning in which other people were occupied with other things.

Darcy did not look towards the door. Neither did Elizabeth. The open door was Jane's solution to a problem none of them had named aloud. It was, she thought, exactly right.

He sat with the slight deliberateness of a man attending to his own behavior, and she thought: he has been preparing for this. The recognition did not soften her. It revised, slightly, the form of her attention.

"You wished to speak before the settlements," she said. "I assume you have a sense of where to begin."

"I have a sense of where I ought to begin," he said. "Whether I manage it is a separate question." He paused; not for effect, she thought, but because he was trying to be accurate. "I should like to speak about Bingley. About what I did."

Elizabeth looked at him. "Then speak about it."

He had thought about how to say this. She could see the thought in it, not the polish of a rehearsed speech, but the effort of a man trying to say something that would not be made tidy, in a way that did not allow him to make it smaller than it was.

"I advised Bingley to quit Netherfield," he said. "He was inclined to stay. His attachment to your sister was genuine, not a passing admiration, not the ordinary pleasure of an agreeable acquaintance, but something real. If he had stayed, he would have proposed. I told him that the attachment was not returned, that your sister's feelings did not appear to match his own, and that the connection was, on balance, unsuitable. He trusted my judgment. He left."

She said nothing. He continued.

"My grounds were these: I had observed your sister at Netherfield for some weeks. She was warm and pleasant in company; she received his attentions without clear discomfort; she was interested, cheerful, and seemingly at ease. And I concluded from all of it that she felt nothing particular for him." He stopped. Then, at the same even pace: "I now believe that what I read as insufficient attachment was restraint. That her manner — composed, careful, not inclined to display more than occasion required — I mistook for the behavior of a woman who was not in earnest. I was wrong." Another pause, and then the thing he had clearly decided he would say plainly: "The error was not innocent. I had reason to look more carefully, and I chose not to, because the simpler version of events was more convenient for the advice I had already decided to give."

The room was quiet. Somewhere above them a door opened and closed; her mother's voice rose briefly and was muffled by walls and distance.

"Why," said Elizabeth, "was it convenient."

Not a question, quite. He heard that.

"Because Bingley is not well-served by attachments that are not returned. That is the honest answer... the honest beginning of the answer." He was looking at her steadily. "But the fuller answer is that I had already formed a view of the match as unsuitable, for reasons that had more to do with the situation of your family than with your sister's feelings. And having formed that view, I found it easier to believe what supported it than to look closely at what might not." He let that sit. "I did not want to see it. That is the sum of it."

She absorbed this. She had come into the room with a prepared position. she had identified the points she required him to address, and had anticipated, despite herself, the ways in which he might diminish each one. She had a response ready for each anticipated diminishment. He had not diminished. She set the responses aside.

She had expected a qualified concession, that he had perhaps acted too hastily, that Bingley's happiness was of course his primary concern, that the situation of her family had been a natural and understandable complication. The kind of accounting that took responsibility with one hand and redistributed it with the other. He had not done that. He had named the mechanism of his error precisely: the prior judgment, the preference for evidence that confirmed it, the choice not to look too carefully at what might not. He had called it by its accurate name. He had not wanted to see it, because seeing it would have required him to do something harder than what he did.

She found she did not know what to do with that. She had not prepared for it. She filed it, not as exoneration, not as anything that changed the outcome for Jane, but as a fact about the man that was different from the fact she had arrived with. She was honest enough with herself to note that the difference existed.

"Jane did not know," she said. "For a long time, she did not know what had happened or why. She knew only that Mr. Bingley left Netherfield, and she had no information that allowed her to assign the cause correctly. So she assigned it to herself, to something she had done wrong, or said, or been, without being able to identify what, and she spent a considerable time in that."

Darcy said nothing.

"She would not tell you this. She does not make complaints, she does not apportion blame. She would receive you with perfect civility if you walked through that door this moment, and she would mean it. That is entirely her own, and I have no criticism of it." Elizabeth's voice did not change in temperature. "But you should know what was actually happening to her while you were comfortable in your certainty. She spent months believing herself not sufficiently loved, when the truth was that she had been made invisible by someone who had decided in advance that she did not matter enough to look at properly."

He took that without flinching. She had watched to see whether he would.

"Yes," he said. "I know it. That is... yes."

The yes had something in it that was not quite composure. She registered it and moved on.

"What do you intend to do about it?"

"I have written to him." His voice had resumed its steadiness, though she thought it cost him something now, where before it had been simply his register. "He knows what I did and the grounds on which I did it. He knows that I was wrong and that I will not interfere again. He knows that any choice he makes regarding your sister will have my full support and no qualification from me." A pause. "He has not removed the friendship. That is a reflection of his character, not mine."

"He is forgiving."

"Excessively," Darcy said, with a quality that was not quite dryness but was adjacent to it. "More than I had any right to expect."

Elizabeth looked at him for a moment. "I want Bingley to return to her, if he wishes to, genuinely, as his own choice, without your having arranged it so that refusal becomes awkward for him. I want it to be his wish and hers, arrived at freely. Not a correction made to a problem you created." She said it without heat, as a statement of position. "Can you give me that?"

"He is already returned to Netherfield. Of his own decision, made before I wrote." Darcy held her gaze. "I did not arrange his return. I arranged only that he had the truth about my interference, so that whatever he chose, he chose with full knowledge. The return was his."

She looked at him. Then: "Good."

One word. No warmth in it, but no coldness either. The word of a woman who had received accurate information and taken its measure, and who would not dress the reception as more than it was. He seemed, she thought, to understand exactly what it was. He did not look as though he had expected more, and he did not look relieved at receiving less. He looked like a man who had said what he came to say and was waiting to hear what came next.

"I will tell you what I require," she said. "Not as formal conditions. We are past formal conditions, but as a statement of what I expect from this arrangement, now that I understand more of what it contains."

"I want to hear it."

She had thought about this without allowing herself to rehearse it. Rehearsal invited counter-argument, and she did not want a debate. What she wanted was to say three things clearly enough that they could not be mistaken for negotiable, and then to see how he received them.

"I will not be managed. I know you are accustomed to managing situations, information, people, and outcomes. I understand it is not malice; it is what you have always done, and mostly you have done it in the sincere belief that it was useful. But I am not a situation. I am not a problem that benefits from being resolved without being consulted." She kept her eyes on him. "If there is something I need to know, about this family, about your decisions, about anything that now concerns both of us, I want to know it when you know it, not when you have decided I am ready to hear it."

He said: "Yes."

"I want to be certain you understand what that means in practice. It means you will sometimes have to tell me things before you have determined how they should be resolved. It means I will have opinions about the resolution. It means — " she paused, and chose the next sentence carefully, "it means that the instinct to protect by withholding is one you will have to actively work against, because it will not feel like withholding to you. It will feel like sense."

He was quiet for a moment. "You are describing a habit I am uncertain I know how to break."

"I know," Elizabeth said. "I am not asking you to have broken it. I am asking you to try, and to tell me when you have noticed that you have failed to try."

Something moved across his face brief and too controlled but she thought it was not displeasure.

"The second thing," she said. "Jane. What you did to her situation cannot be undone. I am not asking you to undo it. I am asking that whatever you do going forward be a real thing rather than a gesture. If Bingley returns to her properly, he does so freely, which you have told me is already the case. I am asking that you not allow your guilt about it to turn the resolution into another act of management. Let it be theirs."

"Yes," he said again. "I understand the distinction."

"The third thing." She stopped, and gathered the sentence. "I accepted your proposal because my situation required it. I have not forgotten that, and I see no reason either of us should act as though it were otherwise. I do not know yet what this marriage will be. I know what it is now; an arrangement made under pressure, with honest terms, between two people who have chosen to be truthful with each other when it would have been easier not to be." She looked at him steadily. "Whether it becomes more than that will depend on what both of us do. I am not in a position to promise you that it will."

"I am not asking for that promise."

"What are you asking for?"

He took his time. She had learned to attend to that, the pause that meant he was looking for the accurate answer rather than the presentable one.

"Permission to try," he said. "To — " he stopped. Tried again. "I have been in the habit, for a long time, of conducting myself in ways I believed to be correct without verifying whether they actually were. The consequence of that habit you have described with some thoroughness." The quality of dryness again, not quite irony, but the edge of it. "I am asking to be told when I am wrong. Not spared the knowledge because it would be awkward to deliver. I am asking for an honest account."

Elizabeth looked at him. The request was more specific than she had expected. She had prepared for something vaguer: assurances of good faith, general expressions of goodwill, the kind of open-ended commitment that left all the particulars to be disputed later. He had not offered vagueness. He had offered a concrete and somewhat self-exposing request, which happened to be the same concrete request she had just made of him, arrived at from the opposite direction.

She was, she realized, going to have to revise her understanding of him again. It was becoming a habit.

"I think," she said, "that we may be able to manage that between us."

They sat for a moment in the altered room. Not comfortably - they were not yet comfortable - but the quality of the silence had changed from the silence at the start of the interview. They had each said the thing they had come to say, and neither had flinched, and that was its own information.

Elizabeth was not ready to call it trust. She was precise about words and she knew the difference between trust and the recognition that a person might be trustworthy. One was a conclusion; the other was a direction of travel. She was somewhere on the road, not at the end of it.

"I should like to bring Bingley to call," he said. "Not today. Within the week, if that is agreeable."

"It is."

"And the solicitor comes Friday. I will have everything prepared." He picked up his gloves from the arm of the chair. Then he stopped. She had not expected him to stop, because he was a man who moved through rooms and through conclusions with equal directness, and he turned back.

"Elizabeth." He said it with deliberateness. It was the first time he had used her name and he knew it, and she knew it, and neither of them drew attention to the fact. "I am aware of the terms on which you accepted at Hunsford. I know what they were and I know what they were not." He was looking at her in the way she had come to recognize as his version of candor, direct, undecorated, and slightly uncomfortable with its own exposure. "I intend to give you reason to find it was not the wrong choice. I cannot offer more than an intention. But I want you to know that it is a real one, and that I understand what it costs me nothing to say and will require something to actually do."

Elizabeth looked at him for a moment.

"That," she said, "is a more honest formulation than most people manage."

He went out. She heard his footsteps in the passage, the front door, the sound of his horse and carriage on the gravel drive, and then the ordinary quiet of a house that had gone on being itself throughout.

Jane returned to the room after Darcy left. "He stayed longer than I expected," she said.

"There was a great deal to say."

Jane nodded. She picked up her needlework again, smoothed the cloth across her lap, and did not ask what had been said. Elizabeth sat down in the chair Darcy had vacated. It was still slightly warm, which she noticed and set aside, and looked at her hands.

She had gone in with three things she required of him. She had come out with all three, not in a form of assurance but in the form of demonstrated understanding. She had prepared for qualified versions, for the half-concession that kept one hand free, for the apology that repositioned the fault at the edges rather than the center. He had not done any of those things. He had looked at what he had done and declined to make it smaller.

"Jane," she said.

Her sister looked up.

"Bingley is at Netherfield." Elizabeth watched her face. "He has returned of his own choice, I believe. I am told he is there now."

Jane's expression did not change dramatically. It did something quieter: a slight release, like a breath held for so long that the holding had become ordinary and the release was only remarkable by comparison. She looked back at her needlework.

"I see," she said.

"I do not know what he intends," Elizabeth said. "I do not know what you intend. I am only telling you what I was told, because I thought you should know it."

"Yes," Jane said. "Thank you."

They sat together in the quiet of the room. At length Elizabeth stood and went to the window. Outside, the drive was empty, the morning light flat and white over the garden. It was her father's garden: his beds, his paths, the particular arrangement of the kitchen plot that had been his preference and no one else's and the word *his* had not yet adjusted itself to the past tense in her mind. She suspected it would not for some time.

She thought about what her father would have made of this interview. She could construct his response with some confidence; wry, oblique, a single accurate observation delivered as if it were a general remark about human nature. He would have said something that appeared to be about Darcy and was actually about Elizabeth, and she would have understood, and they would have said nothing further on the subject. They had always managed that economy between them.

He was not there to make the observation. That was the state of her grief on a day like this: not the large, dull ache of absence, which she was learning to carry, but the precise small moment of reaching for something and finding the shelf empty.

She did not allow herself to stay at the window for long. There was too much to do, and the grief, when she let it, had a way of making the practical things feel very far away. The practical things needed to remain close.

She turned back to the room. Jane had resumed her needlework, her head bent, her needle moving in and out of the cloth with a steadiness that Elizabeth recognized as its own form of composure.

Behind her, she heard her mother reach the landing.

Chapter 11: The Settlements

The carriage from Gracechurch Street to Gray's Inn Road took twenty minutes longer than it should have, owing to a dray cart that had shed its load at the corner of Holborn and showed no signs of remorse. Mr. Gardiner used the delay to review his notes. Elizabeth used it to look out the window at London waking: stone and commerce and too many chimneys, nothing like Hertfordshire, and making no apology for it.

"You have read the draft provision?" Her uncle asked, without looking up.

"Last night. Yes."

"Any questions before we go in?"

She had questions, but not the kind the solicitor would answer. "None that pertains to the documents," she said.

Mr. Gardiner closed his notes. He had the good sense not to ask what the other kind of question was.

He had been, throughout this entire business, the person she had most relied upon without having to say so. He did not treat her presence at the solicitor's table as a concession requiring management. He had written to ask whether she wished to attend, received her reply in the affirmative, and written back with the address and the time. The exchange had contained no remarks about the unusual nature of the request, no gentle suggestions she might find it taxing. She would remember that.

Darcy was already in the room when they arrived. He stood at the window with his back to the door, hands clasped, and turned when he heard them with no expression of surprise. He had known she would come. Whether he had expected it, she could not say.

The solicitor was a small man named Fitch with ink on his left cuff and a habit of directing all remarks to the nearest male body regardless of who had asked the question. He produced the settlement papers from a leather folder, laid them on the table, and addressed the air between Mr. Gardiner and Darcy with an explanation of the document's structure. Elizabeth drew the nearest page toward her and read.

Fitch's gaze went to Mr. Gardiner.

Mr. Gardiner looked at Elizabeth.

Elizabeth read the page.

She read slowly, which was not her usual habit but seemed appropriate here. The figures were in order: her pin money, set at a level that acknowledged she had opinions and would need the resources to act on them; the jointure, generous and clearly not calculated to the minimum; the provision for children, standard in form. Competent. More than competent. She turned to the second page.

The provision for her mother and sisters was the third item. She read it twice. The figures were what Darcy had named at Hunsford, and they were more than necessity required, but it was the fourth item that stopped her: a two-year lease on Longbourn, at a rate that was correct rather than lavish, the agreement already reached with Mr. Collins's solicitor pending her signature.

She looked up.

Mr. Gardiner was watching her with the expression of a man who had already read the document and formed his opinion.

"When was this arranged?" she asked Darcy.

"Only a few days ago," he said. "Collins required some time to consider the framing."

She could imagine exactly how the framing had been managed. Collins would have been made to feel that leasing Longbourn to his own cousin's family was the action of a man of consequence and Christian feeling. He would have agreed and believed himself generous.

She put the document down. "It will matter a great deal to my mother," she said.

Darcy said nothing. He already knew this.

She read to the end of the document. Nothing surprised her after the third page, except a single clause near the signature line that gave her the right to receive correspondence directly rather than through Darcy's household. It was not a standard provision. It could only have been inserted because someone had thought to include it, had looked at the standard document, found it wanting in one specific respect, and corrected it.

She put the papers down.

Across the table, Darcy had not moved since they entered. He stood with the stillness of a man who was being patient.

Fitch was explaining something to Mr. Gardiner about the registration process. Darcy was watching Elizabeth in the way he occasionally watched her: not intrusively, not with anything she would call softness, but with attention that did not look away when she looked up.

She looked up. He looked back.

"I have no objection," she said, and looked at Fitch, who looked at Mr. Gardiner, who looked at Darcy.

"Nor do I," Darcy said.

The signatures were affixed. The copy for the Bennet family solicitor was produced and sealed. Elizabeth stood, put her gloves back on, and said nothing more until they were in the carriage and moving south toward Mayfair.

"He is thorough," Mr. Gardiner said, after a moment, meaning Darcy.

"Yes," Elizabeth said.

Her uncle nodded once, as if something had been confirmed, and looked out his window at the street.

Darcy's London house was in Brook Street, which Elizabeth had known in the abstract and now knew in the specific: the proportions of the entrance hall, the color the afternoon light went when it came through the south-facing windows of the drawing room, the smell of beeswax and cut flowers that meant someone had been preparing for guests since morning. The rooms were well-kept and not ostentatious, arranged in a way that suggested the person who had chosen the furniture had also actually sat in it.

The evening was his first formal entertainment as an engaged man. The social calendar had made it obligatory before either of them had thought to object, and Elizabeth had spent an afternoon accepting that she was now a figure in Darcy's social world, not merely a fact within it. She had dressed accordingly, which in her present circumstances meant black crepe over black silk, relieved by nothing except the plainness of the cut. Mourning gave no latitude for ornament, but it permitted good tailoring, and she had made use of that.

She had arrived with the Gardiners, which was to say she had arrived as she had spent most of the day; under the quiet, practical shelter of her aunt and uncle's company. She had gone ahead into the drawing room while Mrs. Gardiner spoke with the housekeeper, intending to form an impression of the room before the room formed an impression of her, and she was aware, without vanity, that the severity of her dress would itself make an impression whether or not she intended it.

Miss Bingley was not among the guests. She had sent a note of congratulation so precisely correct in every word that its hostility was only perceptible to someone already looking for it. Elizabeth found herself admiring the craft.

Lady Catherine's absence would be noted by everyone and explained by no one. It was, in this way, the loudest thing in the room.

The other guests were Colonel Fitzwilliam, easy and warm as he always was; a Sir Edmund and Lady Morrow, whose connection to the Darcy family was old and whose manner toward Elizabeth was pleasant in the way of people who are genuinely curious but too well-bred to ask anything useful; and the Gardiners, who entered last and filled the room, as they always did, with the ease of people who are comfortable wherever they are. Mrs. Gardiner took in the Brook Street drawing room with the calm appreciation of someone who knows good things when she sees them and does not feel the need to say so aloud.

Elizabeth had not expected Darcy to include the Gardiners. He had not asked her whether he should. She noted that too, alongside everything else she had been noting since that morning.

At dinner, Mr. Gardiner was seated across from Darcy, whether by chance or design Elizabeth could not determine, and opened with a question about the Pemberley water levels that was obviously an inquiry into whether Darcy was worth talking to rather than a genuine inquiry about water. Darcy seemed to understand this, because he answered with more detail than the question warranted and then returned one of his own. They worked toward each other across the table with the patience of two men willing to take the long route, and Elizabeth ate her soup and watched them do it.

By the fish course, they had arrived at fishing.

They remained there through the meat course and the remove. Beside her, Mrs. Gardiner caught Elizabeth's eye once, briefly, with an expression that communicated the whole of her assessment without requiring a word, and then returned her attention to Sir Edmund, who was telling her something about his estate in Wiltshire that she appeared to find genuinely interesting. She had a talent for that, Elizabeth's aunt. She could find the interesting thread in almost anyone, and pull it.

Colonel Fitzwilliam, on Elizabeth's other side, had been a courteous and undemanding dinner companion for most of the first two courses. During the remove he leaned in.

"I have not heard him talk that much at dinner in five years," he said, in an undertone, meaning Darcy. "You should feel no pressure to account for it."

"I take no credit," Elizabeth said. "My uncle has a gift."

"Your uncle has found the one subject on which Darcy will always expand, and has done so within ten minutes of sitting down. That is not a gift. That is reconnaissance." He paused, and then, with the expression of a man stepping carefully: "Miss Bennet." The name landed with the particular care of someone aware it would not serve much longer. "Are you quite all right?" Not the social version of the question. The actual one.

She considered it honestly. "I have been in a solicitor's office this morning and a London drawing-room this evening," she said. "Both of them exercises in reading the same information from different angles. I am well enough."

Fitzwilliam laughed — not the polished version he deployed in Lady Catherine's drawing room, but something shorter and more involuntary. "I think," he said, "that you will do."

She did not ask what he meant. He seemed to mean something specific by it, and she did not require his elaboration.

Across the table, her uncle was describing the stretch of the Lambourne where he had once lost a fish so large it had become, over the years of retelling, a fish of genuinely mythological proportions. Darcy was listening with what appeared to be real attention, and Elizabeth watched his face for the condescension she had once found so legible there and could not locate it.

He caught her watching. His expression did not change. He returned his attention to Mr. Gardiner.

She ate her pudding.

At the Gardiners' door in Gracechurch Street, Darcy handed Mrs. Gardiner down from the carriage. Mr. Gardiner followed and turned, and Darcy shook his hand; not the brief grip of obligation but something more deliberate, accompanied by a remark Elizabeth was too far back on the step to hear. Mr. Gardiner replied with one of his short, decisive nods that meant he had decided something. Then he and his wife were inside, and the door was closed, and Elizabeth stood in the lamplight on the pavement and looked at Darcy.

He looked back. She had the impression, not for the first time, that he was storing the picture of her. Not admiring it, exactly, but committing it to something more permanent than an impression. She had not decided what to make of that habit.

"The settlement provision," she said, "for my mother and sisters. You submitted the amount before the Gardiners' solicitor had named a figure."

He did not deny it. "Yes."

"It was more than I would have asked for."

"I know."

She studied him in the way she had learned to study him, without the overlay of what she had once believed, without supplying his motives from old inventory. "Was it an argument," she said, "or a statement of intention?"

He was quiet for a moment. The lamp on the post behind him moved in the wind and the shadow shifted across the pavement between them.

"I am not certain I understand the distinction," he said.

"An argument suggests you wanted me to find it in the papers and think better of you. A statement of intention suggests you calculated what they would need without reference to how it would read."

He considered this with the seriousness he brought to things that deserved it. The consideration, she had come to recognize, was genuine. He did not speak until he had arrived at something he meant. "I calculated what they would need," he said. "Whether you thought better of me was not something I believed I could engineer."

She received this and filed it where the other fact had gone — into the category she was still constructing, for which she did not yet have the right word. Not trust. Something adjacent to trust, with trust's general direction.

"Then it was a statement of intention," she said.

"Yes."

The carriage was waiting. She said good night and went inside.

Her aunt was already pouring when Elizabeth came in.

Elizabeth sat down and accepted the offered cup. "He likes Uncle Gardiner," she said.

Mrs. Gardiner considered this. "Edward liked him too, I think."

"I did not doubt that." Elizabeth turned the cup in her hands. "What I mean is that Darcy did not know he would. He went into the evening with one set of expectations and came out of it with different information, and he received the difference without any apparent difficulty."

Her aunt was quiet for a moment. Outside, they could hear the carriage moving away from the street.

"That is not a small thing," Mrs. Gardiner said, "in a man of his position."

"No," Elizabeth said. "It is not."

She drank her tea. The fire was low. Her aunt did not press her further, and Elizabeth did not volunteer more, because she was not yet certain what the more would be, only that there was some, and that it was growing in a direction she had not mapped.

Chapter 12: Darcy and Bingley at Longbourn

Darcy had not told her he was bringing Bingley.

He had not concealed it precisely. He had simply not mentioned it, which was a distinction he recognized as insufficient even as he made it. The visit had been arranged two days prior; Bingley persuaded over a long evening and a shorter breakfast, and in neither conversation had it occurred to Darcy to write to Elizabeth about it. He told himself this was because the plan was not yet fixed. He recognized, on the morning of the visit, that this was not the entire truth.

He had also not told Bingley what to expect. Not because it would have been improper to say so, but because he was uncertain he could describe it accurately: a house in full mourning, quieter than Bingley remembered it, the ordinary noise of the Bennet household muffled under crape and closed curtains and the particular atmosphere of rooms that have lost their organizing principle. Bingley had called at Longbourn only when Mr. Bennet was alive and the house was loud. Darcy had been once since for the interview with Elizabeth, which had been its own kind of difficult, and the difference was not something he had forgotten.

He watched Bingley in the carriage, the familiar restlessness of his knee, his gaze moving between the window and the middle distance. Darcy had seen that alertness before. He knew what it meant and what it did not yet mean.

"She may not receive callers," Bingley said. "Given the mourning period—"

"Mrs. Bennet receives callers," Darcy said. "She always has. The house is not under strict seclusion."

This was true, and also - he would not say this to Bingley - something Elizabeth had observed aloud when he called last month. She had said it in passing, without particular emphasis: Mrs. Bennet's mourning has not extended to her drawing room. He had taken it at face value. He suspected now she had meant it as more than a social observation.

"Still," Bingley said. "We ought to be brief. It would not be appropriate—"

"We will be appropriately brief," Darcy said. He looked at the road. "Bingley. She will be glad to see you."

Bingley's knee stopped moving. He said nothing for a moment. Then: "You cannot know that."

"No," Darcy said. "But I know more than I did a year ago, and that is what I believe."

Mrs. Bennet met them in the hall.

She was in black from collar to hem, as were the two youngest girls visible behind her; the house had all the trappings of mourning correctly applied: crepe on the knocker, the hall mirror sheeted, a quiet that sat uneasily on rooms designed for noise. Her face carried the combination of genuine grief and genuine relief that Darcy had observed in her before: the grief for Mr. Bennet was real, he believed that, but Mrs. Bennet was not a woman who processed grief as a private experience, and the arrival of her daughter's betrothed and Mr. Bingley had evidently provided an occasion that superseded, if only temporarily, her awareness of loss.

She welcomed Bingley with a warmth that was not quite propriety: too eager, too immediate, insufficiently tempered by the black she wore, but which contained, beneath its surface, the genuine desperation of a woman who understood that her family's prospects had survived only by a narrow margin. Darcy read this correctly. He did not require her to be graceful about it.

His own welcome was marginally cooler and more correct, which he preferred.

Elizabeth was in the drawing-room. She rose when they entered. She was in full mourning still, as she had been when he called days earlier, but he read her differently now than he had then. Then he had been watching for signs of her terms being met or refused. Now he was watching her watch Bingley's face when Bingley registered Jane across the room, and the way she took in what the visit meant before she looked at him.

She looked at Darcy.

He held her gaze without comment.

Jane had not come downstairs for callers in the first weeks after their father's death, or so Mrs. Gardiner had written in the letter that reached Elizabeth at Hunsford while she was still working out the arithmetic of her situation. By the time Elizabeth returned to Longbourn, Jane had resumed the ordinary motions of the household with the competence of someone who had been managing them alone and did not intend to make a grievance of it. Elizabeth had understood this with no need to ask and had simply joined her.

She was seated near the window, her needlework in her lap. She was also in black, the color severe against her fairness, and she had not, Elizabeth observed, reached for the needlework in some time. When Bingley came through the door, Jane rose in the unhurried way she did everything and said "Mr. Bingley" with the careful warmth of a woman who had had several weeks to decide how she would conduct herself in exactly this contingency and was now conducting herself accordingly.

Bingley said, "Miss Bennet" in a voice that cost him something.

Lydia, across the room, exhaled with theatrical impatience. She was sixteen, in mourning for a father she had not quite known how to grieve, and finding the domestic confinement that mourning imposed on unmarried girls aggressively unreasonable. "At last," she said, at a volume that carried.

Mrs. Bennet said "Lydia" without conviction.

Elizabeth said nothing. She was watching Jane.

Darcy stayed near the window.

The room had the atmosphere that mourning houses acquired when they were also drawing rooms expected to function as normal: furniture in its proper arrangement, the fire laid properly, tea available—but everything slightly muted, the usual conversational ease somewhat effortful. Mrs. Bennet managed it by ignoring it. Bingley managed it by bringing his ordinary warmth to bear on whatever topic presented itself. Jane managed it with a composure that was, Darcy understood, her characteristic mode under pressure.

He managed it by remaining peripheral and observing.

He was watching Lydia when he heard the name.

She was talking to Kitty, a separate and considerably less restrained conversation running alongside the main one, and she dropped it without preamble: Wickham, the assembly, the regiment. The name fell into the room the way an irregular sound falls into a quiet space, not loud, but locating something the ear had been, without knowing it, attuned for.

Darcy did not move. He adjusted nothing. He kept his attention on the middle distance and heard the rest of it: the assembly at Meryton, half the regiment invited, Wickham described as the most agreeable man among them. The careless endorsement that required no real feeling to produce, only proximity and a tendency to call any man agreeable who smiled readily.

"He said the rooms will be full," Lydia continued, to Kitty. "And I intend to go. I do not see why mourning should mean we are imprisoned forever. Papa would not have wanted—"

"Lydia." Mrs. Bennet's voice was sharper this time.

Lydia subsided with visible resentment. The resentment, Darcy had noted, of a girl who believed she was being constrained by rules that applied more harshly to her than to the sister who had become engaged during the same period of grief. He recognized this assessment as accurate and without a ready solution.

He looked at Elizabeth.

She was already looking at him. Her expression told him the name had reached her as clearly as it had reached him.

Elizabeth made the tea.

It gave her hands a purpose while she thought. She moved through the routine of it—pot, cups, the correct order of things—and noted, without looking up, that Darcy had positioned himself where he could observe the room. She had learned to read this as deliberate rather than antisocial, which was a revision she had not expected to make.

She handed him his cup without comment. He took it the same way.

Jane came to her side as she poured for the others, drawn by the same long habit of finding each other in overcrowded rooms.

"He looks well," Jane whispered. She meant Bingley.

"He does."

Jane was quiet for a moment. She was watching Bingley talk to Mrs. Bennet about something with the ease of a man who had never found social navigation effortful and who had, never been required to feel guilty about his sociability. "Elizabeth. Did you know he was coming?"

"No."

"Darcy arranged it."

It was not a question. Elizabeth looked at Darcy across the room—he was examining a watercolor above the mantel, or appearing to—and considered what the correct answer was.

"I believe so," she said.

Jane said nothing immediately. She took her cup. Her profile showed more of what she was carrying, the grief still fresh, the uncertainty about her own prospects not fully resolved, the habitual gentleness deployed over something less easy. Then: "That was good of him."

Elizabeth agreed, silently and did not yet know what to do with it.

The visit lasted rather more than an hour, which was longer than strict propriety might have encouraged given the family's circumstances, but which no one present moved to curtail. Mrs. Bennet's sense of occasion had overcome her sense of decorum, and Bingley was constitutionally incapable of leaving a room that still wanted him.

Darcy watched Bingley and Jane with the attention of someone reviewing a calculation he had previously gotten wrong. The conversation between them was formally about nothing: neighborhood weather, Netherfield's spring, Jane's inquiry after Caroline Bingley delivered with the perfect neutrality of someone who required no particular answer, but conducted at the temperature he recognized. The temperature he had observed at Meryton, at Netherfield, in the weeks before he had exercised his judgment.

The difference now was that Jane was conducting something at the same temperature in return. She had not been doing that before; or she had been, and it had not been visible to him because he had not been looking for it, because he had decided in advance that her feelings did not constitute a serious attachment and had not troubled himself to verify this against the evidence available.

He observed this recollection without attempting to minimize it.

He observed Lydia, restless in her chair, her black dress making her look younger and more confined than she appeared. Her boredom was the boredom of a girl who had always expected the world to move around her and was currently being asked, by circumstances she had not created, to sit still. He understood why this produced resentment. He did not underestimate what it might produce if the resentment found an external object to organize itself around.

He would need to speak to Elizabeth about Wickham, or she would raise it herself. She had seen his face when the name was said; he was nearly certain of it, and Elizabeth did not overlook things she had seen. The difficulty was that what he could tell her was almost nothing. He could tell her Wickham was dangerous. He could not tell her why without a full account he was not yet prepared to give, and a partial account would raise questions he could not answer, and unanswered questions from Elizabeth had a way of becoming positions she held against him.

Elizabeth walked them out.

Mrs. Bennet appeared at the drawing-room door, assessed the situation, and retreated with the occasional good sense she deployed when self-interest pointed in the same direction as discretion. Bingley had found a reason to linger in the hall - something he had forgotten to mention to Jane about a book - and Jane had accompanied him with the visible composure of a woman who knows she is being given a moment and intends to use it correctly.

The front step was cold. Elizabeth had not brought a shawl, and the black of her dress offered no warmth. She folded her arms and looked at the lane.

"You did not tell me," she said.

"No." He did not qualify it.

"You ought to have."

"Yes."

The elm was thick with summer growth now; the lane shadowed and close. Collins had been through once already to assess the grounds briefly, and apparently with satisfaction, and Elizabeth thought the trees must have seemed to him like inventory.

"I saw what you did," she said. "About Bingley. Bringing him here."

Darcy said nothing. He was, she had learned, capable of waiting without discomfort, which was a discipline or a disposition, and she had not yet determined which.

"Jane did not deserve what happened. This does not—" she stopped. Restarted. "It does not balance against it. What it is, is what it is."

"Yes."

"But it is something."

"I know."

The quiet between them held for a moment without becoming uncomfortable, which was itself a change from what quiet between them had once meant. Below them, Bingley's voice carried from inside the house, and then Jane's, lower.

"I saw your face," Elizabeth said, "when Lydia said his name."

Darcy did not ask which name. He said nothing.

"I do not know what I saw," she continued, more carefully. "I do not know whether it was something specific or simply an old dislike. Lydia has mentioned him before. She thinks him very agreeable."

"I know what Lydia thinks of him."

The flatness of it was not dismissive. It was something else; contained, in the way he became contained when he was managing something he did not intend to put down. Elizabeth looked at him directly.

"Is there something I ought to know?"

He was quiet long enough that she understood the answer was yes and the question was only how much. "He is not a safe acquaintance for your sister," he said at last. "I cannot say more than that at present."

She received this without expression. It was, she thought, precisely the thing she had told him she would not accept: protection without information, a conclusion delivered without its reasoning. And yet his face, when Lydia had said the name, had not looked like condescension. It looked like something she did not have a word for yet.

"At present," she repeated.

"Yes."

"That implies there will be a point at which you can say more."

He looked at her. "Yes."

She did not push further. Not because she was satisfied - she was not - but because she was still reading him, and what she was reading suggested that the withholding was not careless. She did not yet know what it was instead. She filed it alongside the other things she did not yet know, which was becoming a considerable list.

"Then I will watch Lydia," she said, "and you will tell me more when you are able. And when that time comes, I will want the whole, not the portion you have decided I can manage."

It was sharper than she had intended. He did not flinch from it. "Yes," he said. "The whole."

The door behind them opened and Bingley appeared, shrugging on his coat, his face carrying the specific brightness of a man who has had two minutes of private conversation and is calculating what they might mean. He looked between Darcy and Elizabeth with his characteristic transparency.

"Ready?"

"Yes," Darcy said.

He looked at Elizabeth once more and went down the steps. She stayed on the threshold until the gate closed behind them; the cold coming through the thin wool of her sleeve, Lydia's voice already rising again somewhere inside the house.

In the carriage, Darcy looked at the road. Bingley said nothing for some time and then said: "She is well. Considering."

"Yes," Darcy said.

"They all are. Considering. It cannot be easy, with the house—" Bingley gestured vaguely, meaning Collins, meaning the entail, meaning the entire apparatus of dispossession that politeness prevented him from naming directly.

"No," Darcy said. "It is not easy."

He did not explain what he had arranged about Bingley, or what he and Elizabeth had discussed on the step, or what he intended to do about Wickham. There was nothing that required explaining to Bingley. There was only the fact of what had been arranged, and that Elizabeth had seen it, and that she had told him what she needed from him in return.

This struck him, somewhere past Meryton, as the most honest transaction he had been party to in some time.

Chapter 13: The Wedding

The morning came in stages.

First the birds, then the gray light pressing through the curtains, then Mrs. Bennet's voice from the corridor. She didn't discern words, only tone, and a pitch that announced consequence rather than catastrophe.

Lydia was somewhere below, clattering. Mary's footsteps crossed the landing with their customary deliberation. Jane knocked once at Elizabeth's door and, receiving no answer, said her name quietly through the wood, as if she understood that some kinds of morning required no assistance.

Elizabeth was already dressed.

She had risen before the housemaid could bring water, before any of them had organized their expectations of her. The mirror showed a woman she recognized: upright, composed, wearing the expression she had been developing over the past weeks for occasions that required composure she did not particularly feel. She had become, she thought, quite accomplished at it.

The gown was pale gray, half-mourning, as was proper, as she had insisted when a note from Rosings arrived suggesting lavender. Lady Catherine had not signed it herself; she had delegated the suggestion to a companion, which Elizabeth had taken as a sign that the battle was beneath Darcy's aunt's direct attention. Elizabeth had written back in three sentences. The subject had not been raised again.

She stood at the window while the housemaid dressed her hair. The garden below was still in the early morning: the beds her father had never bothered with, the path to the kitchen door that had always needed raking and never received it. A thrush was doing something practical in the near hedge. She watched it until her hair was done.

Jane appeared at last, fully dressed, a small sprig of white flowers from the garden in her hand.

"You do not need those," Elizabeth said.

"I know," Jane said. "I brought them for myself." She set them on the dressing table between them and looked at her sister with a steadiness that required no softening. "How are you?"

"Present," Elizabeth said. "Alert. Aware of what day it is."

Jane waited.

"I am not frightened," Elizabeth added, because it was true, and because Jane would have noticed the omission. "I am simply -" she stopped. The right word was not available. "I am going to do this correctly."

"Yes," Jane said. "I know you will."

There was nothing more to be said, and so they said nothing, which was one quality Elizabeth valued most in her sister. Jane picked up the sprig of flowers again and turned them in her fingers, and Elizabeth looked at the garden once more. The thrush had gone, and the morning was assembled and waiting.

The church was small; the party was smaller. Mr. Collins had made himself useful in the matter of the ceremony, a usefulness that took the form of an extended commentary on the privilege of witnessing such an alliance between Rosings Park and Longbourn; a commentary that Darcy received with the expression of a man who has decided, once and permanently, to hear nothing that will require a response.

Elizabeth watched him from across the churchyard.

He was speaking with Mr. Gardiner. She could not hear the words, only the register, which was lower and less guarded than he used at Rosings. Mr. Gardiner had a way of making conversation feel like conversation rather than assessment, and Darcy appeared to understand this. His shoulders had dropped a degree since she had last observed him. He was listening to something Mr. Gardiner had said with the attention of a man who has found, unexpectedly, that he is being spoken to rather than spoken at. He said something in return. Mr. Gardiner laughed.

She turned away before Darcy could catch her watching.

He looked well. She had noted this on each occasion since the engagement and had not yet decided whether noting it was useful or merely habitual. Today, he looked like a man who intended to be married and had dressed accordingly, which was all she had required of him. She filed this and turned her attention to the yew hedge at the churchyard's edge, which wanted cutting.

Colonel Fitzwilliam found her before she was called in. He bowed with warmth and said, "Mrs. Darcy-to-be," as if testing whether the title would amuse her.

"Not yet," she said.

"Within the hour." He smiled. It was a genuinely kind smile. She had come, over these weeks, to appreciate the distinction between his kind and his social smiles, which were different animals. "Are you prepared?"

"I am dressed," she said, "and I know the words."

Fitzwilliam laughed, a real one. "That is more than most people manage." He offered her his arm into the church, which was the sort of thing he did without requiring acknowledgment. She took it.

They walked through the porch and into the cool interior. Candles at the front, plain glass in the windows, the smell of old stone. Her mother was already seated, her handkerchief in hand for an emergency that had not yet arrived. Lydia was whispering something to Kitty. Mary sat with her hands folded, her posture the posture of someone who believes she is being observed and finds this morally improving.

Darcy was already at the front when she entered.

She registered him in pieces: the set of his back, the precise angle at which he held himself: not rigidly, which would have been fear, but with the controlled stillness of someone who has decided where his attention will go and is keeping it there. He did not turn until she was beside him.

When he did, she looked back. She had decided some days ago that she would look at him with accuracy rather than arrange her face for the room, and she kept this resolution now.

He was, in fact, afraid.

Not visibly, not in any way the room would read - but she had been watching him for weeks, and she knew the slight contraction around his eyes when something mattered to him more than he intended to allow. He had it now. He composed his expression almost immediately, with the practice of someone who has been composing expressions since childhood, but the moment before composition was there and she had seen it. She thought, *He believes I might still change my mind.*

She found she had nothing useful to do with this information. She faced forward.

The clergyman had a kind voice. There was something deliberate in his delivery that she appreciated, as if he had decided that the people in front of him deserved to hear what they were actually agreeing to. She paid attention. She had decided she would pay attention, rather than retreat into her own thoughts and emerge to find it done. She owed herself that much. She owed him that much, which was a new and mildly inconvenient thought.

When they came to Darcy's part, his voice was level, low, and entirely clear. He said each clause as if it were a separate act: *I, Fitzwilliam, take thee, Elizabeth, to my wedded wife, to have and to hold.* He did not rush. He did not dress the words in ceremony, he simply inhabited them, which was, she was beginning to understand, the difference between a man who had learned to say the correct thing and a man who had learned, at some cost, to mean what he said.

She said hers.

She had said her own name hundreds of times, and it had never struck her as particularly remarkable until she said it here, in this arrangement of words, beside this man. *I, Elizabeth, take thee, Fitzwilliam.* The name sounded strange in her mouth. She had not used it before, had thought of him as Darcy so long that using his given name felt like addressing someone else, a younger and less armored person who might or might not exist. She filed this as the sort of thing that would require an adjustment, along with the half-dozen other adjustments the next months would require, and continued.

To love and to cherish.

She said it.

The ring was cold, then warm.

It was done. Mrs. Bennet, in the second pew, produced the handkerchief.

The breakfast at Longbourn was, in the main, Mrs. Bennet's production.

She had organized it with the energy of a woman who has been managing catastrophe for three months and has just been handed something to celebrate instead. The flowers were excessive. They were cut from the garden and supplemented with whatever Meryton's modest florist could supply on a week's notice, arranged in a fashion that suggested enthusiasm rather than expertise. The food was plentiful in the wrong proportions: too many pastries, not enough of anything substantial, the cold meats placed at an angle that required stretching to reach. Elizabeth had not slept well and was consequently hungry, and spent the first twenty minutes of her own wedding breakfast navigating the table without drawing her mother's attention to the difficulty.

Mrs. Bennet introduced Elizabeth, across the first hour, as "Mrs. Darcy, my eldest daughter... well, second eldest, but the first to be married, and to such advantage," the phrasing adjusting with each iteration in ways that suggested she was editing toward a final version. Darcy was addressed by her as "Mr. Darcy" and also, twice, as "son," which produced in him an expression of such careful neutrality that Elizabeth, catching it from across the room, was briefly grateful she had not been closer.

He bore it. She watched him bear it throughout the breakfast, which was the most consistently illuminating hour she had spent in his company. He was not actively unpleasant about any of it; he simply existed alongside the occasion without contributing to its excess. When Lydia pulled him into a discussion of his carriages, specifically the number of them and whether any were suited to a journey to London, he answered her questions. When Mr. Collins arrived at his elbow with further reflections on the honor of the day, he stood it out. At one point Mrs. Bennet took hold of his arm to steer him toward the wedding cake, and he went with her without visible objection, allowing himself to be positioned and admired. Elizabeth observed his expression from the other side of the room: composed, patient, and underneath those things, the specific quality of a man who has contracted for something he intends to honor.

She found she could respect it. It was not what she had expected to find.

Lydia made a speech that began as a toast and became a description of the journey she intended to make to London once she was invited. Kitty laughed at the right moments. Mary quoted something about matrimony that Elizabeth suspected was not from scripture. Mr. Collins offered a supplementary reading, which no one had requested, on the duties of a wife, which Elizabeth received by examining the arrangement of flowers near her with careful attention.

Jane stood beside Mr. Bingley, who was radiantly cheerful and nearly competent at concealing it. Jane's hand rested in his for a moment before they both appeared to remember the room, and the hand was quietly returned to a more proper arrangement. Elizabeth thought: *Darcy did this.* Bingley's presence, his intention, the renewed warmth between him and Jane; Darcy had arranged all of it before he had asked her a single thing about her feelings on the matter. It was the kind of act that was difficult to know what to do with: not staged for her to witness, not designed to earn credit, simply done because it needed doing and he was the one who could do it.

She had not yet decided what to do with that fact. She continued not deciding.

Mr. Gardiner found her near the window in the second hour and said nothing in particular, only asked how she was getting on. She said tolerably.

He nodded as if this were precisely the correct answer and moved away to find his wife, which was, she thought, the mark of an intelligent man who had learned not to press his luck with the women in his family.

Darcy appeared at her side not long after. He stood for a moment in silence, looking at the same section of wall she was looking at, before he said:

"Your uncle asked me about the fishing at Pemberley."

"And what did you tell him?"

"The truth." A pause. "He seemed pleased."

"He always is, when people answer direct questions directly."

Darcy considered this. "A useful quality in a family," he said. There was something in his voice that was not quite dry. It was more careful than dry, more deliberate and it landed between them as the closest thing to ease they had managed in each other's company since the engagement.

Elizabeth did not quite smile. She came near enough to it that he looked at her differently, not with surprise, exactly, but with attention, the particular quality of his attention that she had come to recognize as meaning he was revising something.

The afternoon light came through the window at a low angle and rested on the table between them, and Mrs. Bennet discovered a new relative of consequence to introduce Darcy to, and the moment closed.

The carriage north left before four o'clock.

Collins said something at the door; Elizabeth received it without hearing it. Mrs. Bennet wept, in the way of someone for whom weeping was a form of triumph rather than grief. Her handkerchief had been at the ready since the ceremony, and she deployed it now with the satisfaction of a woman whose plans had arrived at their intended destination. Lydia called after the carriage until the bend in the road took her voice away. Kitty waved from the step with genuine feeling; she had, Elizabeth thought, a better heart than she was ever given credit for. Jane stood at the gate and watched until the road curved, and Elizabeth watched Jane watching for as long as she could see her, which was not long enough.

Then the gate was gone, and there was only the road.

Darcy sat across from her. The carriage interior was well-appointed. She noticed this in the way she had been noticing everything about Pemberley by proxy, building an inventory of what his choices looked like when no one had required him to justify them. The seats were good leather, dark, without ornament. The fittings were brass rather than silver. The whole had the quality of something chosen for use rather than display, and she turned this over in her mind as the last of Meryton's buildings gave way to open road and the horses found their pace.

They sat in silence for some time. It was not an uncomfortable silence; it was the silence of two people who had nothing yet to say and had the wit to recognize this. The afternoon light moved across the floor of the carriage. A village passed, then fields, then a long stretch of road between hedges going brown with the season.

The road developed a rut at some point north of Hertfordshire, and the carriage tilted with it. Both of them reached for the strap on the same side at the same moment, their hands arriving simultaneously on the same leather loop.

They did not look at each other.

His hand moved to the other strap. She kept hold of the first one . Outside, the road leveled.

She watched the hedgerow for a moment. He looked at something on his side — the passing fields, a barn going dark in the late light.

After some minutes, Darcy said: "Are you comfortable?"

"Adequately," she said.

Another silence. He appeared to be constructing something. She had come to recognize when he was building a sentence rather than simply producing one, the small pause that preceded anything he had decided to say carefully.

"The house at Pemberley," he said, "is kept at a particular temperature in the spring. Mrs. Reynolds keeps fires going in the rooms she expects to be in use. If you find it wrong, too much or not enough, you should tell her directly. She will adjust without requiring a reason."

It was a practical thing to say. She turned it over, looking for what it was actually conveying.

"Why are you telling me this?" she said.

He looked at her. "Because it will be your house. And because she is more likely to adjust it for you than for me."

"Why is that?"

"Because," Darcy said, with something in his voice that was not quite self-deprecation but was adjacent to it, "she has been adjusting it for me for twelve years and I have never once mentioned being cold."

Elizabeth looked at him. She was looking for irony and found something plainer. He was not making a joke. He was telling her, in the precise and oblique way he had of conveying what he found difficult to state directly, that the house would be more responsive to her than it had been to him; that there was, in some practical sense, space for her within it that had not existed for anyone else in a long time.

She said: "I will tell her."

"Good," he said.

Outside, the light was fading. The lamps inside the carriage had been lit at some point; she had not noticed when, and the windows were dark beyond the glass. She looked at the flame for a moment, the small, steady thing, and then returned to the middle distance, which she had found to be the most navigable place to fix her attention when she had more to think about than the immediate landscape required.

The road ahead was long, and they had contracted to travel it together. Outside, the last of the daylight drained from the sky. Inside, the lamp held. Neither of them spoke again for some time, and neither of them found this to be a difficulty.

Chapter 14: Pemberley, First View

The road through the park was longer than Elizabeth had expected, which gave her more time than she wanted to think about what she was arriving at.

She had formed a picture of Pemberley over the past weeks assembled from documents and descriptions, and Darcy's own sparse references to the place, the way one constructs any fact one has not yet encountered. She had heard it described by solicitors with the dry precision of men who valued land by the acre, and once, at considerable length, by Lady Catherine, who had wanted her to understand its consequence. The picture had been adequate for the purpose. It had allowed her to sign her name to papers, to pack her trunks, and to travel north with reasonable composure.

What she had not accounted for was when the picture would be replaced by the thing itself.

The drive curved. The water came into view first; a broad, still expanse that caught the afternoon light and then the house beyond it, larger than she had calculated and set into the landscape as though it had always been there and the landscape had arranged itself accordingly.

Elizabeth put her hands flat on her knees and looked at it.

She looked at it without speaking. It was large, and she had prepared herself for large, but there was something in the proportions that she had not expected: nothing straining, nothing proving itself. The stone was the color of old honey in the afternoon light; the grounds arranged in the way of places old enough to have settled into their own preferences. The river below the house moved without urgency. The trees had been allowed to grow how they wished. She was aware of Darcy across the carriage, watching her with the attentive restraint she identified as his version of anxiety, and she turned from the window before her expression could tell him anything she had not decided to tell him.

"It is very beautiful," she said, because it was, and because it cost her nothing to say so.

"Yes," he said. He did not elaborate. She thought he might have said more if she had given him a different opening, and she was not quite ready to give him a different opening yet.

The carriage stopped. A footman appeared. The door was opened, and the morning air came in, cooler than she expected and sharp with the smell of the grounds, grass and turned earth and something floral she could not name, and Elizabeth descended into her new life with the composure of a woman who had spent the last several weeks practicing composure as a professional skill.

Mrs. Reynolds was waiting at the top of the steps.

She was a woman of fifty or thereabouts, with the unhurried manner of someone who has been managing a large household for long enough that managing it no longer requires visible effort. She greeted Darcy with the ease of long and genuine affection: not servile, not familiar, but simply warm and turned to Elizabeth with the measuring gaze of a person who has taken a great deal of information in quickly and is now deciding what to do with it.

"Mrs. Darcy." The words were offered with full weight, as if Mrs. Reynolds intended her to understand that the title had been held in waiting here, that it meant something specific in this house.

Elizabeth said she was glad to be arrived. It was not untrue, which was the best she could say for it.

The housekeeper showed her the principal rooms with the thoroughness of someone who takes the house personally. She did not describe the furniture. She described decisions: where things had been moved from their original positions and why, which rooms caught light in which season, which grates drew well and which required patience in wet weather. She spoke of the house as a living system that had to be managed rather than a set of beautiful objects to be displayed, and Elizabeth found she could listen to this for a long time without losing attention.

She spoke of Mr. Darcy in the third person, in passing, with the ease of someone for whom the subject is simply a feature of the landscape, and the things she said in passing were the things Elizabeth had not been told directly. He had always been particular about the servants' quarters being in good repair; he had always insisted that the tenants' drainage concerns come to him directly rather than through the steward; there had been a year - Mrs. Reynolds named it without sentiment - when the harvest had gone badly and the rents had been suspended for two terms, and she said this the way she said everything else, as a fact of the place rather than a tribute to its owner.

Elizabeth listened and said very little. She was building something; a second portrait of Darcy assembled from evidence she had not collected herself, and she wanted the lines to be clean before she let herself draw conclusions from them. It was possible that Mrs. Reynolds was loyal past accuracy. It was possible that a household spoke well of a master it had learned to manage rather than one who deserved management. She did not know yet. She was noting what she saw and leaving the verdict open.

What she saw in the rooms themselves was a house that was used. The library had books in the positions of interruption, not display. Several of them were open, two of them stacked with papers inserted among the pages. The music room held an instrument that was tuned; she pressed three keys and found them even, which meant someone played it regularly and cared whether it was right. The guest rooms were neither oppressively grand nor neglected. The mattresses were good. The fireplaces were cleared and laid.

These were small things, and she knew they were small things. She also knew that small things, maintained consistently over years, were a more reliable guide to character than grand gestures made once for a particular occasion. Anyone could rise to an occasion. The state of the fireplaces told her something more specific.

She found the portrait gallery on her own, which was perhaps how Darcy had intended it. He had mentioned it once and then said nothing further, which she suspected was his version of an invitation that he would not press.

The family ran back several generations. There were Darcys who had clearly understood that a portrait was an argument, and had composed their faces to make it; there were others who seemed to have sat still and allowed themselves to be recorded without editorial. Elizabeth moved along the wall with the leisurely attention of someone with no destination.

She found his portrait at the end of the second wall. A younger Darcy, nineteen, perhaps, or twenty, painted before whatever in him had settled into its current form. He looked the same in the essential lines, but the pride was less finished. It had not yet learned to be quiet. There was something in his mouths set that was closer to uncertainty than she had ever seen in his living face, and she stood in front of it for longer than she had stood in front of the others, thinking that this was what he had been before the world had taught him that the safest expression was none.

She moved on.

Georgiana arrived before dinner, earlier than expected, and Elizabeth had enough time, watching the carriage come up the drive from a first-floor window, to understand that she had spent the past week preparing herself for the wrong thing.

She had readied herself for extreme shyness and found instead a young woman whose shyness was one layer over something considerably more observant. Georgiana watched people with the quiet attention of someone who has learned, by necessity, that watching carefully is preferable to trusting quickly. She was sixteen, which Elizabeth had known in the abstract and felt more concretely when she saw her step down from the carriage with the combination of height and uncertainty that belongs to a person not yet fully inhabiting their own body.

She greeted Elizabeth with correct warmth. It was not the warmth of someone going through a courtesy, not hollow, but careful, the warmth of someone who has decided to hope and is not yet certain the hope is safe.

"I am very glad you are here," she said, and then glanced at at Darcy, as if checking that she had said it correctly.

"So am I," Elizabeth said, and meant it, which was not what she had expected to mean when she had imagined this moment.

Darcy watched them from the other side of the room. Elizabeth was aware of him doing so without looking at him directly, the way one is aware of a fire without staring into it. His expression was not possessive, not relieved, not proud in any of the ways she had initially assigned to him. It was something closer to cautious hope; the look of a man watching to see whether something he values will be handled with care, and she found she did not want to disappoint him, which was a new feeling and one she put aside for later examination.

At dinner, Georgiana spoke more than Elizabeth had expected. She was shy in company, Mrs. Reynolds had said, but this was not quite company. This was the first dinner of a strange new household arrangement, and apparently Georgiana had decided to make an effort, which showed in the effort. She asked about Jane. She asked about the assembly rooms at Meryton with the careful curiosity of someone who has heard of such things as a social fact rather than experienced them, the questions of a young woman whose education had been thorough in every direction except the ordinary ones.

Elizabeth answered with more specificity than the questions strictly required, because the longing was real and deserved real information in return. Darcy listened to this exchange without interjecting. Toward the end of dinner, when Georgiana laughed at something - a story about Lydia and a hat that should probably not have been told, but was too good to withhold - he looked at Elizabeth across the table with an expression she could not entirely interpret except to say that it was not the expression of a man who regretted the arrangement he had made.

The estate office was at the back of the house, past a corridor that smelled of old paper and beeswax and something that might have been the grounds coming in through a window left open. She had not been directed there. She found it the following morning by opening the wrong door while looking for the garden, and then, because a closed room is always more interesting than a corridor, going in.

The room was orderly in the way of a space used by someone who prefers to find things where he left them. The correspondence on the desk had been sorted and weighted with a smooth stone that had no obvious origin. Account books occupied a shelf in a sequence that was almost certainly chronological. A large map of the estate hung on the left-hand wall, annotated in a hand she recognized as Darcy's: small, precise notations about drainage, about a field boundary, about something she could not read from the doorway.

On the wall to the right of the window, framed in plain wood, was a letter.

She stepped closer to read it.

It was from a tenant - a man named Caldwell, by the signature - and it was dated three years prior, written in the fall following a poor harvest. The handwriting was careful in the way of someone unaccustomed to formal correspondence: each letter formed with effort, each sentence considered. He thanked Mr. Darcy for the suspension of rent that fall, not as if it were expected, but as if it were the difference between one kind of winter and a far worse kind. He was specific, which was what struck her: he named what had been preserved. His eldest son's apprenticeship fee, already promised to the craftsman. His wife's lying-in costs, due in December. The seed grain for spring, which could not be purchased on credit. He listed these things plainly, without drama, and then he thanked Darcy by name and said he would not forget it.

The letter was in a plain wooden frame, on the wall of the estate office. Not in the entrance hall. Not in any room a visitor would see. Here, in the room where Darcy sat to manage the accounts, where he signed letters and reviewed figures and dealt with the unglamorous mechanics of the estate. Here was where he had chosen to keep it.

Elizabeth read it twice.

She stood with her hands at her sides and looked at the letter and thought about what it meant that a man had framed this and hung it here in this room, where only he would see it regularly. There were two possible explanations, and they led in opposite directions. The first: that this was a man who kept a record of his own virtue as a kind of private accounting, who needed to see the evidence of his goodness in order to continue believing it was real. The second: that this was a man who had done a thing for a family in difficulty, received their thanks, and kept that thanks where he could see it because it mattered to him that it had mattered to them. He did not want to forget that the figures in his account books were attached to people who wrote letters like this one.

She could not determine which explanation was correct. The inability to determine it was, she recognized, itself a form of progress: three months ago, she would not have entertained the second possibility at all.

She was still standing in front of the letter when she heard the door.

Darcy stood in the threshold with the expression of someone who has walked into a room and found it occupied when he did not expect company: not alarmed, not affronted, but caught at something. She understood what he had been caught at: this was the room where he kept his actual self, where nothing required managing, and she had found it without being shown.

"I was looking for the garden," Elizabeth said.

"It is in the other direction."

"I see that now." She looked at the letter, then at him. "The Caldwells, are they still your tenants?"

He looked at the wall, briefly, as if reminding himself which letter she meant. "Yes. Three sons now. The eldest is established in his trade."

She considered asking him why the letter was framed. She decided against it, because the question would require him to explain himself, and she was not sure she wanted the explanation. The explanation might be less interesting than the fact.

"The garden," she said.

"Through the second door on the left, past the morning room."

She went out. He did not follow immediately.

He stood in the estate office for a moment after she left, looking at the letter on the wall with the attention of someone attempting to see a familiar thing as a stranger might see it. He had not thought about the letter in some time. He had hung it there years ago because Caldwell had written it and it had seemed worth keeping. Hhe could not have said why, precisely, only that the specificity of it had struck him, the way Caldwell had named each thing the money had made possible, as if he wanted Darcy to understand that the gesture had not disappeared into a general debt but had attached itself to specific consequences in specific lives. Darcy had found that he did not want to forget this. He had framed it and put it where he would see it.

It had not occurred to him, until this morning, that anyone else might ever read it.

He could not tell what she had made of it. He had been unable, for some weeks now, to tell what she made of most things. She observed, she filed, she occasionally offered him a conclusion when she had finished arriving at it, and the conclusions, when they came, were accurate. He had learned to wait for them rather than press. Pressing Elizabeth toward a judgment she had not finished forming was, he had discovered, a reliable method of receiving a less favorable judgment than she would otherwise have reached.

He went to find her in the garden.

She was on the south path, moving with the unhurried attention of someone under no obligation and temporarily glad of it. The morning was cool, the light flat and even. She had not taken a wrap and appeared not to miss one.

He fell into step beside her without preamble, which she permitted. The grounds were quiet and they walked without speaking past the kitchen garden, past the stone wall that marked the formal beds from the working ones, past a section of path that wanted regrading and that he had been meaning to address since the spring.

"How large is the kitchen garden?" Elizabeth asked.

He told her. She asked about the succession planting, and he told her that too. She asked who managed it. He told her the head gardener's name was Birch, and he had been at Pemberley for eleven years.

She asked whether the kitchen garden supplied the house entirely through winter or whether provisions were also bought in from the market at Lambton. He answered these questions with the pleasure of someone whose knowledge is finally being asked about rather than admired from a distance, and she listened with the attention she gave to things she intended to remember.

"I will want to speak with Birch," she said.

"He will be pleased. He has opinions about the asparagus beds no one has yet asked him to share at length."

"Then we will get along very well."

They turned at the far end of the path and came back toward the house. The light had moved while they walked; the stone had gone from honey to something cooler, and the windows on the south face caught the sky rather than the garden.

Elizabeth looked at the house as they approached it, and Darcy watched her look at it. He did not know what she was thinking. He was aware this was likely to remain his general condition: not knowing, watching, waiting for the conclusions she would eventually share, and he found that he had made a kind of peace with it. What he had made less peace with was the question of what he wanted the conclusions to be: not merely a favorable verdict on the house, or on the estate's management, or on his behavior over the past months, but something he was not yet certain how to name, because naming it felt premature and because Elizabeth had a gift for perceiving premature hopes and finding them faintly ridiculous.

"You should tell me," she said, "which rooms are used and which are not."

It was not the question she had been sitting with. He knew that. She knew he knew it. He had found, where the surface question and the real question coexisted without either being acknowledged, and the skill was in answering the surface question in a way that did not foreclose the real one.

"The east wing is for family. The west when there is company."

"And now?"

"East," he said. "We are family."

She looked at the house for another moment. The windows held the light.

Chapter 15: The Education of Darcy

He had expected, without precisely admitting it to himself, a version of domestic life that resembled the life he already knew.

The expectation was not unreasonable. Pemberley had run on the same principles for a generation before him, and the principles were sound. He knew what an efficient household looked like, what a contented staff looked like, what order cost and what disorder cost more. He had governed this house since he was two-and-twenty with only Georgiana's comfort added to the sum of his responsibilities, and the addition had been considerable but had not disrupted the underlying structure. He had expected, he could see clearly now in the flat way one sees an error once it has passed, that a wife would behave like a more complex Georgiana. A consideration. A presence at the other end of the table. A weight placed carefully on a scale he already understood.

Elizabeth had not read the balance sheet. He was not certain she would have adjusted her conduct if she had.

The first thing he had misjudged was the silence.

He had assumed she would fill it with conversation, social application, the polite performance that other women of her situation seemed to produce as naturally as breathing. He had braced for it, in fact, without being aware that he was bracing. What he received instead was a woman who carried quiet as a deliberate instrument, who could sit in a room with him for a full hour over books and not speak unless she had something to say, and who, when she did speak, said it as if she had already decided what the words were worth.

The first week, he had taken this for disapproval. He knew what her disapproval looked like. He had been its subject before. He had watched for her to stop listening. At Netherfield, when she had finished calculating him, her attention left the room while her courtesy remained. It did not happen here. The silence was not withdrawal. It was, he eventually understood, simply how she thought.

He found this significantly more unsettling than hostility would have been.

The second thing he had misjudged was what she would do with Pemberley.

He had expected, and the expectation was vivid in retrospect, lavish in its presumptions, that she would require guidance. That Mrs. Reynolds would manage the household and Elizabeth would be managed by Mrs. Reynolds, and Darcy would stand at the necessary distance from both. This was approximately how his mother had operated, from what he remembered of her; it was certainly how his aunt operated, though with considerably more volume; it seemed to be the customary arrangement.

Elizabeth had spent the first three days learning the house. Not touring it; she had done that on arrival, receiving the full architectural presentation with the composed attention of someone absorbing useful information rather than admiring scenery. What she did in the days that followed was different. She asked the footmen their names and remembered them. She visited the stillroom, not to inventory it but to ask Mrs. Phelps how the apothecary jars were kept up, and whether the arrangement changed when the family was away in London.

She did not attempt to reorganize anything. She was not making her mark. She was, Darcy concluded, reading the room.

What she learned from it, he could not always see. But when she began to make decisions - small ones, at first; a change in the rotation of the linen; a shift in when certain guest rooms were aired - they were the right ones. He would not have known they were the right ones without her making them. That was the part he could not quite account for.

Georgiana's face, the afternoon they spent together over the pianoforte, had told him something else that required accounting.

He had watched it happen through the library doorway. He had not intended to watch; he had come looking for a letter he had mislaid, and had stopped at the sound of his sister's voice doing something it rarely did in the company of anyone but him. It was not what she was saying because he could not hear the words from the doorway. It was the absence of the careful enclosure she wore in company, the quality of ease he had seen Elizabeth show only with Jane, or perhaps her father, and which she was showing now, without apparent effort, to Georgiana.

Elizabeth was asking her something about the music. Not complimenting it, which Georgiana had learned to receive with polite deflection, but asking something that required an opinion, and receiving the opinion as if it were genuinely wanted.

He withdrew before they saw him. He stood in the corridor for a moment with his mislaid letter entirely forgotten, and tried to understand what he had done when he had arranged this marriage.

He had arranged it for the Bennet family's survival and his own. He had not examined the second motive too carefully. The transaction had been clear, and the terms had been stated. But he had not considered that Elizabeth Bennet at Pemberley might become something that Pemberley had never quite had before. Someone with claims not on the house or its income but on the people in it.

He was not sure what to do with this. He went back to find the letter.

He had sent it to Bingley.

Four sentences. He had written it on the morning following Elizabeth's first real walk around the home farm, when she had returned with mud on her hem and the name of a tenant family whose roof needed attention before winter, information he had not had and could not explain how she had gathered in the course of a two-hour walk. He had not sent her out to gather it. She had gone walking because she wanted to walk, apparently, and had come back with a family name and a specific description of the state of the north-facing chimney stack.

He had asked how she knew about the chimney stack.

She had looked at him with the expression she reserved for things she considered obvious. "Mrs. Hollis mentioned it. She was very polite about it. She would have said nothing to anyone she thought would feel obliged to act on it. I gave the impression of having no authority whatsoever, and she became quite forthcoming."

He had sat with this for a moment. The implication was not that the tenant had been concealing the problem; Mrs. Hollis had likely assumed it was being managed by the estate agent in the ordinary way, or that it was not severe enough to trouble the family directly. The implication was that Elizabeth had understood this, and had managed the conversation and had come home with accurate information that she then gave to him without drama or conclusion.

He had ridden out the next morning to look. She had been right. The roof was in the state she described, the family in the circumstances she had indicated without being able to know the Darcys' full accounting of the situation. He had spoken with the steward and arranged the repair.

He came back to his study and sat for some time before writing. He wrote to Bingley that he would not interfere again, that his previous interference had been a failure of judgment for which he had already given account, and that he had every confidence in Bingley's own assessment of a situation Darcy had no business adjudicating. It was not an apology. It was the closing of an account, stated plainly.

He sent the letter. He did not tell Elizabeth.

He thought about telling her. He considered the various arguments in favor of it: she would want to know; it was, in its way, the completion of something she had asked of him at Longbourn in those three careful lines. He considered the arguments against, which reduced to a single argument that he was uncertain, still, of the distinction between what was due her as information and what would be using her as an audience for his own good conduct.

He did not tell her. He thought this was probably correct.

The third thing he had misjudged was himself.

He had believed - he had not stated this belief even to himself in those terms, but it had governed him - that satisfaction in this marriage would come from its orderly execution. He would provide what he had promised in the settlements and some considerable addition. He would manage the Bennet situation with competence and discretion. He would be a decent husband in the legal and social sense, and Elizabeth, who was intelligent and did not require flattery, would recognize this for what it was and arrive at a reasonable contentment of her own.

He had not anticipated that watching her read would become a difficulty.

This was not an edifying thing to admit. He knew that there was nothing about a woman reading in a chair by the east window that should constitute a difficulty for a man of sense and self-possession. He had watched Georgiana read for years without incident. He had sat in the same room with Caroline Bingley when she was ostentatiously reading for his benefit and had experienced no feeling at all.

Elizabeth read as if the book had something it needed to tell her, and she intended to find out what. She folded herself into the chair in a way that Lady Catherine would have found ungraceful. She turned pages without looking away. When she encountered something she disagreed with, he was learning to read this, there was

a stillness before she went back to re-examine a passage and she made a small sound that was not quite a word.

He had asked her, the third time this happened, what the book had done to her.

She had looked up. For a moment the expression that belonged to her reading face, concentrated, and a degree past polite, was still there, and then she registered the question and the expression shifted into something else, something that started as amusement and deepened as she considered that he had actually asked.

"It is arguing in favor of a principle I cannot agree with," she said. "And doing it well enough to be annoying."

"Which principle?"

She told him. He disagreed with her assessment of the argument. He said so. She looked at him as if he had just become unexpectedly useful and said, "Then explain."

They had argued about it for forty minutes. She had not conceded his position. He had not expected her to, and had not wanted her to, which was also, he recognized, a thing he had not expected to want. He was accustomed to conversations that resolved with Bingley into good-natured agreement; with Fitzwilliam into a draw that both parties found satisfying; or with his aunt into a performance of deference that left everyone's position intact and nothing examined. He was not accustomed to being argued with by someone who had read the same texts and had considered opinions about them and was not interested in softening those opinions to spare him.

He had ended the conversation feeling that his position had not been defeated but had been genuinely tested, which was different from either winning or losing and considerably more useful than either.

He had gone to bed thinking about her counterargument. He had woken up still thinking about it. He had, at breakfast, come at it from a different angle that he had not had time to find the night before, and mentioned it, and she had put down her coffee cup and said, "That is actually a stronger objection," with the composed honesty of someone who did not consider it any kind of concession to acknowledge a good point.

He had not known what to do with this either. He was developing a list of things about Elizabeth Bennet - Elizabeth Darcy - that he did not know what to do with, and the list was longer than the list of things he felt he had correctly anticipated, and growing.

In the fifth week of their marriage, she rode out with him on the estate.

This had not been planned. He had been going to visit the south field boundary, where a fence dispute with a neighboring property required his personal assessment, and she had been standing in the stable yard when he came for his horse, and she had said, without preamble, that she would like to come if he did not object. He had not objected. He could not have explained, quickly, why the prospect was not merely unobjectionable but immediately preferable to riding alone.

She rode competently, which he had known from Hertfordshire and confirmed. She was not a showy rider. She sat correctly without making an exhibition of it, which was a distinction he had had occasion to observe mattered to her in all things. She also did not fill the ride with conversation, which he had half expected and did not receive. They rode out through the home wood and across the lower pasture in a quiet that was, after a short while, simply the quiet of two people on horseback who did not need to announce themselves to each other.

At the boundary fence, she listened to the dispute's particulars from the steward and asked one question that neither he nor Redpath had thought to ask, about the date of a particular agreement relative to a different one, and which superseded which. The steward did not know. Darcy did not know. They went back and had Redpath check the estate records.

She had been right. The older agreement superseded the newer one. The dispute resolved itself from there, in Pemberley's favor, in a way that settled the matter without requiring any of the hostility that had been building in that quarter for the past several months, nor any legal proceeding that would have cost more than the fence was worth and left a neighbor who was disagreeable.

He rode back beside her and thought that she had done in one question what two months of correspondence had failed to accomplish, and that she had done it without having been asked, and without drawing attention to the fact that she had done it. There was no glance at him to confirm that he had noticed. She had asked because she had seen a gap, and it was the natural thing to do with a gap.

"You will find," he said, after they had gone some distance in silence, "that I am accustomed to managing the estate affairs without consultation."

"I know," she said. She did not look at him.

"I should perhaps have made clear —"

"You did not make it unclear," she said. "I asked if I might come. I came. If the question was of no use to you, you may say so, and I will know better next time."

"The question was of considerable use."

She looked at him then, assessing, as she always was, but with something added to it, something that took his measure rather than merely finding it deficient. He had the impression of someone revising a figure slightly upward.

"Then we will say that I will ask questions when I have them," she said, "and you may tell me whether they are useful."

"That seems workable," he said.

"It does," she agreed, in a tone that did not ask for more from him, and settled her attention back on the road.

He looked at the road as well. They rode back to Pemberley in the middle of the afternoon, and the house came into view between the trees at the exact moment it always did, and had the exact quality it always had in that light, but Darcy, looking at it, found he was seeing it differently than he usually did. Not as a charge or an inheritance, or the externalization of a family's weight on a man's shoulders. He was seeing it as a place someone else had begun to think of as hers.

He was not entirely certain when he had decided this was what he wanted. He was certain, by the time they reached the stable yard, that it was.

He had expected gratitude and received partnership. He had expected compliance and received terms. He had entered into a contract designed to be sufficient and found that sufficient was no longer what he was interested in.

This was, he recognized, a problem entirely of his own making, and one he did not know how to solve. He was also aware, with the clarity that Pemberley in the afternoon had always given him, that it was not a problem he wanted to stop having.

He left her at the garden path. Inside, he could hear Georgiana at the pianoforte.

A phrase picked apart and set back together, picked apart again. He stood for a moment at the edge of the path and did not go in immediately.

The letter to Bingley was already sent. There was nothing more, tonight, to correct.

He went inside.

Chapter 16: Jane and Bingley

The letter arrived while Elizabeth was in the library.

She had gone there after breakfast with no particular purpose. Darcy was with his steward; Georgiana was at the pianoforte in a room far enough away that only the bass notes reached and she had taken down three books in succession and opened none of them. It was a Pemberley habit she was still acquiring: the right to be idle in a room without accounting for it.

The letter was from Jane. She knew the hand before the footman had retreated.

She broke the seal standing at the window, where the light was good and the grounds were going about their midsummer business, the trees heavy with leaf and indifferent to the house behind her.

He is returned to Netherfield, Jane wrote.

He called yesterday with Mr. Hurst. Mama received them both and I... Lizzy, I did not know what to say and so I said very little, which I believe was correct, and he seemed... I cannot say what he seemed. I hope I did not behave oddly. I do not think I behaved oddly.

He asked after you. I told him you were well and settled at Pemberley, and he looked very glad.

Elizabeth read to the end of the page, then read it again, and then she went to find Darcy.

He was in the estate office with Crane, the steward, a ledger open between them and a second spread to one side in the way of a man who keeps two sets of figures in view to be sure they agree. Darcy looked up when she appeared at the door and must have seen something in her expression, because he said something quietly to Crane, who collected the ledgers and left without requiring further instruction.

"Jane's letter," Elizabeth said. She held it out.

He read it. He was not a quick reader in the way of someone who skips ahead. He was a quick reader in the way of someone who has already trained the same habit of attention onto a page that he put on everything else.

He handed it back.

"Good," he said.

"Is that all you intend to say?"

"I thought Bingley had better judgment than he has sometimes shown. I am glad to find I was right."

Elizabeth looked at him. He was not going to elaborate; she had learned this about him over the weeks at Pemberley, that when he had said the thing he meant, he considered it said. There was no further layer of feeling waiting to be drawn out by the right question. It was disconcerting and, she had begun to notice, efficient.

"You wrote to him," she said. Not a question.

"I told him the truth of what I had done and why I had done it. I told him that my reasons had been worse than I acknowledged and that Jane's indifference was a conclusion I had reached on insufficient grounds."

"And he simply... returned."

"He is not a complicated man, Elizabeth."

"No," she said. "But a generous one."

Darcy looked at the window, where Crane had disappeared around the corner of the stable block. "I should have said so earlier."

Elizabeth folded Jane's letter and did not answer this directly, because there was nothing useful she could add to it that he had not already understood. She asked whether he would want to go north for Jane's sake, whether he thought the timing of a visit would help or hinder, given how new it all was, how careful Jane was being.

He considered it properly. That was another thing she had noticed: he did not give immediate answers to questions that required more than courtesy.

"A week," he said. "Give it a week. Then go if you want to. I'll come with you or not, as you prefer."

She said she would prefer him to come, and was surprised, as she turned back toward the hall, that this was true.

They went to Netherfield at the end of the following week, on a gray Thursday with frost on the upper windows and the road from Pemberley still solid enough for them to move quickly.

Elizabeth had dressed that morning with more attention than she usually gave it, which annoyed her when she noticed. The black crepe was confining in a way that wool was not, the bodice fitted close and the sleeves narrow; it had been made for Hunsford, for the weeks immediately after, and she had since had two more gowns made up in Derbyshire with better fabric, and a better cut, but they were still black, still the clear and unambiguous black of full mourning, and they would be for months yet.

She had not minded at Pemberley, where no one was watching for anything specific. She minded now, and then minded that she minded, because Jane would be in half-mourning still, and that was grief enough, and vanity had no legitimate business in a carriage on the way to Hertfordshire.

She put it out of her mind before the first gate.

The road between Longbourn and Netherfield was not long enough for Mrs. Bennet to finish what she had to say about it, which meant she was still saying it when Bingley came out to meet them in the drive.

He had not waited inside, which Elizabeth had come to recognize as simply how he was built. He was the kind of man who met people at the door because standing still while someone approached was not a thing he could manage. He handed Mrs. Bennet down from the carriage with a good humor that did not waver even as she informed him, before her second foot had touched the gravel, that the last quarter mile wanted attention.

"I have said so to Jane," Mrs. Bennet told him. "Have I not, Jane? I said the road was very bad."

"You did, Mama," Jane said.

"And here it is. Very bad." She looked around the drive with the expression of a woman confirming a long-held position. "But the house is just as I remembered. A very good house, Mr. Bingley. I have always said so."

Bingley said he was glad to hear it, and turned to Darcy with the warmth of a man genuinely pleased to see his friend, and then to Elizabeth, and his expression shifted as it found her — not pity, which she would not have liked, but a care that was almost gentle.

"Mrs. Darcy," he said. "How do you do, truly?"

It was the right question. "Better than I was," she said. "And glad to be here."

He led them inside. Mrs. Bennet took his arm before he had quite offered it and began telling him what she had said to Mrs. Phillips about

Netherfield, which was, Elizabeth gathered from the portion she could hear, considerable.

Jane fell into step beside her.

"He came out to meet us," Jane said, low.

"He did."

"He need not have done."

"No," Elizabeth agreed. "He need not have done."

Jane looked at the gravel. Elizabeth did not say anything further, because nothing further was required.

The sitting room had been arranged with the kind of care that does not wish to appear as care: roses from the garden in a blue jug, the tea things ready, the chairs positioned so that the party could be comfortable without having been obviously prepared for. Elizabeth catalogued it and understood that Bingley had thought about this visit, and that the thinking had expressed itself in roses and a good fire rather than in anything he would have known how to say.

Mrs. Bennet settled herself into the best chair with the authority of prior claim and looked around the room.

"This is a very well-proportioned sitting room," she said. "I have always felt that a sitting room ought to be well-proportioned. Jane, do you not find it well-proportioned?"

"I do, Mama."

"Mrs. Darcy — Lizzy — you must tell me whether Pemberley's sitting rooms are well-proportioned. I have been telling everyone they are, but I have not had your confirmation." She directed this at Elizabeth with the air of someone calling in a debt. "Mrs. Long asked me just last week, and I said I was quite certain they were."

"They are," Elizabeth said. "You were right to say so."

Mrs. Bennet received this with satisfaction and turned to Bingley to tell him what Mrs. Long had said in response, which allowed Elizabeth to take the chair beside Jane, and Jane to pour, and the two of them to be briefly, provisionally, alone within the general noise.

"You look well," Jane said, which meant: *the mourning has not got the better of you.*

"I am well," Elizabeth said. "Are you?"

Jane's attention went, briefly and involuntarily, to Bingley, who was attending to Mrs. Bennet with a patience that Elizabeth was beginning to think was not performance but genuine character. "I think I may be," she said. "It is still very new."

"You have been prudent about it in every letter for a fortnight," Elizabeth said. "You are allowed to say he came back."

"He came back," Jane said; and the plain fact of it, said aloud, did something that no careful correspondence had managed.

They were not left with it long.

"Jane," said Mrs. Bennet, "you must show Lizzy the morning room. I told her in my letter about the morning room. The color, Lizzy. Mr. Bingley has had it painted a very decided yellow." She looked at Bingley with the approval of a woman whose aesthetic judgments have been publicly vindicated. "I have always felt yellow was undervalued."

"I am glad it meets with your approval, ma'am," Bingley said.

"It does. It does very much." She paused, and then, with the careful casualness of someone who has been waiting to say a thing for some time: "Of course, the mistress of the house will have her own opinions about color, when there is one. That is only natural." She looked at the ceiling. She looked at her tea. She looked, briefly, at Jane, and then away again, with the elaborate unconcern of a woman holding a very large card face-down on the table.

The room absorbed this. Darcy looked at the window. Bingley's ears went slightly red. Jane found something absorbing in the middle distance. Elizabeth drank her tea.

"More tea, Mama?" she said.

"Thank you, Lizzy. Yes."

The visit found its footing after that, or at least its rhythm. Mrs. Bennet talked, as she always did, with the energy of someone who had a great deal to say and was aware that time was finite. She covered the road, the yellow morning room, the late Mr. Bennet's library which she described as very large, larger probably than Netherfield's, though Netherfield's was quite good for a house of this size, and what she had told Mrs. Phillips about Pemberley, which she then required Elizabeth to confirm in several particulars Elizabeth had never shared with her.

"The library," Mrs. Bennet said. "I told Mrs. Long it was the largest in Derbyshire. Is it the largest in Derbyshire, Mr. Darcy?"

"I could not say," Darcy said. "I have not measured the others."

Mrs. Bennet considered this. "Well," she said, "it can hardly be contradicted. I shall continue to say so."

In the interval that followed, while Mrs. Bennet accepted more cake and directed her attention toward Bingley's opinion of a mutual neighbor, Jane leaned toward Elizabeth by the width of a teacup.

"He would have liked it," she said, in the tone that meant *Papa.* "The library."

Elizabeth looked at her cup. "He would have had a great deal to say about the arrangement of the shelves," she said. "And then spent three weeks reading the books he found badly organized."

"He would have been right about the arrangement."

"Almost certainly."

They sat with that for a moment, tucked inside the general noise of Mrs. Bennet explaining to Bingley that the late Mr. Bennet had been a great reader, which was true, and that this quality was one she had always particularly admired in a man, which was less verifiable.

"I still catch myself composing things to tell him," Elizabeth said. "Small observations. The sort of joke that only he would have found funny. And then I have to stop." She set her cup down. "The habit outlasted the person."

Jane refilled her cup and said nothing, which was the correct response. Then: "Write it to me instead. What he would have said. I should like to read it."

Elizabeth looked at her. It was such a Jane thing to offer, practical and generous and not trying to be either. "I will," she said.

Bingley led Darcy to the study off the library, which still smelled of the Hursts' tenure and needed work. The shelves were half-empty, and the arrangement had no logic. He poured two glasses of wine that were neither the hour nor the occasion for and handed one over, anyway.

"I was glad you wrote," Bingley said.

"I should have written in August. In July."

"Yes, but you didn't, and here we are." Bingley said this without reproach, which was its own reproach, though Darcy suspected Bingley did not intend it as one. "She didn't know," Bingley said. "About me, I mean. About what I thought she thought."

"No. The fault there was mine, as well."

Bingley turned his wineglass by the stem. "I don't suppose you want to talk about it more than that."

"Not especially."

"Good," Bingley said. "Neither do I." He looked up, and his expression was the one Darcy had known since they were twenty-three: uncomplicated pleasure in the existence of a friend. "She's steady, Darcy. Not quiet. Steady. There's a difference."

Darcy said he had noticed.

"And Elizabeth?" Bingley asked. "How is she, actually? Not the letter version."

Darcy was quiet for a moment. He thought of Elizabeth in the estate office that morning, holding the letter, the black of her sleeve against the white paper, the way she had watched him read with a quality of held-breath composure that he recognized as the particular grief she carried. She had lost her father four months ago. She had married a stranger two months ago. She was at Pemberley now, which was not nothing, but was also not home in the way that the word meant when spoken by people who had always had homes.

"She is managing a great deal," he said. "She does not make it visible."

"No," Bingley said. "She wouldn't." He hesitated. "Jane wrote to her about Mr. Bennet. About missing him. Did Elizabeth say anything to you? I mean, does she speak of it?"

"Not often," Darcy said. "When she does, it is specific. Not general grief. Particular things she has lost."

Bingley nodded, as if this was exactly what he expected and was glad to hear it confirmed. "She is all right, then," he said. Not a question.

"I believe she is," Darcy said. He did believe it; and he found, as he said it, that he was also aware of how much he wanted it to be true.

The women were still by the fire when Darcy and Bingley returned, the tea cold now but neither of them having moved to refresh it, and the conversation had settled into the easy, unaccountable flow that happens between sisters who have not been in the same room for too long. Bingley suggested a walk. He always suggested a walk, finding stillness difficult, and they went out onto the Netherfield grounds, Bingley and Jane ahead, their conversation inaudible, their pace unhurried, and Elizabeth and Darcy behind at a distance that was neither engineered nor quite accidental. Mrs. Bennet stayed behind to plan her letters.

"She seems well," Darcy said, of Jane.

"She is being careful," Elizabeth said. "Which is sensible. But she was very glad, I think."

"Bingley is not capable of disguising gladness. It's one of his more useful qualities."

Elizabeth looked at the path, which was uneven with frost-heave. "He was not angry with you?"

"No."

"Were you expecting him to be?"

"I thought it was possible he would be cooler than he was. That I would have to work harder to be in the same room with him." He paused. "He is not built that way."

"And you find that surprising?"

"I find that instructive," he said. Which was not what she had expected, and she thought about it for some time afterward.

They caught up with Jane and Bingley at the gate to the kitchen garden, which was stuck and required Bingley's shoulder.

"Very bleak," Bingley said cheerfully of the gardens that had not been planted since the house had not been more than minimally occupied.

"It will be something next April," Jane said.

Elizabeth looked at Darcy. He was watching the garden with an expression she could not have named six weeks ago and could not quite name now, except that it was not absent. He was here, in this barren kitchen garden, with Bingley's shoulder and Jane's hope and he was paying attention to all of it.

"Yes," he said, to no one in particular. "It will."

The party broke up with the usual courtesies, Mrs. Bennet extracting from Bingley a half-promise about the road that Elizabeth was confident he would forget by morning and equally confident Mrs. Bennet would not, and pronouncing herself quite restored by the tea. Bingley handed her into the Darcy carriage with the good humor that appeared to be simply how he was made, and then handed Jane in after her, and said goodbye to Jane with a bow that lasted a beat longer than strictly necessary and conveyed, Elizabeth thought, a very great deal.

The carriage set off. Mrs. Bennet settled into the satisfied silence of a woman arranging what she would tell Mrs. Phillips, and Jane looked out of the window at the Netherfield roses going past and was clearly somewhere else entirely. Darcy looked at the road. Elizabeth looked at her hands and thought about the library, and what she would write to Jane, and how she would begin.

At Longbourn, Mrs. Bennet was handed down and immediately remembered three things she had not yet said to Elizabeth, which she said on the front step in rapid succession while Jane waited beside her with the patience of long practice. Then they went in. The door closed.

The carriage moved on.

After a mile or so, Elizabeth said: "She told him the library was the largest in Derbyshire."

"I heard."

"She will continue to say so. It can hardly be contradicted."

Darcy was quiet for a moment. "I have a letter from my uncle Viscount Matlock somewhere in my correspondence, specifically disputing that claim on behalf of his own collection. He wrote it as a point of family pride."

Elizabeth turned to look at him. "Does your uncle correspond with you about the relative sizes of your libraries?"

"He does when he feels the matter has not been given proper weight."

"And has it not?"

"In his opinion," Darcy said, "never adequately."

Elizabeth laughed, a real one, the kind that arrived before she had decided to produce it, and Darcy looked at her with the expression of a man who had aimed for something and found, slightly to his own surprise, that he had hit it.

Outside, Derbyshire waited. The road north was clear.

The carriage north was dark by the time they reached the Pemberley road, and Elizabeth leaned against the window and watched the fields disappear into early evening, gray into gray. She was tired in the way she was always tired after a day among people who knew her; not depleted, but quieted, the internal conversation that ran under everything finally given room to slow down.

She had been glad, today. She had laughed twice, once with Jane and once with Bingley, whose directness was its own relief. She had sat in a warm room and spoken about her father without the conversation requiring management. These were not small things.

She was also aware, as she always was on the way home from Longbourn or Netherfield, of the specific weight of absence. Her father would not see Jane married. He would not see Bingley returned, would not have the quiet satisfaction of knowing that the sensible daughter had been right about the character of that young man, as she had been right about so many things. He would not see Pemberley. He would not see-- and here she stopped the thought where she always stopped it, because there were things she had not yet earned the right to imagine.

"Thank you," she said, after some miles.

Darcy glanced at her. "For coming?"

"For making it possible to go."

He turned back to the window. Outside, the first Pemberley gates had appeared in the lamp's reach: the stone piers and iron gates with the long drive beyond. She watched his face in profile for a moment, the planes of it steady in the lantern light, and thought that she was beginning to have an idea of him. Not a complete idea. But a working one.

"Jane did not deserve what happened to her," he said. It was not the first time he had said this. It was the first time he had said it without the quality of a point being made; it was simply a fact, offered into the dark.

"No," Elizabeth said. "She didn't."

The carriage went through the gates. The drive was cold and quiet, and the house was lit at the upper windows. Georgiana, probably, who kept late hours with her music when they were away, as if the empty rooms gave her permission to fill them differently.

Elizabeth did not say anything else. Neither did Darcy. There was, she found, nothing further that needed to be said.

Chapter 17: Lady Catherine Calls

The letter arrived on a Tuesday addressed to Darcy. Lady Catherine had spent three months pretending that Elizabeth did not receive correspondence at Pemberley, or rather that any correspondence received there was not Darcy's concern to share. He read it at breakfast without change of expression and set it beside his cup.

"She is coming Friday," he said. "She intends to stay three days."

Elizabeth looked up from her own letter: Jane, cheerful, nothing requiring immediate action. "To what purpose?"

"She does not specify. She rarely does." He picked up his cup. "I thought it right to tell you."

"Yes," Elizabeth said. "Thank you."

She folded Jane's letter and noted that her hands were quite steady.

The preparation for Lady Catherine's visit was, in Elizabeth's observation, one of the more clarifying exercises of her first months at Pemberley. Mrs. Reynolds managed the household with an equanimity that bordered on the scientific; she had, it emerged, prepared for Lady Catherine's visits for twenty years and had a system. Elizabeth asked two questions, received clear answers, and then stepped back. This too was a decision: to let competence work without insisting on a visible hand in it.

Darcy, who noticed most things, noticed this.

"You are not anxious," he said, the evening before.

"I am not," Elizabeth agreed. She was reading; she did not look up. "Should I be?"

He was quiet a moment. "She will say disagreeable things."

"She has already said disagreeable things to my face at Pemberley once. She left without having achieved anything visible, as I recall."

That had been three months ago. The phrasing was precise, not pointed, and she felt rather than saw him register the distinction.

"She has had time since then to develop a strategy," he said.

"So have I," Elizabeth said, and turned the page.

Lady Catherine arrived at half past two on Friday. Her carriage was, as always, exactly what one would expect from a woman who required that every external circumstance legibly communicate her position, which is to say, it was very large and very clean and announced itself on the drive considerably before it came into view.

Colonel Fitzwilliam had arrived that morning. His presence was not accidental; Elizabeth had understood this from the moment Darcy mentioned he would be visiting, without explaining when the arrangement had been made. He greeted her in the hall with his usual ease, and she thought:

you are here in case I need a buffer. She was glad of the thought; she filed it; she did not plan to need him.

She received Lady Catherine in the blue drawing room. She had chosen the blue drawing room because it was not the largest room in the house, and she did not intend Lady Catherine to feel that Pemberley had arranged itself reverently around her entrance.

She was seated when Lady Catherine came in.

"Mrs. Darcy," Lady Catherine said, in a voice that managed to make the title sound like a charge still under investigation.

"Lady Catherine." Elizabeth did not stand. She gestured toward the chair across from her. "Please sit. I've asked for tea."

Lady Catherine sat, which was a small concession and they both knew it. She looked around the room with the practiced eye of a woman cataloguing evidence, though what charge she was building toward remained, for the moment, unclear.

"You have made some alterations," she observed.

"One or two." The alterations were minor: the placement of a reading table near the window, a different arrangement of the chairs to catch the afternoon light. "The room is better for it, I think."

"The room was arranged by Darcy's mother."

"I know," Elizabeth said pleasantly. "Lady Anne had excellent taste. I moved a table."

The tea arrived. Elizabeth poured.

The first twenty minutes were a careful preliminary; two chess players developing their positions before any piece of consequence moved. Lady Catherine asked about the household with the manner of someone who expected to find fault and was mildly disappointed by the absence of obvious material. Elizabeth answered every question directly and without apology.

Then Lady Catherine said: "I have heard from Anne."

"I hope Miss de Bourgh is well."

"She is not well." Lady Catherine set down her cup with more force than the surface required. "She has been unwell since the spring. Since the news reached Rosings." The implication was laid like a card on the table: *your news. Your fault.*

"I am sorry to hear it," Elizabeth said. This was true; she had no quarrel with Anne de Bourgh.

"Anne was promised to Darcy from their infancy."

"I am aware of the expectation," Elizabeth said. "I understand it was an arrangement between their mothers. I understand it was not, in the legal sense, a promise."

"The distinction is contemptible."

"The distinction is the law of England, but I take your meaning." She kept her voice even. "You believe Darcy failed in a duty he owed your family. That is not a view I share, but I understand you hold it genuinely, and I don't intend to argue you out of it."

Lady Catherine looked at her with an expression that had not quite settled into fury. It was still organizing itself, gathering force. "You are very composed, for a woman in your position."

"What position is that?"

"A woman who married above herself under circumstances that no one with any sense of propriety could consider unimpeachable."

Elizabeth put down her own cup. She did it without haste. "Lady Catherine, I am going to answer you once, clearly, and then I would like to speak of something else. I married your nephew honestly, with his full knowledge of my circumstances and his own. The decision was his as much as mine. If you believe him incapable of knowing his own mind, that is a low view of a man you claim to love. If you believe I manipulated a man of his intelligence and character into a decision against his nature, that is also a low view of him, and of me. I will not defend the marriage further. It does not require my defense."

The room was very still.

"You are impertinent," Lady Catherine said.

"You have said so before." Elizabeth reached for the teapot. "More tea?"

Darcy had positioned himself to arrive at a point in the visit when his presence would be reinforcing rather than rescuing. He had told Elizabeth this, obliquely, the night before, *I will come down before the second hour,* and she had understood what he meant without requiring him to say it plainly.

He entered the drawing room to find the tea things in good order, his wife seated without visible distress, and his aunt in the posture of a woman who has been outmaneuvered but not yet admitted it.

"Aunt." He greeted Lady Catherine with the courtesy due her and took the chair beside Elizabeth's. The positioning was not accidental; she was close enough that the fact of their alliance was visible to anyone with the acuity Lady Catherine possessed.

"Darcy." Lady Catherine's gaze moved between them. "I have been speaking to your wife."

"So, I understand." He reached for a biscuit, which was a more comfortable gesture than it might appear from the outside. "I hope the conversation has been agreeable."

"It has been," Elizabeth said, before Lady Catherine could answer. "Lady Catherine was asking about Anne's health."

Darcy looked at his aunt. "I am sorry Anne is unwell. I will write to her."

"You will do more than write," Lady Catherine said. "You have obligations to this family that you have chosen to disregard."

"The obligations I have to this family," Darcy said, with the patience of someone who had thought through this argument in advance and found it unpersuasive, "are those I choose to honor, and I do honor them. My obligation to Anne was always one of affection, not contract. I have not ceased to feel affection for my cousin." He paused. "I have simply declined to marry her."

"On the basis of... this." Lady Catherine indicated Elizabeth with a gesture that stopped short of pointing, though barely.

"On the basis," Darcy said, "of having found someone I wished to marry."

The sentence landed in the room and did not retreat. Elizabeth, who had not been certain what he would say, absorbed it without any visible change of expression; but she registered it. *Someone I wished to marry.* Not the careful contractual language he had used in the early months; not the neutral framing she had grown accustomed to. That was something he had not said before, and not before witnesses.

Lady Catherine heard it too. The knowledge that she had heard it was in her face.

She did not pursue the point. She shifted, instead, to the question of Georgiana's season and whether Darcy intended to present her from Pemberley or from the London house, whether Elizabeth had given any thought to the obligations of her position as hostess, a retreat into territory where she could continue her siege by other means.

Darcy answered the questions about Georgiana. Elizabeth listened and offered one observation, which was accurate, and which Lady Catherine was unable to dismiss without contradicting a fact about Georgiana's preferences that she had herself stated. The observation was not delivered with any particular relish. It was simply correct.

At the end of the visit, Lady Catherine had announced she would not, after all, stay three days; she would depart Saturday morning. Colonel Fitzwilliam collected his hat from the hallway table.

He had been present at dinner, at supper, and now at the moment of departure, and had spent most of the visit being pleasantly unremarkable in the way of men who are genuinely easy in company. He had talked to Lady Catherine about her roses. He had talked to Darcy about a horse. He had talked to Elizabeth about a novel she had mentioned in passing, which he had also read, and they had disagreed about the ending in a way that was, for both of them, enjoyable.

He had not been needed in any defensive capacity. He had eaten a great deal of Mrs. Reynolds's cooking and had, by all observable evidence, an excellent time.

"A successful visit," he said, at the door, with the air of someone testing the temperature of a sentence.

"I thought so," Elizabeth said.

Fitzwilliam looked at Darcy. "She didn't need me."

"No," Darcy agreed.

Fitzwilliam put on his hat. He looked at Elizabeth for a moment with an expression she could not entirely read, though it contained something adjacent to surprise: not the surprise of a man who expected failure, but of one who had assigned rough odds and found them revised.

"Well," he said. "Pemberley suits you, Mrs. Darcy."

He left before she could decide how to answer. She heard his horse on the gravel a few minutes later.

Darcy found her in the library after dinner. She was not reading; she was standing at the window, looking at the grounds in the dark, which told him something about where her thoughts were.

"That was well done," he said.

"It wasn't difficult." She turned from the window. "She is not, as adversaries go, subtle."

"She is very determined."

"So am I." Elizabeth moved away from the window toward the center of the room. "She will write again. She will perhaps come again. But I think she understood this evening that she will not find a different result."

"She will not." He said it without qualification. He had said *someone I wished to marry* in front of Lady Catherine and not retreated from it, and now he was standing in the library saying *she will not* with the same quality of certainty.

Elizabeth looked at him. She had developed, over months, a catalogue of the small differences in his expression, the distinction between the restraint that was social habit and the restraint that covered something he was deciding not to say. This was the second kind.

"What is it?" she asked.

"Nothing requiring action," he said. "I only wanted to say, you did not use Fitzwilliam."

"No."

"I arranged for him to be here in case you did."

"I know." She had known it since the morning of his arrival. "It was a kind thought."

He seemed to consider whether that was a criticism dressed as courtesy, and concluded, correctly, that it was not. "It was not condescension."

"I know that too." She studied him for a moment: his precise, private face, the one the room did not usually get to see. "Darcy. I understand the difference between being protected and being managed. What you did was the first."

He was quiet.

"You will do it again," she said, "and so will I, for you, when the situation calls for it. That is what people who live in the same house do for each other." She moved toward the door. It was late; she had, in fact, no reason to linger and then paused. "You said I wished to marry. In front of Lady Catherine."

He did not look away. "I did."

"Was it," she said carefully, "true when you said it?"

The pause between them was not uncomfortable. It was the kind that precedes a significant answer rather than the absence of one.

"It was true when I proposed," he said. "It has not become less true since."

Elizabeth held that for a moment. Then she said: "Good night, Darcy," and went upstairs.

She did not run through the conversation again in her mind as she lay awake. She lay quietly knowing that something had shifted, and let it settle without requiring it to announce itself further.

She went to sleep before she decided what to call it.

Chapter 18: Georgiana's Trust

The rain had confined them all morning, and Pemberley in the rain was a different house. It was quieter, turned inward, the light at each window a gray particular to Derbyshire. Georgiana had been at the pianoforte since breakfast, working through a passage she had not managed to her own satisfaction, and the house had arranged itself around the sound without anyone remarking on it.

Elizabeth sat with a book she was not reading. When the passage ended and did not begin again, she looked up.

Georgiana was sitting with both hands in her lap, looking at the keys.

"That last movement," Elizabeth said. "The hesitation before the turn, is that in the score, or is it yours?"

Georgiana turned. She had not heard Elizabeth come in, or perhaps she had heard and had not thought it required acknowledgment. "Mine," she said. "It is too much, I think."

"I liked it. It had the quality of someone remembering something mid-sentence."

Georgiana considered this with the seriousness she brought to most things. "My teacher would not agree."

"Your teacher is not here." Elizabeth set the book down and crossed to the chair nearer the instrument. "Play it again. I want to listen."

This was the kind of request Georgiana knew how to receive. She straightened and set her hands on the keys, and the passage came again, the hesitation still in it, the small delay before the phrase completed itself. Elizabeth watched her hands rather than her face. They were more legible: the movement was controlled and confident up to the turn, and then there was a fraction of a beat where the left hand waited, and in that wait was whatever Georgiana was thinking about when she played it.

When it ended, Elizabeth said, "How long have you played?"

"Since I was four. There was a teacher who came to the house; a small woman, very precise about the wrist." A brief pause. "She would not play herself, only correct. I used to wonder whether she could."

"Did you ever ask?"

Georgiana looked at her hands. "No."

"I would have asked."

"I know." The tone was not reproachful. It was, Elizabeth thought, something closer to admiration wearing the clothes of observation.

They sat a moment in the qualified way that had been their habit in the weeks since Elizabeth's arrival, comfortable in the silence, neither of them in a hurry to fill it with more than it required. Rain hit the tall window. On the drive below, a groom walked quickly from one outbuilding to another with his coat over his head.

"What were you reading?" Georgiana asked.

"I was not, particularly. I was listening to you and using the book as an excuse not to seem as if I were listening."

Georgiana looked at her. "Why would you not simply say so?"

"Because you might have stopped."

This landed as Elizabeth intended it, as a small, exact compliment, not inflated. Georgiana looked back at the keys and Elizabeth watched her take it in, the way she received things that were kind: carefully, as though they might still turn out to be something else.

"My brother says you are very direct," Georgiana said.

"Is that what he says?"

"He says it admiringly." A pause. "He is not always direct himself. Not because he wishes to deceive. More because he is accustomed to a room that does not require it of him."

Elizabeth found this precise enough to be worth sitting with. She had noticed it; the way Darcy moved through a conversation as if he had mapped the exits in advance. Not dishonesty. Something more like the habit of a man who had been agreed with for so long that disagreement required preparation.

"He is becoming more direct," Elizabeth said, which was true, and neutral enough to stand on its own without requiring either of them to build further on it.

Georgiana opened the score on the stand, though she did not look at it. "When he is worried," she said, "he becomes very quiet. Quieter than usual. People mistake it for anger."

"I know." Elizabeth said it before she had decided to say it, which meant it was accurate. "I made that mistake myself, in the beginning."

"Most people do." Georgiana's fingers moved on the keys — not playing, only thinking through them. "It is not the easiest habit to live beside."

"No. But it is honest, which is something."

Georgiana said nothing. The silence was different now, not simply comfortable but held, as though she were testing whether the room would change if she put a weight on it.

Elizabeth let it stand.

"There was a time," Georgiana said, "when I wished very much that someone would be direct with me. About something I did not understand." She said it to the window. "It was the summer I left school."

Elizabeth did not move, did not prompt. The fire settled in the grate with a soft sound.

"I had been at school," Georgiana continued, "or rather I had left school, and the arrangement was that I should have a companion in Ramsgate for part of the summer. A Mrs. Younge." The name landed flat, a fact rather than a confidence. "She had been recommended. She seemed... she seemed to know the right things to say about most situations."

"Someone I had known as a child came to Ramsgate," Georgiana said. "He had known my father. He was — he was very easy to talk to. He understood what it was to find certain rooms too large. He did not treat me as if being young were a deficiency." She stopped.

Elizabeth kept her eyes on the fire. Ramsgate. A companion arranged. An easy man from childhood. She was assembling something, and she did not want Georgiana to see her doing it.

"I know now that this was a choice he made deliberately. That the ease was not natural to him. But I did not know it then."

Elizabeth asked, quietly, "What did you want to happen?"

Georgiana looked at her. The question had caught her. "I wanted —" She stopped. Tried again. "I believed I was in love. I believed he was also in love. I agreed to an elopement." A beat. "My brother arrived before anything... before it was completed. He came to Ramsgate without warning and I told him everything because I could not... I could not hold it any longer."

"How did he receive it?"

"He was very pale." Georgiana's hands, still resting on the instrument, pressed down slightly. "He did not raise his voice. He did not reproach me. He asked me three or four questions, very calm, and then he wrote a letter and the man... left. And Fitzwilliam held the whole thing entirely to himself." She said the last part with an exactness that suggested she had weighed it many times.

Elizabeth said nothing. She was thinking about the evening at Longbourn; the name dropped by Lydia into the middle of a crowded room, Darcy's expression changing by the particular degree that only Elizabeth had been placed to see, and then his words to her afterward: he is not safe. Nothing further. She had not pressed him, and he had not offered more. She understood now what he had been holding.

"I believed, for some months afterward," Georgiana said, "that the fault was mine entirely. My brother did not tell me otherwise. I think he did not wish to increase my distress, but neither did anyone correct me." She met Elizabeth's eyes. "It is a strange thing to carry. That weight. One does not quite know whether to put it down or not."

She was learning it now, in this room, from the person who had survived it. The girl who had believed an easy man because he told her she was not a deficiency, lately out of school, handed from one supervised arrangement directly into a badly supervised one, with no interval in which to become harder to read, a specific period of being young. Elizabeth had her own version, which was less dramatic in form and not, in the essential mathematics, very different.

Elizabeth said, "You had just left school. He had been studying the approach for some time before Ramsgate." She let that settle. "The judgment would not look the same on him."

Georgiana was quiet. Elizabeth watched her receive this, not as consolation, which it was not meant to be, but as a recalibration of a fact she had held at the wrong angle for too long.

The clock on the mantel marked the quarter hour. Neither of them had noticed the previous one.

"Mrs. Younge," Georgiana said presently. "I think of her sometimes. Whether she was a willing party or merely careless. I have never been able to decide which would be worse."

"Willing," Elizabeth said. "Carelessness can be corrected. The other is a choice."

Georgiana turned this over. "My brother could have told me that. Instead of simply ending it and saying nothing further."

"He was protecting you from the full picture."

"I know. I wish he had not." Her voice was not resentful, it was measured, the voice of someone who had thought through the question carefully and arrived at a conclusion she did not particularly enjoy. "One manages a thing better, I think, when one can see it clearly. Even when it is unpleasant."

Elizabeth recognized this. It was a version of the argument she had made to Darcy himself, in the formal terms of their early engagement: she would not be managed, she would not be protected from facts that concerned her. Georgiana had arrived at the same position through carrying partial information for too long, which was perhaps the harder route but arrived at the same place.

"I think he has learned that," Elizabeth said. "He is still learning it. But he is inclined to learn, which is not always the case with people."

Georgiana said, after a moment, "He is different with you than he was." She said it carefully, as one states an observation that may or may not be welcome. "Not less himself. More of himself, perhaps. As though a room in the house that was generally kept shut has been opened and found to contain nothing alarming."

Elizabeth looked at her. The image was exact in the way that images are when they have arrived from genuine observation rather than social courtesy. "He is much the same with me," she said. "But he argues his point now, instead of simply ceasing to speak when he does not agree. I count that as an improvement."

Georgiana's expression arrived at something warmer. "He ceases to speak with me as well. I used to think it meant I had said something wrong."

"So did I."

"He came back, the following spring," Georgiana said. The shift was slight but deliberate. She had not finished. "In Meryton. With the militia."

"Yes." Elizabeth said it without inflection.

"Did my brother tell you that?"

"He told me very little." Elizabeth said it plainly. "Only that Wickham was not safe. I did not know why until now."

Georgiana looked at her. "You thought well of him. Of Wickham?"

There was no reproach in the name she had said it herself, which was its own form of courage.

"I formed a very poor opinion of your brother on slight acquaintance," Elizabeth said. "His manner at our first meeting gave me reason enough to dislike him, or so I thought at the time. I did not examine whether the reason was sufficient. I simply proceeded." She kept her voice even. "Wickham's name has reached me only twice, and both times at a remove. I know nothing of him beyond what your brother told me in a single sentence. But I understand what he does: a man who reads what someone has already decided and confirms it. I was the easier target for having decided so much already."

"You do not excuse yourself very much."

"No. Neither do you."

This produced the closest thing to a smile Elizabeth had yet seen from Georgiana, not bright, but real, arriving without preparation. It changed her face considerably.

The rain against the window was lighter now. The gray in the room had shifted by a degree. The score on the stand lifted slightly in the draft from the chimney and settled back.

Georgiana reached out and put her hand flat on the page to keep it still. It was a small gesture, the kind that belongs only to the person who makes it: proprietary, unconscious, entirely legible to Elizabeth as the act of someone who had learned to hold things down before they blew away.

Somewhere in the house a door opened and closed, and then footsteps — Darcy's, Elizabeth knew them by now crossed the hall below, and then were gone.

"Will he know," Georgiana asked, "that we have spoken?"

"Not yet. He will when he sees us, I think. He reads rooms more accurately than he is generally given credit for."

"He does." A pause. "Will you tell him what I said?"

Elizabeth thought about this with the honesty she had required of herself since Longbourn. "If it comes up - if there is something in what you have told me that I need to act on - I will tell you first. Nothing about you travels through me without your knowing."

Georgiana was still for a moment. Then she turned back to the pianoforte and set her hands on the keys. The passage came again with the hesitation before the turn, the left hand waiting, and this time Elizabeth heard it differently. It was not a fault in the playing. It was a small pause before the phrase resolved: the sound of something held back, then given over.

When it ended, neither of them spoke. The fire had settled to a steady burn.

Darcy appeared in the doorway some minutes later. He looked at the two of them, Georgiana at the instrument, Elizabeth in the chair nearby with the unread book again in her lap and Elizabeth watched him take in the room: the ease of it, the stillness, the way it had arrived at something without requiring explanation.

He crossed to the side table, poured tea into two cups, and set one within Georgiana's reach without a word.

He sat in the chair across from Elizabeth, lifted the teapot, and looked at her with an inquiry that was not quite a question.

She held out her cup.

He poured.

Outside, the rain had stopped.

Chapter 19: Wickham Surfaces

They had come south for two reasons, which was one more reason than Darcy generally required and one fewer than Elizabeth would have invented if left to herself. His solicitor was in London; her sister was at Longbourn; Netherfield stood conveniently between the two, and Bingley had been so transparently delighted at the prospect of company that refusing him would have required a harder heart than either of them possessed.

Mrs. Philips's card party was not, strictly speaking, a third reason. It had materialized on their second afternoon in Hertfordshire with the cheerful inexorability of all her aunt's arrangements, expanding outward from a small family gathering until it had acquired dimensions that bore only passing resemblance to the original plan.

The room held more people than a small family gathering strictly required, and several of them were unfamiliar.

Mrs. Philips was a woman of warm feelings and approximate judgment, and she had, in extending the evening's invitation more broadly than strictly necessary, acted from pure good nature rather than any intent to transgress. This was always the difficulty with her aunt. The transgression was real, the intent entirely innocent, and the result the same, regardless.

Darcy noticed the room's composition before Elizabeth did. She felt it in the slight shift of his attention, the way his gaze moved through the faces assembled in the drawing room with a precision that was not rudeness but was not ease either.

She said nothing. They crossed to where Mrs. Philips stood, made their greetings, and Elizabeth watched her aunt glow with the pleasure of someone who has managed to produce the most distinguished guest in Meryton's recent memory.

Lydia and Kitty were already established at one of the card tables with two of the Goulding daughters. Lydia was dealing with the cheerful efficiency of a girl who has waited all week for an occasion and intends to extract full value from it. Her mourning dress of gray wool was respectable but nothing at all like what Lydia would have chosen in other circumstances. It did nothing to diminish her animation.

She had not yet seen the door.

Colonel Fitzwilliam arrived with a man in a red coat.

The arrival itself was unremarkable. Fitzwilliam moved through rooms with an ease that produced no disruption, and the officer beside him had the look of someone accustomed to being introduced into drawing rooms by men of good standing. He paused just inside the doorway, just long enough to read the room without appearing to read it, and then moved forward at Fitzwilliam's side with the unhurried confidence of a man who does not expect to be unwelcome.

Elizabeth watched this entrance from across the room and did not yet know what she was watching.

Fitzwilliam greeted Darcy with the warmth of long habit, and then turned to Elizabeth with the consideration he always showed her, not deferential, just attentive, the manner of a man who takes women seriously as conversationalists because he has found it more interesting to do so.

"Mrs. Darcy. August suits you, somehow."

"August suits no one," Elizabeth said. "You are being generous."

"I am being accurate. Darcy, do you know Lieutenant Wickham? He is newly stationed with the regiment. I ran into him at the posting house this afternoon and could not in conscience leave him to a solitary evening."

It was not Fitzwilliam's fault. He had been in Hertfordshire for four days and had no reason to have assembled the specific history that would have made this introduction impossible. He made it with the easy goodwill of a man doing a small social kindness, and nothing in his expression suggested he had noticed that Darcy had not immediately spoken.

Wickham bowed to Elizabeth with careful respect; not too much, not too little, calibrated to a married woman of consequence.

He bowed to Darcy with a shade of familiarity that was not quite insolence and not quite warmth, but occupied the precise uncomfortable territory between them.

Then Lydia, who had looked up from her cards at the sound of a new voice, caught his eye across the room.

Mrs. Philips took charge of the introduction to the rest of the room in the pleasant, imprecise way of a hostess who is delighted to have a new face and not especially concerned with the mechanism by which it arrived. Within ten minutes, Wickham had a seat at the card table nearest the fire, directly across from Lydia.

This had not happened by accident. Elizabeth had watched her aunt engineer it with the cheerful efficiency of someone who considers herself to be doing everyone a favor, and had been three steps too far from the table to intervene without making the intervention conspicuous.

Darcy did not attempt to intervene. He took a seat at the other table, at Elizabeth's side, and was dealt in with the composure of a man who has decided that direct action will produce exactly the wrong result and that patience, at this moment, is the form of action available to him.

Elizabeth watched Lydia across two card tables and listened to Darcy bid correctly on a hand he was not attending to, and thought: this is going to be a very long evening.

The card play gave Wickham everything he needed. A card table is, in its way, a more intimate social space than a ballroom: the players are seated, proximate, required to speak, and enclosed by the logic of the game from the social obligation to include anyone beyond their four. Wickham used this without appearing to use it.

He was a good player, which immediately interested Lydia, who was a competitive player and had been dealt three indifferent hands in succession and was therefore in exactly the mood to admire competence. He played with easy good humor, praised her when she played well, which she did, when she was attending, and absorbed her mistakes with the indulgent grace of a man who finds everything she does charming.

“You play very well, Miss Bennet,” he said, after she had taken a trick she had not appeared to expect. "You attend to the cards when you choose to, and when you choose to, you play very well indeed."

Lydia laughed. “My father always said I was too easily distracted to be a really good player. But then, he also said Kitty and I would never improve, and Kitty has not improved.”

“Then your father was half wrong,” Wickham said. “Which is a better rate than most.”

It was a small thing, the invocation of Mr. Bennet, handled with just enough lightness to be a compliment without requiring any acknowledgment of the grief that surrounded it. Lydia brightened in the way she brightened when she felt understood. Elizabeth, watching from the other table, recognized the move without being able to fault its execution.

Between hands, Wickham spoke to Lydia in the lower register that the card table permitted without excluding: close enough to be private, not so low as to be remarkable. Elizabeth caught fragments only.

'Spirit', she heard once; Wickham using the word with a particular emphasis that implied Lydia possessed something the rest of the room lacked. Lydia's chin lifted on hearing it, which was exactly what he had intended.

Then, during the shuffle, something else, too low for Elizabeth to catch, that made Lydia laugh and glance around the room as though checking whether the right people had seen her laugh. The right people, Elizabeth understood, were not herself.

When the cards were dealt again and Lydia had had a moment to settle her pleasure into something more composed, Wickham said something that Elizabeth caught more clearly: a word about being misjudged, offered lightly, as if it were a rueful observation on human nature rather than the opening of a particular argument. He did not name anyone. He did not need to. The light self-deprecation, 'I have not always been fortunate in how I am understood, but one learns to laugh,' had the texture of a confession made to someone trusted, and Lydia heard it that way.

Then, during the shuffle, Lydia's attention went to Darcy for a moment as some remark of Mrs. Philips's had included his name, and Elizabeth watched Wickham follow Lydia's glance and then return to her with an expression she could not read from this distance but recognized in its structure: the look of a man introducing a subject without appearing to introduce it.

Darcy had also watched.

He had done so with the contained precision of a man who understands that he is the most visible person in the room and therefore the least able to observe without being observed. He had played three hands correctly, answered two questions from Mrs. Philips about Pemberley that she had asked him before and would ask again, and kept Wickham in his peripheral attention with the practiced skill of someone who had been doing exactly this for years.

The years were, in this moment, very present to him. He had done this calculation before, the specific arithmetic of what revealing Georgiana's history would cost against what concealing it would cost, and the answer had always come out the same way: concealment, because the alternative was worse. The alternative turned a private wound into public currency. It made Georgiana's worst months the instrument of her brother's convenience, and he would not do it.

Wickham knew this. The knowing was itself a weapon. Every room he entered with Darcy in it, he entered carrying the knowledge that Darcy's hands were tied by exactly the thing he would most wish to protect.

He could not say the one sentence that would end Wickham's welcome in this drawing room. He could not cross the card table and remove Lydia from the conversation without producing precisely the kind of scene that would entrench Wickham's sympathetic status with the neighborhood for the next six months. He could not even look at Wickham with the full weight of what he knew without it reading, to a room that did not share his knowledge, as the habitual hauteur of a proud man toward an inferior.

He played his cards and waited.

Across the table, Elizabeth turned a card and then looked up, and she found Darcy already watching her; a moment brief enough that no one else would have caught it. She had seen him watching Wickham. She knew what he was managing. The look she gave him was not reassurance, it was acknowledgment, which was better.

He returned his attention to his hand.

The supper interval redistributed the room. The card tables were abandoned; people moved to the supper table; the fixed geometry of the evening loosened into the more fluid arrangement of people serving themselves and finding where to stand.

Wickham was beside Lydia before anyone had organized themselves. He had moved with the casual promptness of a man who knows exactly where he is going and has arranged to look as though he simply arrived there.

Elizabeth was watching.

She was also speaking with Mrs. Long about the weather and the roads north, which were being compared unfavorably to the roads south, and she sustained this conversation with the portion of her attention it required and devoted the remainder to the supper table.

Wickham spoke to Lydia for several minutes: his back was partly to the room, which was not an accident, and the angle made it impossible for Elizabeth to read his expression. But she could read Lydia's: the tilt of her chin, the quality of her attention, the small movement of pleasure when he said something that made her feel she was being told a truth the room at large was not permitted to hear.

Then his posture changed slightly, and his glance went, just briefly, toward Darcy.

Lydia noticed. Elizabeth saw her notice. The noticing did something to Lydia's expression. It quickened it, gave it a private satisfaction, as if she had just been included in something.

Elizabeth set down her plate.

She found a moment at the edge of the supper room when Darcy was briefly alone. Mrs. Philips had been claimed by the Gouldings, Fitzwilliam had gone to speak with someone, and Darcy stood with a glass he was not drinking from and watched the room.

She came to stand beside him. Not close enough to suggest a private conversation. Close enough to speak without being heard.

"Tell me," she said, under the general noise of the supper.

He looked at her. Something in his expression closed the way it did when he was calculating not whether to speak but how much. "Not here."

"I know not here. Tell me something."

A pause. Then, still looking at the room: "You must trust me. He is not safe."

She wanted his reasons, and looking at his face she understood that she already had them. The cost of the full truth was a name, a specific name, attached to a history Georgiana had given her in pieces in the music room at Pemberley and that name could not be said in a supper room in Meryton without becoming the neighborhood's property before the week was out. This was not evasion. It was the same constraint it had always been, and she now knew its detailed dimensions.

Something in her settled into cold recognition. Not surprise. She had watched this man for four months now, and she knew the difference between the restraint that was pride and the restraint that was protection. This was the second kind.

This was not dislike. This was warning.

She looked back at the supper table, where Lydia was laughing at something Wickham had said. "What do you need from me tonight?"

"Keep her close to you if you can. And say nothing to give him a reason to think he's been read."

"He already knows he's been read."

"Yes," Darcy said. "But there is a difference between knowing it and having it confirmed."

Elizabeth picked up her plate again and returned to the supper table.

The rest of the evening was a careful management of circumstances that were not, in the end, manageable.

Mrs. Philips, who had no idea that any management was required, undermined three separate approaches simply by being herself: she redirected Lydia toward Wickham twice in the space of an hour, once by asking him to explain a point of whist to her niece and once by seating them adjacent at the resumed card table on the grounds that they had been getting on so famously.

Wickham continued to be exactly what the room needed him to be: agreeable, undemanding, lightly amusing, and entirely present to whoever was speaking to him. He was very good at this. Elizabeth could observe his technique with something approaching professional respect while finding nothing respectable in its application.

At one point she attempted a direct approach to Lydia under some pretext to draw her to the other side of the room and Lydia came willingly enough and then drifted back within ten minutes, the current of the evening carrying her where the interest was strongest.

Darcy's efforts were equally unavailing in their own register. He requested Wickham join him and Fitzwilliam at the whist table, which would have separated him from Lydia; Wickham accepted with gracious warmth and then contrived, through the management of the next hand's seating, to be returned to his original position before the rubber was complete. It was done without apparent intention. It was not without apparent intention.

Fitzwilliam, who understood something of the general unease without understanding its specific content, made several well-meant attempts to smooth the evening that had the effect of normalizing Wickham's presence still further. He was not to blame for this. It was simply what happened when a man of good nature operated without necessary information.

In the last half hour, while the card tables were breaking up and wraps were being retrieved, Wickham found Lydia near the window. Elizabeth was close enough to be in the same room and not close enough to be included.

She saw Lydia's chin lift in the way it lifted when she was receiving a compliment she considered her due. She saw the brief, private nature of what he said low and direct, with the confidence that implies a shared understanding. She saw Lydia's response: the brightness of someone who has been handed, not just an evening's entertainment, but a story in which she is the interesting figure.

Then Fitzwilliam's voice reached them from across the room, easy and friendly, and Wickham stepped back from the window with the unhurried ease of a man who has already secured what he came for.

On the way out, Mrs. Philips pressed Wickham's hand and said he must come again, they were always at home on Tuesdays and Thursdays, and she knew her nieces would be very glad to see him, and he must not be a stranger, it was so very dull in the oppressing heat of summer for the young people. Wickham received this with gracious warmth and said exactly the right things, and Elizabeth, standing beside Darcy in the doorway, heard the invitation land and could not find a way to unsay it that would not require an explanation she was not in a position to give.

The carriage back to Netherfield was quiet. Lydia was not with them. She had returned to Longbourn with Kitty and her mother, and Elizabeth and Darcy sat across from each other in the dark interior with the specific silence of two people who have been managing separately all evening and have not yet had occasion to debrief.

Elizabeth looked out the window. The lights of Meryton fell away behind them. The road was rutted and uneven and the carriage moved through it with the particular lurch of a vehicle that has had a long day.

"Tomorrow," she said, at length.

Darcy looked at her.

"Whatever you need to tell me. All of it. Tomorrow."

He nodded once.

They did not speak again until Netherfield, which was what they both needed: the relief of a silence that does not require management.

Chapter 19: Wickham Surfaces

They had come south for two reasons, which was one more reason than Darcy generally required and one fewer than Elizabeth would have invented if left to herself. His solicitor was in London; her sister was at Longbourn; Netherfield stood conveniently between the two, and Bingley had been so transparently delighted at the prospect of company that refusing him would have required a harder heart than either of them possessed.

Mrs. Philips's card party was not, strictly speaking, a third reason. It had materialized on their second afternoon in Hertfordshire with the cheerful inexorability of all her aunt's arrangements, expanding outward from a small family gathering until it had acquired dimensions that bore only passing resemblance to the original plan.

The room held more people than a small family gathering strictly required, and several of them were unfamiliar.

Mrs. Philips was a woman of warm feelings and approximate judgment, and she had, in extending the evening's invitation more broadly than strictly necessary, acted from pure good nature rather than any intent to transgress. This was always the difficulty with her aunt. The transgression was real, the intent entirely innocent, and the result the same, regardless.

Darcy noticed the room's composition before Elizabeth did. She felt it in the slight shift of his attention, the way his gaze moved through the faces assembled in the drawing room with a precision that was not rudeness but was not ease either.

She said nothing. They crossed to where Mrs. Philips stood, made their greetings, and Elizabeth watched her aunt glow with the pleasure of someone who has managed to produce the most distinguished guest in Meryton's recent memory.

Lydia and Kitty were already established at one of the card tables with two of the Goulding daughters. Lydia was dealing with the cheerful efficiency of a girl who has waited all week for an occasion and intends to extract full value from it. Her mourning dress of gray wool was respectable but nothing at all like what Lydia would have chosen in other circumstances. It did nothing to diminish her animation.

She had not yet seen the door.

Colonel Fitzwilliam arrived with a man in a red coat.

The arrival itself was unremarkable. Fitzwilliam moved through rooms with an ease that produced no disruption, and the officer beside him had the look of someone accustomed to being introduced into drawing rooms by men of good standing. He paused just inside the doorway, just long enough to read the room without appearing to read it, and then moved forward at Fitzwilliam's side with the unhurried confidence of a man who does not expect to be unwelcome.

Elizabeth watched this entrance from across the room and did not yet know what she was watching.

Fitzwilliam greeted Darcy with the warmth of long habit, and then turned to Elizabeth with the consideration he always showed her, not deferential, just attentive, the manner of a man who takes women seriously as conversationalists because he has found it more interesting to do so.

"Mrs. Darcy. August suits you, somehow."

"August suits no one," Elizabeth said. "You are being generous."

"I am being accurate. Darcy, do you know Lieutenant Wickham? He is newly stationed with the regiment. I ran into him at the posting house this afternoon and could not in conscience leave him to a solitary evening."

It was not Fitzwilliam's fault. He had been in Hertfordshire for four days and had no reason to have assembled the specific history that would have made this introduction impossible. He made it with the easy goodwill of a man doing a small social kindness, and nothing in his expression suggested he had noticed that Darcy had not immediately spoken.

Wickham bowed to Elizabeth with careful respect; not too much, not too little, calibrated to a married woman of consequence.

He bowed to Darcy with a shade of familiarity that was not quite insolence and not quite warmth, but occupied the precise uncomfortable territory between them.

Then Lydia, who had looked up from her cards at the sound of a new voice, caught his eye across the room.

Mrs. Philips took charge of the introduction to the rest of the room in the pleasant, imprecise way of a hostess who is delighted to have a new face and not especially concerned with the mechanism by which it arrived. Within ten minutes, Wickham had a seat at the card table nearest the fire, directly across from Lydia.

This had not happened by accident. Elizabeth had watched her aunt engineer it with the cheerful efficiency of someone who considers herself to be doing everyone a favor, and had been three steps too far from the table to intervene without making the intervention conspicuous.

Darcy did not attempt to intervene. He took a seat at the other table, at Elizabeth's side, and was dealt in with the composure of a man who has decided that direct action will produce exactly the wrong result and that patience, at this moment, is the form of action available to him.

Elizabeth watched Lydia across two card tables and listened to Darcy bid correctly on a hand he was not attending to, and thought: this is going to be a very long evening.

The card play gave Wickham everything he needed. A card table is, in its way, a more intimate social space than a ballroom: the players are seated, proximate, required to speak, and enclosed by the logic of the game from the social obligation to include anyone beyond their four. Wickham used this without appearing to use it.

He was a good player, which immediately interested Lydia, who was a competitive player and had been dealt three indifferent hands in succession and was therefore in exactly the mood to admire competence. He played with easy good humor, praised her when she played well, which she did, when she was attending, and absorbed her mistakes with the indulgent grace of a man who finds everything she does charming.

"You play very well, Miss Bennet," he said, after she had taken a trick she had not appeared to expect. "You attend to the cards when you choose to, and when you choose to, you play very well indeed."

Lydia laughed. "My father always said I was too easily distracted to be a really good player. But then, he also said Kitty and I would never improve, and Kitty has not improved."

"Then your father was half wrong," Wickham said. "Which is a better rate than most."

It was a small thing, the invocation of Mr. Bennet, handled with just enough lightness to be a compliment without requiring any acknowledgment of the grief that surrounded it. Lydia brightened in the way she brightened when she felt understood. Elizabeth, watching from the other table, recognized the move without being able to fault its execution.

Between hands, Wickham spoke to Lydia in the lower register that the card table permitted without excluding: close enough to be private, not so low as to be remarkable. Elizabeth caught fragments only.

'Spirit', she heard once; Wickham using the word with a particular emphasis that implied Lydia possessed something the rest of the room lacked. Lydia's chin lifted on hearing it, which was exactly what he had intended.

Then, during the shuffle, something else, too low for Elizabeth to catch, that made Lydia laugh and glance around the room as though checking whether the right people had seen her laugh. The right people, Elizabeth understood, were not herself.

When the cards were dealt again and Lydia had had a moment to settle her pleasure into something more composed, Wickham said something that Elizabeth caught more clearly: a word about being misjudged, offered lightly, as if it were a rueful observation on human nature rather than the opening of a particular argument. He did not name anyone. He did not need to. The light self-deprecation, 'I have not always been fortunate in how I am understood, but one learns to laugh,' had the texture of a confession made to someone trusted, and Lydia heard it that way.

Then, during the shuffle, Lydia's attention went to Darcy for a moment as some remark of Mrs. Philips's had included his name, and Elizabeth watched Wickham follow Lydia's glance and then return to her with an expression she could not read from this distance but recognized in its structure: the look of a man introducing a subject without appearing to introduce it.

Darcy had also watched.

He had done so with the contained precision of a man who understands that he is the most visible person in the room and therefore the least able to observe without being observed. He had played three hands correctly, answered two questions from Mrs. Philips about Pemberley that she had asked him before and would ask again, and kept Wickham in his peripheral attention with the practiced skill of someone who had been doing exactly this for years.

The years were, in this moment, very present to him. He had done this calculation before, the specific arithmetic of what revealing Georgiana's history would cost against what concealing it would cost, and the answer had always come out the same way: concealment, because the alternative was worse. The alternative turned a private wound into public currency. It made Georgiana's worst months the instrument of her brother's convenience, and he would not do it.

Wickham knew this. The knowing was itself a weapon. Every room he entered with Darcy in it, he entered carrying the knowledge that Darcy's hands were tied by exactly the thing he would most wish to protect.

He could not say the one sentence that would end Wickham's welcome in this drawing room. He could not cross the card table and remove Lydia from the conversation without producing precisely the kind of scene that would entrench Wickham's sympathetic status with the neighborhood for the next six months. He could not even look at Wickham with the full weight of what he knew without it reading, to a room that did not share his knowledge, as the habitual hauteur of a proud man toward an inferior.

He played his cards and waited.

Across the table, Elizabeth turned a card and then looked up, and she found Darcy already watching her; a moment brief enough that no one else would have caught it. She had seen him watching Wickham. She knew what he was managing. The look she gave him was not reassurance, it was acknowledgment, which was better.

He returned his attention to his hand.

The supper interval redistributed the room. The card tables were abandoned; people moved to the supper table; the fixed geometry of the evening loosened into the more fluid arrangement of people serving themselves and finding where to stand.

Wickham was beside Lydia before anyone had organized themselves. He had moved with the casual promptness of a man who knows exactly where he is going and has arranged to look as though he simply arrived there.

Elizabeth was watching.

She was also speaking with Mrs. Long about the weather and the roads north, which were being compared unfavorably to the roads south, and she sustained this conversation with the portion of her attention it required and devoted the remainder to the supper table.

Wickham spoke to Lydia for several minutes: his back was partly to the room, which was not an accident, and the angle made it impossible for Elizabeth to read his expression. But she could read Lydia's: the tilt of her chin, the quality of her attention, the small movement of pleasure when he said something that made her feel she was being told a truth the room at large was not permitted to hear.

Then his posture changed slightly, and his glance went, just briefly, toward Darcy.

Lydia noticed. Elizabeth saw her notice. The noticing did something to Lydia's expression. It quickened it, gave it a private satisfaction, as if she had just been included in something.

Elizabeth set down her plate.

She found a moment at the edge of the supper room when Darcy was briefly alone. Mrs. Philips had been claimed by the Gouldings, Fitzwilliam had gone to speak with someone, and Darcy stood with a glass he was not drinking from and watched the room.

She came to stand beside him. Not close enough to suggest a private conversation. Close enough to speak without being heard.

"Tell me," she said, under the general noise of the supper.

He looked at her. Something in his expression closed the way it did when he was calculating not whether to speak but how much. "Not here."

"I know not here. Tell me something."

A pause. Then, still looking at the room: "You must trust me. He is not safe."

She wanted his reasons, and looking at his face she understood that she already had them. The cost of the full truth was a name, a specific name, attached to a history Georgiana had given her in pieces in the music room at Pemberley and that name could not be said in a supper room in Meryton without becoming the neighborhood's property before the week was out. This was not evasion. It was the same constraint it had always been, and she now knew its detailed dimensions.

Something in her settled into cold recognition. Not surprise. She had watched this man for four months now, and she knew the difference between the restraint that was pride and the restraint that was protection. This was the second kind.

This was not dislike. This was warning.

She looked back at the supper table, where Lydia was laughing at something Wickham had said. "What do you need from me tonight?"

"Keep her close to you if you can. And say nothing to give him a reason to think he's been read."

"He already knows he's been read."

"Yes," Darcy said. "But there is a difference between knowing it and having it confirmed."

Elizabeth picked up her plate again and returned to the supper table.

The rest of the evening was a careful management of circumstances that were not, in the end, manageable.

Mrs. Philips, who had no idea that any management was required, undermined three separate approaches simply by being herself: she redirected Lydia toward Wickham twice in the space of an hour, once by asking him to explain a point of whist to her niece and once by seating them adjacent at the resumed card table on the grounds that they had been getting on so famously.

Wickham continued to be exactly what the room needed him to be: agreeable, undemanding, lightly amusing, and entirely present to whoever was speaking to him. He was very good at this. Elizabeth could observe his technique with something approaching professional respect while finding nothing respectable in its application.

At one point she attempted a direct approach to Lydia under some pretext to draw her to the other side of the room and Lydia came willingly enough and then drifted back within ten minutes, the current of the evening carrying her where the interest was strongest.

Darcy's efforts were equally unavailing in their own register. He requested Wickham join him and Fitzwilliam at the whist table, which would have separated him from Lydia; Wickham accepted with gracious warmth and then contrived, through the management of the next hand's seating, to be returned to his original position before the rubber was complete. It was done without apparent intention. It was not without apparent intention.

Fitzwilliam, who understood something of the general unease without understanding its specific content, made several well-meant attempts to smooth the evening that had the effect of normalizing Wickham's presence still further. He was not to blame for this. It was simply what happened when a man of good nature operated without necessary information.

In the last half hour, while the card tables were breaking up and wraps were being retrieved, Wickham found Lydia near the window. Elizabeth was close enough to be in the same room and not close enough to be included.

She saw Lydia's chin lift in the way it lifted when she was receiving a compliment she considered her due. She saw the brief, private nature of what he said low and direct, with the confidence that implies a shared understanding. She saw Lydia's response: the brightness of someone who has been handed, not just an evening's entertainment, but a story in which she is the interesting figure.

Then Fitzwilliam's voice reached them from across the room, easy and friendly, and Wickham stepped back from the window with the unhurried ease of a man who has already secured what he came for.

On the way out, Mrs. Philips pressed Wickham's hand and said he must come again, they were always at home on Tuesdays and Thursdays, and she knew her nieces would be very glad to see him, and he must not be a stranger, it was so very dull in the oppressing heat of summer for the young people. Wickham received this with gracious warmth and said exactly the right things, and Elizabeth, standing beside Darcy in the doorway, heard the invitation land and could not find a way to unsay it that would not require an explanation she was not in a position to give.

The carriage back to Netherfield was quiet. Lydia was not with them. She had returned to Longbourn with Kitty and her mother, and Elizabeth and Darcy sat across from each other in the dark interior with the specific silence of two people who have been managing separately all evening and have not yet had occasion to debrief.

Elizabeth looked out the window. The lights of Meryton fell away behind them. The road was rutted and uneven and the carriage moved through it with the particular lurch of a vehicle that has had a long day.

"Tomorrow," she said, at length.

Darcy looked at her.

"Whatever you need to tell me. All of it. Tomorrow."

He nodded once.

They did not speak again until Netherfield, which was what they both needed: the relief of a silence that does not require management.

Chapter 20: The Truth About Wickham

The morning was already warm when the carriage left Netherfield. Darcy had arranged the hour; Elizabeth had not asked for an early start, and he had not explained the hour. She did not need him to. She knew he intended to have this conversation before the day had any further claims on either of them.

They were alone. The road to Longbourn was familiar by now in the way all roads used repeatedly become familiar: not quite noticed, there when required.

Elizabeth waited. She had learned something over the preceding months about the difference between Darcy gathering himself and Darcy avoiding. The present silence was the former. She let it run its course.

He began with Wickham's father.

The elder Wickham had been Pemberley's steward, a position of genuine trust, held for many years and held well. Darcy's own father had regarded him with real warmth. George Wickham had grown up at Pemberley accordingly: not quite a son of the house, but not otherwise either, and aware of both the privilege and its limits.

"My father left him a legacy," Darcy said. "A living was promised: Kympton, if he wished to take orders. He did not. He applied instead for the value of it in money, on the grounds that he intended a career in law. I paid it. Three thousand pounds."

Elizabeth said nothing. She was watching the road ahead and he had learned by now what her stillness meant when she was listening.

"The law career did not materialize. Two years later he wrote again to claim the living itself, on the grounds that his circumstances had changed and he was now prepared to take orders. I refused."

"On what grounds?" she asked.

"On the grounds that he had already received the value of it. And on others that I could demonstrate but had chosen not to make public." He paused. "Wickham's debts in that period were considerable, and their nature was not consistent with a man preparing for orders. I knew this. I had not found it necessary to say it."

"Because of your father's feeling for his?"

"Yes."

It was a single word and she did not push past it. There was, she thought, an entire education compressed into that refusal to speak ill of a dead man's son, a kind of loyalty that had cost him more than he had intended to pay, and that he would probably practice again in similar circumstances, because it was how he was made up.

He told her the rest in the same measured way: the pattern of debt across the following years, the occasional letter with its demands and expectations, the sense that Wickham understood Darcy's silence as a resource and intended to continue drawing on it.

Then he stopped.

The hedgerows on both sides were thick with late summer growth, the sky a hazy white above them.

"There is more," Elizabeth said. It was not a question.

He looked at her directly. "Yes."

"I know," she said, "that there is more. I want you to understand that before I tell you how I know."

Darcy went still. Not visibly, nothing about his posture changed, but she had spent enough time in his company to distinguish stillness from rest. He was recalibrating.

"Georgiana spoke to me," Elizabeth said. "At Pemberley several days ago. I did not seek it, and I did not press her. She moved toward it herself, in her own time, and I let her do so at the pace she chose."

She paused. "I have held it since because it was hers to give and not mine to distribute. I am telling you now because you have a right to know she gave it, and because I will not manage information about your family from you in one direction while objecting to your managing it from me in the other."

A long silence.

"What did she tell you?" His voice was even.

"That a man she knew in her childhood had found her again when she was still young and inexperienced and without adequate guidance. That he had persuaded her she was in love with him. That you arrived and he did not remain." She looked at him. "I inferred the rest from what she did not say."

"What did you infer?"

"That the man's name was Wickham. That the reason you have said nothing publicly in Hertfordshire, or at the Philipses', last night is that speaking would require speaking it. And that you have calculated, repeatedly, that her history is not yours to spend in a room full of people looking for something to repeat."

Darcy turned to face the window. When he spoke again he chose his words with the care of a man who had not said them before. "She was not yet sixteen. I had trusted her companion selection to a recommendation I should not have trusted. By the time I understood what was happening, the design had been in place for some weeks."

Elizabeth did not speak.

"She was prepared to elope with him. She believed herself in love. I arrived before the thing was concluded - two days before - and I confronted Wickham. He left." A pause. "I told Georgiana only that the engagement could not proceed and that she was to have nothing further to do with him. I did not explain why."

Elizabeth was quiet for a moment. "She does not know why he left."

"No."

"You decided she was not to be told."

"I decided she was too distressed to hear it." He said it with the flatness of a man who has rehearsed a justification until he can deliver it accurately and no longer believes it entirely. "I told myself it was protection. I have wondered since whether it was easier than the conversation."

Elizabeth did not answer immediately. She thought of Georgiana at Pemberley and the way she had spoken of Wickham as a figure she had known and lost without understanding the loss, carrying a bewilderment she had never been given the means to resolve.

"She carries it rather well," Elizabeth said at last. "Better than you may know. But she would carry it better still with the truth."

He looked at her then, with an expression she had no name for yet.

"She trusts you," he said.

"She does. I intend to be worth it."

He turned back to the window. The statement did not require a response and he did not offer one, which was the correct answer.

The gates of Longbourn came into view. The house sat in the bright morning light, unchanged, exactly as it had always been. Elizabeth looked at it and thought of her father's study, the door she did not open anymore, and then let the thought pass.

"Last night," she said. "When you watched him with Lydia, you could not warn her."

"No."

"You could warn me now. Now that I know why."

"Yes." He turned to face her fully. "He will pursue her. He has nothing to lose and something to gain: leverage, money, the satisfaction of it. He will pursue her carefully because he is a careful man, and the principal obstacle to his being believed is that the only proof I have cannot be given without Georgiana's consent, which I have never asked for and do not intend to ask for."

"Then we manage it without the proof," Elizabeth said.

"That has been my intention. I have not been successful so far."

"You have been managing it alone." She said it without accusation. It was an observation. "That is what we are correcting now."

He held her gaze. She met it without looking away.

"Yes," he said. "That is what we are correcting."

The carriage stopped. A groom appeared at the door. Elizabeth gathered her things, but Darcy descended first and offered his hand, which he had stopped doing early in the marriage because she had told him it was unnecessary and he had listened.

She took it this morning.

He did not remark on it. He steadied her descent and released her hand when she was on solid ground, and they walked toward the door of Longbourn together through the warm August morning, and neither of them said anything further, because the conversation was complete and what came next was work, not words.

Inside, they could already hear Mrs. Bennet.

Chapter 21: Prevention Fails

They had a plan. This was perhaps the first thing wrong with it.

It had not been named a plan exactly. They had conducted it rather as two people who arrived at identical conclusions and proceeded without ceremony. Darcy would speak to Colonel Forster before returning to Pemberley, pointing obliquely to some prior difficulty of Wickham's character. Elizabeth would remain at Longbourn for a week or two, managing what could be managed on that front: her mother's nerves, Lydia's social calendar, the general disorder that Mr. Bennet's absence had left with no one to quietly contain it. She would write to Darcy with what she observed. He would write back with what he had accomplished.

Two weeks later, Elizabeth evaluated the results.

The results were not good.

Darcy's letter arrived on a Thursday, four days after he had written it from Pemberley. He had seen Forster before leaving Hertfordshire. The meeting was described in two paragraphs that told her everything she needed to know about its outcome without requiring him to say so directly. Forster had received his communication with every appearance of attention, thanked him for his concern, and done nothing that Elizabeth could see. Wickham remained.

Mourning had reduced the Bennet girls' social latitude to private card parties and family suppers, which was to say, to exactly the rooms Wickham had chosen. He was at the Phillipses' table on Tuesday evenings, where Mrs. Philips pressed cold meat and warm wine on every officer who came through the door and counted herself the regiment's principal patroness. He remained in Lydia's company with a persistence that was almost administrative in its regularity.

Darcy's assessment, written in his characteristic precision, was this: a commanding officer who had received no formal complaint and observed no documented misconduct would find reasons not to disrupt a popular member of his company on the word of a private gentleman, however well-connected. The fact that the private gentleman was now also the elopement-risk's brother-in-law made it, if anything, more awkward. Forster might conclude that family feeling was the primary engine of the concern.

He will not act on suggestion, Darcy wrote. He requires evidence, or a formal application, or Wickham to do something visible enough that it cannot be ignored.

Elizabeth folded the letter and looked at the parlor fire for a long moment.

Wickham had been visible enough to be admired. He had been precisely, calculatedly, nothing further.

She had spoken to Lydia in the second week, choosing her moment with the care she usually reserved for more consequential tasks. She had picked an afternoon when Mrs. Bennet was resting and Kitty had gone to Maria Lucas's, when the house was quiet enough that a conversation might be had without an audience.

Lydia had asked, within the first two minutes, whether Wickham had done something improper.

Elizabeth said she could not explain the particulars.

Lydia told her that was precisely what a married woman would say, delivered with the satisfaction of someone who had made a very good observation.

She was not entirely wrong. It was what a married woman in Elizabeth's position must say. But the logic landed nowhere useful. Lydia took her reticence as evidence that there was nothing to be reticent about, or that whatever there was to be cautious of, she had already calculated and dismissed it. She had also decided, somewhere in the preceding weeks, that Elizabeth was attempting to manage her, which she objected to on principle. The marriage had rearranged the family's social geometry in ways Lydia felt without being able to articulate, and Elizabeth's concern read to her as authority without justification: Mrs. Darcy, very grand now, unwilling to let anyone enjoy themselves.

She had said this to Kitty. Kitty had repeated it, with the faithful accuracy of a younger sister, to Elizabeth.

Elizabeth had written all of this to Darcy in her second letter, without heat and without expecting that it would produce any remedy. It was accurate, in the way Lydia's observations sometimes were; surface correct, conclusions wrong.

His reply came back in five days. The observation about management is not without logic from her position, he had written, which Elizabeth had read twice, because it was not the sentence she had expected. She cannot be warned by a consequence she cannot be shown. This is the constraint we are both inside.

She had put that letter in her writing case beside the first one.

The thing about Wickham, Elizabeth had come to understand, was that he did not require much. He did not need to manufacture opportunity; he only needed to recognize where doors had been left ajar by other people's habits and walk through them. Mrs. Bennet's approval was a door. Colonel Forster's indifference was a door. Lydia's grievance, the sense she had carried, evidently for some weeks, that Elizabeth's marriage had reorganized the family's attention around Elizabeth and left Lydia somewhere to the side of it, was a door so wide he had not even needed to push it. He had stepped through, complimented the interior, and made himself at home.

Elizabeth had watched him do it at the Phillipses' and at two subsequent card parties, going for precisely this purpose. At each one, his attention to Lydia followed the same pattern. Admiration first, which Lydia accepted with the ease of someone accustomed to it. Then a small, careful confiding. Nothing that could be repeated and damage him, but something that made Lydia feel chosen, made her feel she was being given access to a private register other people could not reach. And then, last, the needle-thin suggestion of injury done by persons of consequence who could not be named directly, which Lydia could carry home and turn over and feel herself very wise for understanding.

Lydia was not stupid. This was what made it difficult to watch. She was quick and she read rooms well, in her fashion. Under different management, such as from her father, years younger and actually attending, she might have been something rather sharper than she was. But she had been trained, by long habit and Mrs. Bennet's ambition, to direct her intelligence entirely at the question of being admired, and this had left her with no instinct for recognizing when admiration was a tool being used on her rather than a tribute being paid.

Wickham admired her the way a card player watches his hand. Lydia, watching him watch her, saw only the watching.

It was the Darcy-Forster meeting that Elizabeth could not stop returning to, in the way one returns to an arithmetic that keeps producing the wrong answer.

She had not been present, but she could construct it well enough from Darcy's account and from what she knew of both men. Forster would have been correct, attentive, and entirely uncompelled. Darcy would have been precise, and she knew, he would have restrained himself from the one sentence that would have made the case unanswerable, because the one sentence that would have made the case unanswerable cost Georgiana her privacy in a room it could not be guaranteed to stay in. So, he had gone in with half his evidence and came out with nothing.

She had written asking him as much. His reply had been brief: Yes. That is where we are.

Words that described, without editorializing, the same constraint she was living on her side. She had the information and could not deploy it. He had the authority and could not use it without making its source public. Between them, they were very well-equipped and entirely hamstrung.

She wrote back: Then we watch and wait for him to do something provable.

His reply, when it came: Yes. I have also written to two contacts regarding Wickham's posting. I will let you know what comes of it.

What came of it arrived the following Wednesday, in a letter from Darcy that she read standing at the hall table before she had taken off her pelisse.

Wickham had, two weeks prior, made his own arrangements to extend his current posting. The paperwork had been filed correctly and accepted. There was nothing to be done about it for at least another month, possibly two.

He had expected interference. The precaution would have cost him very little.

Elizabeth refolded the letter. She was still holding her gloves. Outside, Lydia was somewhere in the garden with Kitty, laughing at something in her full voice. Elizabeth had stopped, some days ago, attempting to identify what Lydia found worth laughing at. It covered too much territory.

She put Darcy's letter in her pocket and went to find her mother.

Mrs. Bennet could not be addressed about Wickham directly. This had been decided early, confirmed by every subsequent attempt at an oblique approach. She had found him agreeable, which in her vocabulary was a term that required significant elevation before it became a concern. He was an officer, which proved he was respectable. He had been introduced at the Phillipses' by persons of good standing, which proved he was connected. He had shown attention to Lydia, which proved he had taste.

Elizabeth had tried three different registers. In each one, her concern reached her mother and was translated, with great efficiency, into evidence that Elizabeth had grown proud since the marriage. Mrs. Bennet did not dislike Darcy. She liked him a great deal, was proud of him, mentioned him to the neighborhood at every available opportunity, but she attributed any anxiety Elizabeth expressed about Lydia to the corrupting influence of Pemberley's consequence. Fine-lady airs. That was the phrase.

She was not susceptible to logic on this subject, and she was not susceptible to feeling. She was susceptible to authority, which Elizabeth did not have over her, and to social consequence, which Wickham had in the form of his red coat and his easy manners, and to the evidence of her own eyes, which showed her a daughter being admired, and Elizabeth could not compete with any of that without the one instrument she did not have.

She sat in her father's study one afternoon. She went there sometimes, for no reason except that it was the one room in the house that still felt quiet in the way it used to and she looked at his chair and thought about what he would have done.

He would, she suspected, have done very little. He would have made a dry remark to Elizabeth in private and retreated behind a book. This was not useful to contemplate, but it was honest.

She picked up his letter knife, which was still on the desk where he had left it, and set it down again.

The letter from Bingley went to Pemberley though Elizabeth did not know this until later. Darcy read it, set it on his desk for an afternoon, and wrote back to say he would come.

What Elizabeth knew, on the morning in question, was that a note had arrived by messenger from Netherfield inviting the Bennet women to dinner that evening. Mr. Bingley's compliments; he hoped they were all well; he would be very glad of their company and hoped they might come.

Mrs. Bennet was in favor of going. Lydia was in favor of going. Kitty was in favor of going. Jane read the note twice and said she thought they ought to accept.

Elizabeth looked at her sister's face and said yes, she agreed.

She was the last down the stairs at Netherfield, having stopped to see to a loose button on her cuff, and so she came into the drawing room behind her mother and sisters and did not have, from the doorway, a clear view of the room's full occupancy.

She heard Bingley's voice: warm, immediate, the pitch he used when he was pleased to see people. She heard her mother. She heard Lydia. She came around the edge of the door, and she saw Darcy standing by the window.

Her first thought, formed and completed in approximately two seconds, was that something had happened. Wickham. Lydia. Some development she had not been told of, something Darcy had learned and come south to manage without time to write first. He had come because there was a crisis.

She crossed the room toward him and said, low enough not to be heard over Mrs. Bennet's greetings, "What has happened?"

Darcy looked at her. Something in his expression adjusted; not quite amusement, but adjacent to it. "Bingley asked me to come."

She held his gaze for a moment. "That is all?"

"That is all."

She took a breath and let it go. Bingley was behind her now, pressing her hands and saying how glad he was she had come, how glad he was they could all be together, with a gladness that meant he was containing something larger than an ordinary dinner invitation.

She looked at Jane.

Jane was already looking at Bingley.

Elizabeth took a seat near the fire and said nothing further.

Dinner was Bingley at his most animated, which was very animated indeed. He directed his attention around the table with an energy that was not quite random — it landed on Mrs. Bennet often enough to keep her satisfied, on Lydia often enough to keep her from competing for it, on Darcy with the ease of long practice, and on Jane with a frequency that required no analysis. Darcy was beside Elizabeth, which was where he generally ended up at Bingley's table, and he spoke to her in the low, direct way he had lately. It was not ceremony, just address, and she answered in kind, and they managed between them a version of the dinner conversation that was comfortable in a way Elizabeth could not have predicted, six months ago, would ever be available to them.

After dinner, when the ladies had removed and the gentlemen had sat over their port for rather less time than usual, Bingley appeared in the drawing room doorway with an expression Elizabeth associated with men who have rehearsed something and found the rehearsal has not entirely survived contact with the room.

He asked whether Miss Bennet might walk with him in the gallery.

Mrs. Bennet went very still. Lydia looked at Kitty. Elizabeth looked at her hands.

Jane rose and went with him.

The gallery was not heated. This was something everyone in the drawing room understood and no one mentioned. Mrs. Bennet took up her needlework and set it down again. Lydia began a sentence and thought better of it. Darcy stood by the mantelpiece and looked at the fire.

They were gone fifteen minutes. Elizabeth counted without meaning to, marking time against the clock on the mantel and the behavior of the coals and the specific character of her mother's silence, which was the loudest silence Mrs. Bennet was capable of producing.

When the gallery door opened and Jane came back through it, her color was high and her composure was the deliberate kind, the kind she put on over things she did not want to say in front of Lydia and Kitty and their mother all at once.

Bingley came in behind her and announced, to the room, that Miss Bennet had done him the very great honor of accepting his hand, and that he hoped they would all wish them very happy.

Mrs. Bennet made a sound that was not quite a word.

Lydia shrieked something congratulatory and embraced Jane with her whole body. Kitty burst into tears of the sympathetic variety. Mrs. Bennet recovered herself sufficiently to take both of Bingley's hands and tell him that she had always known he would come back, always, from the very first, she had said so to anyone who would listen.

Elizabeth looked at her sister.

Jane was not crying. She was standing very still by then with Bingley's hand in hers, and her expression was the one Elizabeth had no precise word for, the one that meant she had been hoping for something for long enough that its arrival required a moment to be made real before she could be glad of it.

Elizabeth went to her. She said, in Jane's ear, that she was very happy.

Jane held on for a moment longer than was strictly required.

Later, when Mrs. Bennet had been settled in a chair with Bingley's full attention and Lydia had claimed Kitty for a private conference in the corner, Elizabeth found herself near the window with Darcy beside her, not by arrangement, simply because the room had sorted itself and this was where they ended up.

"You knew," she said.

"Bingley wrote asking whether I might come. He did not specify why. I had a reasonable inference."

"And you said nothing in your letters."

"It was Bingley's to tell."

She looked across the room at her sister, who was listening to something Bingley was saying to her mother with the expression of someone who is genuinely, privately happy and is not yet trying to conceal it.

"He might have failed his nerve," Elizabeth said.

"He might have."

"You came anyway."

"He asked me to come."

She considered this. Darcy had traveled from Pemberley - two days, at minimum - on the strength of Bingley's letter and a reasonable inference, and he had stood in this room for however long it had taken them to drive from Longbourn, holding the information in, saying nothing to her when she had come through the door and looked at him as if the sky were falling.

"You were here when I arrived," she said.

"Yes."

"I thought something had happened. With Wickham."

He looked at her. "I know. I saw it in your face."

"And you let me think so for approximately three seconds."

"Two," he said. "It was two seconds. I corrected the misapprehension immediately."

She did not quite smile. Across the room, Bingley laughed at something her mother said, and Jane turned her head at the sound, and the expression on her face was entirely unguarded.

Elizabeth watched it. She had no instrument for what was happening in her chest at this moment, and she did not try to find one.

Outside, the grounds were dark. Inside, nobody was in any hurry to end the evening.

Chapter 22: Lydia Is Gone

The express arrived before breakfast.

Elizabeth was at the writing desk when she heard Darcy's step in the corridor, a quicker than normal pace that meant something had come, and that he had read it before deciding what to do with it. She set down her pen. There was news.

He opened the door and held out the letter.

She took it. She saw Jane's hand on the direction and read the first three lines and did not read further.

Lydia. Gone. Wickham's name. 'Gone' was a word she had not been waiting to see written down.

She put the letter flat on the desk. Darcy had not moved from the doorway. Outside the window, the grounds were gray and still; a mist had come in overnight and had not lifted.

"When did it arrive?"

"An hour ago. I waited until —"

"No." she said it without looking up. "In the future, you do not wait."

He did not argue. She read the rest of Jane's letter, which covered two pages and contained very little beyond what the first three lines had told her. Jane's composure worked against her, as it always did when things were worst. Mrs. Bennet had taken to her room. Mr. Gardiner had been written to. No one knew where they had gone or how long they had been gone, only that Lydia had left a note saying she would be married from Scotland and that they were not to worry.

Elizabeth thought about Lydia writing that note. The hand that had written it: round, hurried, still childish at the letters, and the face behind it, flushed and convinced. She thought about the Philipses' card evening, the way Lydia had left in the carriage already living in the story Wickham had built for her, already the heroine of it, already convinced she had found her own adventure under Mrs. Darcy's very nose. Lydia had been sixteen years old and had not once in her life been given a reason to distrust a man who smiled at her.

Elizabeth set the letter down.

"He will not marry her." She said this to the desk, not to Darcy, because it was not a statement she was making to him. It was a fact she was confirming to herself. "Not without considerable inducement. He has nothing, and she has less, and he has done this before." She looked up. "He planned it. The timing of it. He placed himself in that room at the Philipses' because he chose to, and he chose Lydia because she was the easiest target available to him, and because she was mine to protect." The last words came out with an edge she had not entirely intended, but she did not retract them.

Darcy crossed the room and took the chair across the desk from her; not beside her, not standing over her. He sat down. It was, she thought, exactly the right thing to do.

"I will go to London," he said. "Today, if the roads allow it. Wickham has creditors there - men who know where he goes when he needs to disappear - and I know the name of at least one. It will take time, but it can be done."

"So will I."

The silence was brief.

"Elizabeth —"

"I know what you are about to say." She folded Jane's letter and held it in both hands. "You are going to say that you can move faster alone. That the negotiations will be easier without me present. That it is not appropriate —" She stopped herself there, because she had not meant to use that word, with its freight. "You are going to say that it would be better for me to go directly to Longbourn."

"I was going to say," Darcy said, "that the journey is faster by post and the post does not accommodate two."

She looked at him.

"I can arrange a second carriage within the hour," he said. "You would arrive at Gracechurch Street by evening. Your aunt and uncle will want you there, and your being there will give your uncle better intelligence than any letter could provide. He should know what we know about Wickham before he is approached." A pause. "This is not a separation. It is a division of effort."

It was, she thought, a considerable distance from what she had expected him to say. She turned this over.

"You will not act without telling me. Not before... not the price, not the negotiation, not who you contact, and what you offer. You will write to me at Gracechurch Street the same day."

"Yes."

"If he makes a counteroffer you are not prepared to meet, you will not answer it until I have seen it."

Something crossed his face. Not resistance; something more like recalibration. "That may not always be practicable."

"Then you will make it practicable." She met his eyes steadily. "This is my family. I am not asking to be protected from the particulars of my family's crisis. I am asking to be a party to decisions made in their name."

The word party landed in the room with the weight of something legal, which was precisely why she had chosen it. He understood this, and she could see that he understood it. He did not try to make it smaller than it was.

"Agreed," he said. "All of it."

She nodded. She stood and went to the window. The mist had shifted; the line of the far trees was just visible now, the leaves gone russet and dull gold at the edges, beginning their slow release. It occurred to her that Lydia did not know it was September, or rather did not think of it as September. Lydia would think of it as the month she had done the thing no one thought she would dare to do. She would not have considered what came after. She had never, in Elizabeth's memory, considered what came after.

"She is not stupid," Elizabeth said. "That is the part that... she is not stupid, and she is not bad. She is seventeen years old, and she has been told all her life that the thing she is best suited to do is make a man admire her. She did exactly what she was prepared to do." She pressed the heel of her hand briefly against the window glass. Cool. "And Wickham knew it."

Darcy said nothing. He did not offer comfort, which was one thing she had come, slowly, to value in him. He did not try to make grief into something more manageable than it was.

She turned back to the room. "I need an hour to pack. I will write to my aunt before we leave."

"I will see to the carriages."

He stood. He moved towards the door. Then he stopped, not dramatically, not with any gestures toward weight or significance, and he said without turning: "I should have had him reassigned in August. I had the means, and I delayed because I did not want to appear I was acting in personal interest." A moment. "That was a mistake in judgment. I want you to know I know it."

Elizabeth held the letter in her hands and considered this. It was not an apology organized to receive absolution. It was an accounting offered to someone who deserved the true number.

"Yes," she said. "It was. We will discuss it properly when this is resolved."

He left. She went to the wardrobe and opened it and looked at the gray dresses, the lavender, the white: the vocabulary of half-mourning that she moved in now as naturally as she had once moved in color. She chose the gray wool, for the journey. She chose the dark bonnet, for the wind.

She had been packing for three minutes before she understood that she was also, in some very small part of herself, grateful. Not for the crisis. For the fact that when she had said so will I, he had not said no.

She locked the trunk.

Below, in the stable yard, she could already hear Darcy giving instructions; not his voice, but its register, the particular brevity that meant he was working through a problem in sequence. The carriage would be ready.

She picked up her pen and began the letter to her aunt.

Chapter 23: London

The Gardiners' house on Gracechurch Street smelled of coal smoke and boiled mutton and, underneath both, the damp of a house that had been shut against September rain. Elizabeth noticed these things because she was noticing everything. It was the only way she knew to keep her mind working in a straight line.

Her aunt had met her at the door, taken one look at her face, and said nothing beyond 'come in.' That was, Elizabeth thought, one of the most useful things a person could do for another person, and she had filed it away in the place where she kept things she would remember later, when later arrived.

They sat in the front parlor. Mrs. Gardiner poured tea. The sound of the rain against the window was steady and uninspiring.

"He found them yesterday," her aunt said. "He came here first, before he went. I thought you would want to know that."

Elizabeth set down her cup.

"He came here?"

"He did. He sat in the chair you are sitting in now and asked your uncle for Wickham's likely associates in London: men from the militia, anyone Wickham might have borrowed from. Your uncle told him what he knew." Mrs. Gardiner looked at the window. "He was very composed. That is not criticism."

"I know what it is," Elizabeth said.

She had ridden from Pemberley in the carriage Darcy had arranged, with a maid she had not asked for and a letter of instruction to the Gardiners she had not been told about. She had read the letter when her aunt handed it to her. It was two pages in Darcy's hand: clear, precise, anticipatory. He had written out the addresses of two solicitors, a description of Wickham's likely financial situation, and a sentence at the end that said: Mrs. Darcy is to be told everything I learn, at whatever hour I learn it.

She had read that sentence three times.

"Is my uncle with him now?" she asked.

"They went together this morning. To a lodging house in Southwark." Mrs. Gardiner paused. "Your uncle insisted. Mr. Darcy did not argue."

The lodging house was a narrow building on a street that had once been respectable and had since made other arrangements. Darcy had the address from a man who owed Wickham money and was consequently delighted to provide it. He stood in front of the door with Mr. Gardiner beside him and looked at the paint peeling in long strips from the frame and thought about Lydia Bennet, who was barely seventeen years old and had never been more than thirty miles from Meryton, and he knocked.

A woman answered. She looked at Darcy's coat and Mr. Gardiner's expression and stepped back without speaking.

Wickham was in the back room.

He had a bottle and a chair, and the ease of a man who has decided that the worst has already happened. When Darcy came through the door, he looked up and the ease went out of his face completely, and for one moment, the duration of one breath, Darcy saw the boy he had grown up with, the one who had known him before he learned to be careful, and then that was gone too, and there was only Wickham in a hired chair in a bad room with nowhere to go.

"Darcy," Wickham said. His voice was entirely steady. That, at least, had not changed.

"Where is she?"

"Upstairs." He did not move. "She's perfectly well. In case that was your next question."

"It was not."

Wickham looked at Mr. Gardiner, standing in the doorway. Something shifted in his expression. Not shame, Darcy thought, but a recalculation. "I didn't expect the family."

"You didn't expect a great deal," Darcy said. "Sit down."

"I am sitting."

"Then stay there."

He crossed the room and stood at the window. The street below was wet and empty. He had rehearsed none of this. He had found, when he was honest with himself, that there was nothing to rehearse, that the thing which needed doing was simply the thing which needed doing, and the words would either come or they would not.

"Tell me what you want," he said. He was still looking at the street.

"I beg your pardon?"

"You heard me." He turned. "You chose Lydia Bennet. Of all the choices available to you, you chose the one woman whose ruin would cause the most damage to the one person whose damage you most wanted to cause.

That is not a coincidence, and I will not treat it as one. Tell me what you want."

Wickham was quiet for a moment. Then something that might have been a smile crossed his face, not warm, not even amused, just the reflex of a man who has been found out and has found some amusement in it rather than none. "You always saw things clearly," he said, "when you chose to look."

"What do you want?"

"Marriage." He said it flatly. "A proper settlement. A commission somewhere sufficiently far away that I don't have to look at your face again." He picked up the bottle, considered it, and set it down. "And the debts. You know which ones."

"I know which ones."

"Then we understand each other."

Darcy looked at him for a long time. Not with anger; anger had a texture that was almost comfortable, and he did not want to be comfortable. He was looking at Wickham the way you look at a sum that does not balance, trying to find where it went wrong. He had never found it. He suspected now that there was nothing to find, that Wickham had not gone wrong anywhere in particular but had simply always been what he was, and that the boy he had mourned for twenty years had never existed.

"Yes," he said. "We understand each other."

Mr. Gardiner had not been invited. He had simply stood at the Gracechurch Street door that morning and said, 'I'm coming with you' in the tone of a man who has decided the matter, and Darcy had looked at him and recognized the tone and said nothing at all. There was a table in the back room and Darcy had gestured him toward it without explanation, and Mr. Gardiner had sat down and folded his hands and prepared to watch, which was, Darcy came to understand over the next two hours exactly what he was meant to do.

Wickham's first terms were not serious. They both knew this. He named a figure for the debts that was a quarter too high and attached to it an immediate cash payment of five hundred pounds "for expenses incurred," which was, given the state of the room, either brazen or delusional, and Darcy had spent enough time with Wickham to know it was neither. It was a test. Wickham wanted to see how much Darcy needed this done.

"No," Darcy said.

"The debts alone —"

"Are not that figure. I have spoken to three of your creditors this morning. I know what the debts are." He had paper in his coat, and he took it out and set it on the table between them. He had written the names and the amounts in a column. "I will settle these. I will not settle invented ones."

Wickham looked at the paper. He did not touch it. "You spoke to my creditors."

"Before I came here, yes."

Something moved in Wickham's expression: not anger exactly, but the recalibration of a man who has understood that the ground is different than he mapped it. He picked up the paper. He read it. He set it down.

"Carson is not on there," he said.

"Carson is not a creditor. Carson is a man you cheated at cards in Brighton. That is a different category of obligation and not one I intend to dignify."

"He'll come after me."

"He will, yes. That is a consequence of cheating at cards and not my concern." Darcy retrieved the paper. "The debts on this list. A commission. A settlement on Miss Lydia Bennet sufficient to make the marriage respectable. Those are the terms."

Wickham leaned back in his chair. He had a way of doing this, of making any posture look like comfort, like ease, like he was precisely where he had intended to be, and Darcy had known him long enough to understand that it was a performance and to find it no less grating for knowing so.

"The commission," Wickham said. "Where?"

"The north."

"How far north."

"Far enough."

Wickham's mouth curved. "I'd like a name."

"Newcastle."

The curve flattened. Newcastle was not glamorous. Newcastle was cold and militarily unglamorous and offered very few of the social opportunities that Wickham had spent his adult life cultivating. Darcy had chosen it for precisely these reasons and had spent no time feeling badly about it.

"That's punitive," Wickham said.

"It is practical. There is a regiment assembling and a position available, and I can have you placed within a fortnight. You may consider the geography a coincidence."

"I won't."

"I know."

Wickham looked at the window. Outside, a woman was shouting at someone two floors up, and the sound of it came through the glass flat and ordinary, and neither of them acknowledged it.

"The settlement on Lydia," Wickham said. "What figure?"

Darcy named it.

Wickham said nothing for a moment. Then: "That's generous."

"It is adequate. It is what will make the marriage legible to her family and to society. It is not generous. It is the minimum required to prevent your wife from being embarrassed by your financial habits for the remainder of her life, which I suspect will be considerable work regardless."

The word *wife* landed in the room. Wickham looked at him.

"You don't like this," Wickham said. Not an accusation. Something almost like observation.

"No."

"Paying for it."

"Paying for your choices is not something I enjoy, no. I have done it before. I expect I will not be required to do it again." Darcy held his gaze. "Because if I am required to do it again, for any reason, in any form, however small, the commission in Newcastle will look considerably more appealing than the alternative."

There was a silence.

"Is that a threat?" Wickham asked.

"It is information. I am giving you information because I have found that you make better decisions when you have it."

Wickham looked at him for a long moment. He had the look, Darcy thought, of a man taking inventory, assessing what could be used, what was fixed, where the edges were. He had been the subject of that look since they were boys, and he was tired of it in the way you tire of something that has simply been going on too long.

"The full debt figure," Wickham said. "Not what's on your list. The full figure, including Carson."

"No."

"Then I'd like the cash payment."

"No."

"Darcy —"

"No," he said it without heat. He picked up his pen. "You will take what is on this paper; you will marry Miss Lydia Bennet; and you will go to Newcastle. Those are the terms. I am not interested in your counter-terms, and I will not develop an interest in them. If you would like to spend the next hour attempting to discover otherwise, I will wait. I have nowhere else to be this afternoon."

Wickham's jaw moved. He looked at Mr. Gardiner, who had been sitting at the table for fifty minutes and had not moved, and who now looked back at him with the steady, incurious patience of a man who imports goods for a living and has negotiated with people rather worse than this in rather worse rooms.

Wickham looked back at Darcy.

He picked up the pen from the table.

He signed.

Darcy watched him do it. He did not feel what he had expected to feel, relief, or satisfaction, or the release of a thing concluded. He felt tired. He felt the specific weight of an afternoon in a bad room paying for someone else's damage with money that was not the thing Wickham had actually wanted from him, which was acknowledgment, which was the knowledge that he could still reach Darcy from across whatever distance Darcy put between them. He had it. Darcy had handed it to him by coming here. There was nothing to be done about that now.

He took the signed paper and folded it.

"Lydia," Mr. Gardiner said, from the table.

Both men looked at him. It was the first thing he had said in forty minutes.

"What does the girl want?"

Wickham blinked. It was not a question he had expected. Darcy was not certain it was a question he himself would have thought to ask.

"She wants to be married," Wickham said, after a moment.

"To you specifically?"

A pause. Something in Wickham's face moved that was harder to name. It was not guilt, not quite, but a younger thing than guilt, something that still knew the difference between what it was doing and what it ought to do. "She seems to think so," he said.

"Then she will have it." Mr. Gardiner looked at him with the steadiness of a man delivering a verdict rather than a request. "And you will treat her with decency. That is not a term I will allow to be negotiated."

Wickham opened his mouth. Closed it. He looked at Darcy.

Darcy said nothing. He was watching Wickham look for a way out and finding none, and he let him look.

Wickham nodded once.

Mr. Gardiner looked at Darcy. Darcy looked at the paper in front of him.

"I'll draw up the full settlement," he said. "By tomorrow morning."

Lydia came downstairs while Darcy and Mr. Gardiner were putting on their coats.

She was wearing a dress that was not quite appropriate for the hour, and her hair was done badly, and she looked, for one unguarded moment when she first appeared in the hallway, very young and very uncertain. Then she saw her uncle, and the uncertainty became something else; relief, defiance, calculation, all of it moving across her face in the span of a second.

"Uncle Gardiner," she said, with the brightness of someone with confidence they do not entirely feel.

"Lydia." He crossed the hallway and took her hands. He did not say anything else. She looked at him for a moment, and her chin wobbled once, quickly, before she controlled it.

Darcy picked up his hat. He looked at Lydia, and she looked back at him, and there was nothing comfortable in it on either side.

"He has agreed to marry you," Darcy said. "The arrangements will be drawn up by tomorrow. Your uncle will see you settled."

Lydia lifted her chin. "I knew it would come right. I told Wickham —"

"Yes," Darcy said. "Quite."

He went out. The rain had stopped. The street was cold and smelled of wet stone and horse traffic, and he stood on the pavement and let the cold come in and did not move for a moment.

Mr. Gardiner came out behind him and pulled the door closed.

They stood there together. A cart went past, the horse's hooves loud on the cobblestones.

"You did not have to do this," Mr. Gardiner said. Not an accusation. Not quite gratitude.

"She is my wife's sister." Darcy looked up the street. "She is my wife's sister, and I knew what Wickham was, and I did not act soon enough. Those are related facts."

Mr. Gardiner was quiet for a moment. "Elizabeth will want to know that you said that."

"I will tell her myself."

He started walking. Mr. Gardiner fell into step beside him, and they walked back toward Gracechurch Street through the wet streets without speaking, which suited them both.

She was waiting in the front parlor.

She heard the door and she heard her uncle's voice in the hallway, and she put down the letter she had not been reading and stood up. When Darcy came through the parlor door, she looked at his face and read it quickly, the way she had learned to read his face over the course of months in which reading his face had been a necessary skill.

He was tired. He was intact. It was done.

She let out a breath that had been waiting since Pemberley.

"Sit down," she said. "I'll get you something."

He looked at her. "You don't need to —"

"Sit down."

He sat. She found the whiskey her uncle kept in the cabinet by the bookcase and poured a measure and brought it to him and he took it and did not drink it immediately, just held it, and she sat across from him.

"Tell me," she said.

He told her all of it - Wickham's face when the door opened, the negotiation, the figure, the commission, Mr. Gardiner at the table asking, 'what does the girl want?' in a voice that had stopped the room. He told it plainly, in the order it happened, without editorializing. She listened without speaking.

When he had finished she asked: "How much?"

He told her.

She looked at her hands in her lap for a moment. Then: "You should not have had to do this."

"I was the one who could."

"That is not the same thing."

"No." He looked at the glass in his hand. "No, it is not."

She wanted to say something more. She had several things to say, and she had been turning them over since the carriage, sharp and exact. She put them aside. They would keep. There would be time, later, for the full accounting of what he should and should not have done, and for her part in it, and for all of the ways the thing could have gone differently if either of them had been different people at an earlier moment. That conversation would happen. She could afford to wait for it.

What she could not do was leave him sitting here with the weight of the afternoon on him and nothing said.

"Wickham knew what he was doing," she said. "He chose Lydia deliberately. To reach you through me."

"Yes."

"You knew that before you went."

"Yes."

"And you went anyway." She paused. "You paid it anyway."

He looked up. She held his gaze. There was no warmth in her face. Not yet, not exactly, but there was the thing that had been building for months, the thing that was not gratitude because gratitude was not what she felt, the thing that had no name she had found yet in the available vocabulary.

"I told your uncle," he said, "that I had known what Wickham was, and that I did not act soon enough, that those were related facts."

She looked at him for a long time.

"You did not have to tell him that."

"No."

Outside, Mrs. Gardiner was speaking to someone in the hall. The clock on the mantle marked the half-hour. The fire needed building up, and neither of them moved to do it.

"There will be more to manage," Elizabeth said. "The settlement. The ceremony. My mother." She paused. "Lydia's certainty that she has arranged a romance."

"Yes."

"We will manage it."

He looked at her. The 'we' sat in the room between them, and both of them heard it, and neither of them remarked on it.

"Yes," he said.

She stood and picked up the glass from his hand. He had not touched the whiskey, and she put it on the table. She went to the fire and built it up herself, because the room was cold and they were both still here and there was no particular reason for the cold.

Mr. Gardiner shook Darcy's hand at the door at half-past nine.

It was not a long handshake. It was not accompanied by a speech or a formal expression of gratitude. It was a handshake of the kind one man gives another when the accounting has been done, and the sum is clear and there is nothing left to do but acknowledge it.

Darcy looked slightly surprised.

He recovered. He nodded once, and went down the steps to the carriage, and the door of the house on Gracechurch Street closed behind him.

Inside, Mr. Gardiner went back to the parlor where his wife was sitting with her work, and he sat down in his chair, and he picked up his book, and he said nothing at all.

Mrs. Gardiner looked at him over her needle.

"Well?" she said.

He found his page. "Leave the fire," he said. "It will keep."

Chapter 24: Lydia Returns

Bingley had pressed the invitation before they left London; there was a room made up, he said, it was no trouble, Netherfield was three miles from Longbourn and that was near enough to be useful.

Darcy had accepted without consulting Elizabeth, which she had overlooked because she was exhausted and three miles from Longbourn was, in fact, just close enough and just far enough.

They had arrived late. The house was dark except for the hall. Bingley met them himself, which was characteristic; took one look at their faces, and asked nothing beyond whether they had eaten. They had not. He fed them cold meat and bread in the library and talked about nothing of consequence for twenty minutes, and Elizabeth thought she had never been so grateful for Bingley in her life.

Darcy left in the morning, before she was properly awake, to return to London and the solicitor. He had told her the night before what remained to be done: the agreements drawn up, the figures confirmed in writing,

Wickham bound to them by something more durable than his word. He would collect Lydia and bring her back to Longbourn. Wickham would make his own way.

Elizabeth went to Longbourn at ten.

The house had the feeling of a place holding its breath. Mrs. Bennet had been at the window since breakfast, Kitty reported, except for the interval when she had rearranged the parlor and then put it back. Jane was in the kitchen with the cook, establishing what dinner would be and at what hour, which was the most useful thing anyone could do and therefore the thing Jane was doing.

Elizabeth found her there, and they stood together for a few minutes while the cook addressed a question about the fish.

"He is bringing her himself?" Jane asked, when the cook had gone.

"Yes."

Jane considered this. She did not say what the consideration produced. After a moment she asked: "And Wickham?"

"He'll come for dinner. Beyond that, I don't know his arrangements." Elizabeth looked at the window. "He is not her husband yet."

"No," Jane said. "Not yet."

They left it there. Jane went back to the question of the fish.

Lydia arrived at half-past two, in Darcy's carriage, which she had apparently spent the journey from London treating as her due. She came in talking and did not stop. She embraced Mrs. Bennet, embraced Kitty, turned to Elizabeth and said she was looking very well for a married woman, and turned back to Mrs. Bennet before Elizabeth could reply, which was perhaps just as well.

Darcy followed. He greeted Mrs. Bennet, who received everything from him as warmth and always would. He nodded to Kitty. He said something quiet to Jane that made her look at him with the steadiness she reserved for things she intended to remember. Then he crossed the room to Elizabeth.

She asked, low: "The solicitor?"

"Done," he said.

Wickham arrived twenty minutes later, in a hired chaise, and came in with the ease of a man who had arranged himself for an entrance. He greeted Mrs. Bennet warmly, Kitty cheerfully, Jane with correct politeness. He turned to Elizabeth with the smile she remembered from the card parties, unhurried, carrying its suggestion of private understanding, as if the two of them shared some pleasant joke the room had not been let in on. She received it and said the correct things. His eyes moved to Darcy.

"Darcy."

"Wickham." Darcy's voice was level and without warmth, and not unkind, which Elizabeth now understood was the most precise form of social censure available to a man of his self-control. He held Wickham's eye for exactly the right amount of time and then turned to answer something Bingley had said.

Wickham turned to Kitty with a question about the neighborhood, easy and interested, as though her answer genuinely mattered to him.

He was very good at this. He had always been very good at this.

Dinner was noisier than it needed to be, which was the condition of any meal at which Mrs. Bennet was the ranking hostess and Lydia was in the room. Lydia talked. Mrs. Bennet amplified. Kitty laughed at intervals in the manner of someone who has learned that laughing keeps her in the conversation without requiring her to contribute to it.

Wickham was a pleasant dinner companion. He knew how to be. He spoke to Mrs. Bennet with appropriate attention, to Bingley with easy good humor; Bingley, who did not know the full extent of what Wickham had done and whose natural warmth could not be suppressed by the weight of what others in the room were carrying. He asked Jane something about Bingley's plans for Netherfield, deferring to her as though her answer carried authority. He said two things to Elizabeth that were entirely unremarkable.

He said nothing directly to Darcy.

Darcy said nothing directly to Wickham.

Between them at the table, Wickham at Mrs. Bennet's right, Darcy at Elizabeth's left, there was a distance of perhaps six feet and a history that could not be named in any dining room in England. Elizabeth watched Darcy manage it from the corner of her eye: the set of his jaw, the precise degree to which he engaged with the surrounding conversation, the way he listened to Bingley's account of a disputed fence line with every appearance of interest. He was doing considerable work, and none of it showed. She had an entirely new appreciation for how much work he had always done that she had once simply called coldness.

At the far end of the table, Lydia was talking about Wickham's colonel.

"Everyone thinks very highly of him in the regiment," she said. "His colonel says he has the makings of a real officer. He was not always understood, you know. Some people took against him, Denny told me, without any cause at all. It was nothing but envy." She reached for the bread. "And his situation before that was handled very shabbily. His father worked his whole life for one family, and when he died, there was an understanding about a living, not written, which was the mistake, but perfectly clear to everyone at the time. And then it was simply not honored." She delivered this with the air of someone presenting evidence to a jury she considered poorly informed. "Wickham says it was the earliest lesson he ever had in the difference between what a great man promises and what he actually does."

Mrs. Bennet said it was disgraceful.

Kitty said it was very unfair.

Bingley looked at his plate.

Jane looked at no one in particular, which meant she was looking at everything.

Elizabeth looked at Darcy.

His expression had not changed. He was attending to his dinner with the steady interest of a man who had decided, before he sat down, exactly how much of himself this table was going to get, and had apportioned it in advance. He did not look at Wickham. He did not look at Elizabeth. He turned to Bingley and said something low about the fence line that had not been resolved to his satisfaction, and Bingley, bless him, answered it fully and carried them through the next three minutes without apparent effort.

Lydia, satisfied with her evidence, moved on to the subject of Newcastle's assembly rooms.

Elizabeth picked up her fork.

She was hearing Wickham in every syllable of it: the architecture of the grievance, the careful vagueness about names and dates and checkable facts, the noble suffering that invited sympathy without risking scrutiny. He had told this story so many times that Lydia presented it as her own understanding, with her own indignation, as though she had arrived at it independently. She had not borrowed it. She had absorbed it so completely that the seam no longer showed.

Across the table, Wickham was laughing at something Bingley had said. It was a genuine laugh, full, easy, and apparently unguarded. Elizabeth could not decide whether she found this more or less troubling than his silences. He was either a man who had so thoroughly arranged the world to his benefit that he could afford genuine amusement, or he was a man so practiced at ease that the ease had become indistinguishable from the real thing. She was not certain the distinction mattered.

Darcy refilled her glass without being asked, without looking at her, without breaking the sentence he was completing with Bingley about the fence.

Elizabeth noted it and said nothing.

Bingley was the first to rise from the table, which gave the signal to the room with no one having to manufacture one. Mrs. Bennet entreated everyone to stay in the manner of someone who would be relieved when they did not, and the party separated. Lydia drew Kitty upstairs, Wickham accepted a glass of port from Mr. Bennet's old decanter that Mrs. Bennet had brought out for the occasion, and Darcy stood with Bingley near the window in the kind of conversation that required very little of either of them.

Jane touched Elizabeth's elbow. They slipped into the hall.

"Well," Jane said.

"Wickham is charming," Elizabeth said. "He was charming all evening. He will be charming indefinitely."

"Yes." Jane kept her voice low. "And Lydia?"

"Lydia believes he was wronged at Pemberley. She believes their — " Elizabeth stopped. "She believes he bears no ill will toward anyone. She said at dinner that his greatest quality was forgiveness."

Jane was quiet for a moment. "She said that?"

"She meant it. He has told her a version of his own life that is very complete. She lives in it quite comfortably." Elizabeth looked toward the parlor door. From inside came the sound of Wickham saying something that made Mrs. Bennet laugh. She shook her head slowly. "The cost of what she is about to have is entirely invisible to her. It will remain so."

Jane said: "Perhaps that is the kindest possible outcome."

"I think it may be." Elizabeth watched the door. "Lydia living in full knowledge of what it meant, and what he is... that is not a life I would wish on her. Even Lydia."

Jane looked at her with the steadiness that was Jane's particular form of precision. "I think you know who he is. Darcy."

Elizabeth did not answer immediately. She was thinking about London, about Gracechurch Street, about Darcy telling her the settlement figure with the same directness he brought to everything, not seeking credit, simply honest about what had been done and what it had cost and what he expected in return, which was nothing. She was thinking about the carriage last night, the lateness, Bingley's cold meat and his twenty minutes of easy conversation that had asked nothing of either of them.

"I think I am beginning to know," she said. "Which is not the same thing. But it is more than I had at Hunsford."

Jane accepted this. From inside the parlor, Mrs. Bennet laughed again.

The September night was warm. The carriage was waiting on the drive, Bingley's, brought round for the three miles back to Netherfield.

Darcy said, as they turned out of Longbourn's gate: "She is happy."

"Yes," Elizabeth said. "She is."

He looked out at the dark lane. The carriage lamps threw a narrow light on the hedgerows going past. "I had not expected that."

Elizabeth considered what to say and settled on what was true. "She has what she wanted. She has always been very good at wanting things that are available to her." She paused. "The cost of what she has is entirely invisible to her. It will remain so."

Darcy said nothing for a moment. Then: "That may be the kindest possible outcome."

"I think it is." Elizabeth watched the hedgerow. "Lydia living in full knowledge of what you paid, and what it meant, and what Wickham is... that is not a life I would wish on her. Even Lydia."

He turned from the window. In the low light of the carriage she could see him looking at her. His look was specific and steady, asking nothing in return. "You are more charitable than I am," he said.

"In this particular case only," Elizabeth said. "Do not let it alarm you."

He looked at her a moment longer. Then he turned back to the window, and the three miles ran out, and the lights of Netherfield came into view through the trees.

She hoped Lydia was content with her arrangements.

She thought she probably was.

Chapter 25: The Accounting

The house had resumed its ordinary rhythm by the time they returned from London. The steward came at his usual hour. The housekeeper's report arrived at breakfast. The correspondence sorted itself into its expected categories and waited on the desk in the library. Elizabeth had not expected to find this comforting, the machinery of a well-run household proceeding without crisis, but she did.

She found Darcy in the library that afternoon. He was at the desk but not working; he was looking out the window, which meant he had been thinking about something long enough to run out of room for it.

She sat down and did not lead him anywhere.

"I want to understand something," she said. "Not what you did in London. I know what you did. I want to understand why you did it without me."

He looked at her directly. "I was uncertain it would succeed. I did not want to give you hope I could not deliver."

"That was the wrong calculation."

"Yes."

He did not qualify it. She gave him a moment to try. He did not.

"You told me in London what you had done," she said. "What you paid. I am not asking about that. I am asking why you acted without me? Why the finding of them, and every decision that followed, was concluded before you thought to tell me where things stood."

"I know."

"You kept me at the edge of something that concerned my own family because you were uncertain of the outcome."

"Yes." He held her gaze. "I made the calculation that speed mattered more than consultation. I was wrong about the order. I have not set that aside."

It was the quality of his honesty that she had spent months learning to identify: direct, without the inflation of self-reproach, without the deflection of explanation. It arrived and stayed. She had come to trust it more than she would have trusted something more graceful.

Outside, the grounds were doing whatever grounds do in late summer. The light through the library windows had shifted to its afternoon angle, lower and longer than she had expected when she first arrived here. She had learned the rhythms of this house without meaning to. It had taken longer to notice that she had learned them.

Darcy set down the pen he had not been using.

"There is something I want to ask you," he said. "I am not looking for a particular answer. I am asking because I would rather know the truth of it than continue interpreting things that may mean something other than what I have been taking them to mean."

She waited.

"When you accepted me at Hunsford," he said, "you stated your terms. I agreed to them, and I have tried to honor them. What I cannot determine, from the outside, is whether you are still inside that original arrangement, or whether you have decided, of your own judgment, that this is your life."

She did not speak immediately.

"There is a difference," he said, "between a woman fulfilling the terms she agreed to and a woman who has chosen to be where she is. I am not asking you to say it is true if it is not. But I would like to know which of the two I am looking at."

She looked at him. He was watching her with the focused stillness she had come to recognize as his version of vulnerability; not the open face of a man who displayed his feelings freely, but the concentrated attention of a man who had made himself available to an answer he might not want. It was braver than it appeared. He was asking her to be honest at the direct expense of his own comfort.

"I cannot give you a complete answer today," she said. "Not because the answer is unfavorable. But because I have been forming an opinion and I am not yet finished forming it, and I will not give you a conclusion I have not fully reached."

He was very still.

"What I can tell you," she said, "is that I have stopped keeping accounts. I was, for a long time, very precise about it; what had been done, what was owed in each direction. It was the only way I knew to remain clear-headed about a situation I had not chosen freely. But I think I have stopped." She paused. "I cannot tell you exactly when."

Darcy said nothing. He was being deliberate about not speaking, which she recognized as its own form of attentiveness.

"The word for what this is now," she said, "is one I am not yet prepared to say in an ordinary room on an ordinary afternoon with no particular occasion attached to it, which is, I recognize, an absurd scruple."

Something in his face changed - not broadly, not in any way the room could have read, but she was not the room.

"Then I will not ask you for ceremony," he said. "I will only ask you to tell me when you are ready."

"That is a very reasonable request."

"I am attempting," he said, with a dryness she had not anticipated, "to make reasonable requests. I understand it is not my most practiced mode."

She laughed - the unguarded kind, surprised out of her - and he looked at her as if he had noted it down alongside everything else he had collected since Hertfordshire.

"For what it is worth," she said, when the moment had settled, "I have noticed that you are trying. Not performing an effort at trying. Actually trying. I have noticed it for some time."

"Have you?"

"Do not sound surprised. You have not been subtle about it."

He picked up the pen again, which was the closest thing she had observed him do to collect himself.

She rose and went to the window. The grounds held the last of the afternoon. There was work still to be done before dark. She could see the steward moving toward the east field, unhurried, purposeful. The ordinary operations of a place that did not require a crisis to justify its existence.

She stayed at the window a moment longer than she needed to, and then went to find what the evening wanted of her.

Chapter 26: Jane's Wedding

The morning was cold for the time of year, the kind of fall morning that arrives before the season has properly announced itself: a clear sky, hard light, and the fields on either side of the Longbourn lane already going to copper at the edges. Elizabeth stood at the window of the room that had been hers and was not, quite, anymore. The bed was too familiar, the view unchanged, but everything else was altered in ways she could not have anticipated the last time she slept there.

She was dressed. Jane was not yet.

This was not unusual. Jane had always required more time than Elizabeth, not from vanity but from care. She attended to the small things with the thoroughness of someone who understood that small things mattered. Elizabeth had long ago made peace with being the one who waited. This morning she was glad of it. The ten minutes before Jane was ready were hers, and the window, and the cold light moving across the lane, and the fact of being back in this room on this particular morning.

She heard the door open behind her.

Jane was in white muslin and lavender ribbon, half-mourning translated into the best version of itself, the pale colors that suited her so exactly it was impossible to say whether she had chosen them or they had chosen her. Her hair was simply dressed. She looked exactly as she ought, which was to say she looked like exactly what Bingley was about to promise to spend his life with.

"You are staring," Jane said.

"I am allowed. It is your wedding day."

Jane came to stand beside her at the window. For a moment neither of them spoke. Below, in the lane, one of the Netherfield grooms was walking a horse in a slow circle that appeared to have no particular purpose. They watched him.

"Are you well?" Jane asked. Not the conventional question. Jane's version, which meant something else entirely.

Elizabeth considered it honestly, as she always did when Jane asked. "I think I am becoming so," she said. "Yes."

Jane looked at her. She did not press, which was something Elizabeth valued, the understanding that some answers were entire in themselves and did not require expansion to be believed. She nodded, once, and turned back to the window.

"He made this possible," Elizabeth said. She was not looking at Jane when she said it. "Whatever else, he made this possible."

"I know," Jane said.

"Not as an abstraction. Bingley was persuaded away by specific arguments and brought back by the withdrawal of them. Darcy did that."

"I know that too." Jane's voice was even. "I have thought about it a great deal."

"And?"

Jane was quiet long enough that the groom in the lane had completed another circuit. "I think," she said finally, "that a man who can recognize a mistake of that magnitude and correct it, at cost to his own comfort, is a man worth knowing." She paused. "I think you have been finding the same thing out."

Elizabeth said nothing. Jane did not require her to.

Below, a carriage turned into the lane. Mrs. Bennet's voice rose from somewhere in the lower part of the house, not in distress but in the particular register she used when she had opinions about timing that she intended everyone to receive. They listened to it subside.

"We should go down," Jane said.

"We should." Elizabeth turned from the window. "You look exactly like yourself."

Jane smiled; not the careful smile she used in company but the real one, the one that went all the way. "That is the kindest thing you could have said."

The church at Longbourn was not large. It had been the church of Bennet weddings and Bennet funerals for two generations, and it bore both with equal patience. The same stone walls, the same cold floor, the same light arriving through the same narrow windows at the same angle it always had. Elizabeth had stood here for her own wedding six months ago in a state of such compressed attention that she could recall almost nothing of the building and almost everything about Darcy's voice saying the words. She had not expected to notice that but she had noticed it.

Today she was in the pew beside him, and the words were Bingley's.

Bingley was not a man who concealed his feelings with any success, and he did not attempt it now. He stood at the front of the church looking at Jane with the expression of someone who understood, with complete clarity, that the thing he had wanted and feared he would not have was standing in front of him in white muslin, and the understanding had not diminished the wanting by any fraction. It was, Elizabeth thought, a remarkably legible face for a church full of people who could all read it perfectly.

Jane received it with the composure that was entirely her own, not coldness, not reserve, but a steadiness that came from being genuinely sure of what she felt and genuinely sure of what she was doing. She had had months of uncertainty. The certainty, when it finally came, had settled in her the way conviction settles in a person who has done the full accounting and found the figures correct.

Elizabeth was aware, without looking directly at him, of Darcy beside her. He was still in the way he was still during anything that required sustained attention, not suppressed, simply present. She had learned to read the gradations of this stillness by now. This one was not the stillness of discomfort or social endurance. It was something else. She had a theory about what it was and had not yet decided whether to test it.

The ceremony was brief. At the end of it Bingley kissed Jane's hand with a care that was somehow more affecting than anything grander would have been, and the church, collectively, exhaled.

Beside Elizabeth, Darcy made a sound that was not quite a breath and not quite anything else. She glanced at him. His expression gave nothing definitive away, but she looked at his face and thought about what he had done, what it had cost him, what it had required him to admit about himself, and thought: *he is watching his friend get what he arranged to take from him. And he knows it. And he is glad anyway.*

She looked back at the front of the church.

She filed this, as she filed everything about him now, not as evidence for a case she was still building, but as something she already knew and was simply adding to a record that had grown, over six months, considerably longer than she had expected.

The wedding breakfast at Netherfield was everything the house could offer, and a good deal of what Mrs. Bennet had planned besides that. The rooms were full and warm; the table crowded past its comfortable capacity, and the noise was of the cheerful variety that occurs when a gathering contains more happiness than it can quite hold and everyone is at some level aware of this and pleased by it.

Elizabeth moved through it with the ease of someone who had been, by now, to enough of Darcy's social occasions to have developed a working method. She watched him across the room.

He was talking to Mr. Gardiner. This was, she knew, not accidental. Darcy sought out her uncle in social rooms with the specific intentionality of a man who has met someone he would like to know better and is going about it in the only way available — present, attentive, asking the question that shows he listened to the last answer. She could not hear what they were saying from across the room, but she could see Mr. Gardiner's expression, which was the expression he used when a conversation was going exactly as well as he had hoped.

Mrs. Bennet appeared at Elizabeth's elbow with a plate and an opinion about the cold pheasant.

Elizabeth received both.

Mrs. Bennet's happiness today was of the specific, uncomplicated variety that came from a goal achieved: Jane married, and well, and the world arranged into the configuration she had always intended it to take. That this configuration had arrived by routes she had not planned and at costs she had not been asked to calculate was not something she dwelt on. Elizabeth did not require her to. She watched her mother move through the room, accepting congratulations with the graciousness of someone who feels them entirely due, and found, to her own mild surprise, that she was not irritated. She was something closer to fond.

Kitty was near the window with two of Jane's friends from Meryton, talking with more animation than Elizabeth had expected and less noise than she had feared. There was something slightly different in how she carried herself today, not changed, exactly, but adjusted at some small angle. Elizabeth filed this too.

Lydia was there too, of course. She was Mrs. Wickham now, a fact she had conveyed to the room within the first quarter hour, not by announcement but by the particular way she moved through it, accepting congratulations that were technically for Jane with an air of someone who felt the occasion reflected well on the entire family and herself most specifically. She wore the best of her new things and had her hair done in a style Elizabeth did not recognize and suspected had been copied from a print. She was, in the way she had always been, entirely herself.

Wickham was beside her, or near her, in the easy manner of a man who has learned that a room will accommodate him if he gives it no reason to do otherwise. He was agreeable - he was always agreeable - and he said the right things to the right people with the fluency of someone for whom social spaces had never presented any difficulty. He had kissed Jane's hand at the door with every appearance of warmth. He had shaken Bingley's hand and made some remark that made Bingley laugh. He was doing it now with one of the Netherfield neighbors, two men in easy conversation, nothing to remark upon.

Elizabeth watched him from a careful distance but did not watch too long.

Darcy, she found by the quality of his stillness rather than by looking for him directly. He was near the far end of the table, a glass in hand, in conversation with Colonel Forster in the kind of civil, undemanding exchange that required almost nothing and could be sustained indefinitely. His back was not precisely to Wickham. It was simply not toward him. She understood the distinction.

He did not look at Wickham. He did not look at her. But when a shift in the room's arrangement brought Wickham three steps closer to the table's end, Darcy said something to Colonel Forster, finished his glass, and moved without any appearance of haste to join Mr. Gardiner's conversation instead.

Elizabeth turned back to her mother's opinions about the cold pheasant.

Bingley found her between courses.

"I have been meaning to tell you," he said, without preamble and with his customary impression of a man who had been meaning to say something for some time and has finally arrived at the moment, "that I am very glad of all of it. The whole of it. I know that is... I know it is not a small thing to say, and I don't mean it as a small thing."

Elizabeth looked at him. Bingley was not a man who said more than he meant, which made him, on balance, easier to read than most. "I am glad too," she said. "Jane is happy. That is the whole of what I wanted."

Bingley nodded. He glanced across the room to where Darcy and Mr. Gardiner were still talking, and his expression did something brief and warm. "He is a very good man," he said. "I don't always say it because I don't think he wants it said. But he is."

Elizabeth followed his gaze. "I am beginning to find that out."

Bingley smiled, the full, uncalculated version. "Yes," he said. "I thought you might be."

He went back to Jane.

The rooms thinned toward late afternoon. The cold that had held off all day moved in as the light went, and the party broke into smaller configurations, some staying, some not, the natural sorting of an occasion that has done its work and is now simply winding itself down. Darcy appeared beside Elizabeth with her shawl, which she had left in the morning room and had not yet thought to retrieve.

He said nothing. He held it out. She took it.

They drifted, by no particular plan, toward the garden door.

Outside, the Netherfield garden in October was the kind of beautiful that required no assistance: the late grasses long and pale, the kitchen beds gone to seed, and the ornamental borders reduced to their structural bones. The cold was real now. Neither of them suggested going back in.

They walked along the path that ran beside the east wall. The light was nearly gone. Behind them, through the windows, the remaining guests moved in the warm rooms like figures in a lantern show.

"Bingley was incandescent," Elizabeth said.

"He was." Darcy's tone contained, she thought, more than agreement, something that was not quite amusement and not quite something graver, but occupied the space between.

"He told me you are a very good man. He said he doesn't usually say it because you don't want it said."

There was a pause. "He is not entirely wrong about that."

"About which part?"

Another pause, shorter. "Either."

The path turned where an overgrown apple tree had been left to do what it liked for several seasons. One long branch reached across at shoulder height. Darcy, without breaking stride, raised his hand and held it back for her to pass.

She passed. He followed. Neither of them remarked on it.

The windows behind them held the last of the light. Ahead, the garden wall ran out into shadow. They did not hurry.

Chapter 27: Return to Pemberley

The light came differently in the fall. Elizabeth had not expected that, or rather, she had not thought to expect anything at all, having left Pemberley in the urgency of wedding preparations and returned to it now in a quieter state. The same approach road. The same turn where the trees gave way and the house appeared below. The light was lower now, autumn-flat, and the stone caught it differently than it had in spring. Below, the stream caught it too, and gave it back in pieces. She looked longer than she meant to.

Darcy said nothing. He was watching her, or the road, or both; she did not check which.

The carriage drew up. Mrs. Reynolds met them at the door with the efficiency of someone who had been informed of the exact hour and had organized herself accordingly. Her welcome was warm and correct, and she directed two footmen with the luggage before Elizabeth had removed her gloves. The house received them as a house that had been waiting: fires laid, rooms aired, everything in its place, and Elizabeth walked through the entrance hall and felt, without deciding to feel it, that she had come back somewhere.

She went upstairs to change. The room was the same room, which was obvious enough not to require the observation, and yet she made it privately, standing at the window while the maid unfastened her traveling dress. Longbourn these last two weeks had smelled of close rooms and her mother's brand of domestic upheaval. Pemberley smelled of beeswax and cold air and wood-smoke beginning, and Elizabeth breathed it in and was not sorry to be back.

Mrs. Reynolds was waiting for her when she came downstairs, with the look of a woman who had a list and considered the list reasonable.

The housekeeper's reports were a weekly affair, and Elizabeth had inherited a system already functioning: linen inventories, candle tallies, the cook's order book, the accounting that kept a house of this size running without visible effort. She had spent the first weeks simply learning to read it. The second month she began asking questions. By the time they left for Hertfordshire the first time, back in July, she was making decisions rather than ratifying them, and the difference had been noticed, not unpleasantly, by Mrs. Reynolds and the upper staff.

Now there were a couple of weeks' worth of postponed business to review.

They went through it in the small sitting room off the housekeeper's parlor, which was where Mrs. Reynolds preferred to work, and which Elizabeth had discovered she preferred as well. It was quieter than the main rooms, with a window that looked onto the kitchen yard and let you see the actual operations of the house rather than its public face. The water supply to the east wing laundry needed attention before winter; Elizabeth approved the mason. The arrangement of the spare rooms in the guest wing wanted revising. There were two rooms that were kept permanently in readiness that had not been used in three years; Elizabeth suggested reducing this to one and repurposing the second as a sitting room for Georgiana, who currently had no private space of her own beyond her bedroom. Mrs. Reynolds wrote this down with the expression of someone who thought it was obvious and was glad it had been said.

There was a matter regarding one of the kitchen maids; a situation requiring some delicacy, which Mrs. Reynolds described with the concision of a woman who trusted her listener to complete the picture without additional diagrams. Elizabeth asked two questions, both practical, and they settled it between them in under ten minutes.

Darcy passed the doorway once during this and did not come in. She was aware of him pausing in the corridor, registering that the conversation was in progress, and continuing on his way. When the housekeeper's reports were finished and Mrs. Reynolds had gathered her papers, Elizabeth went to the library and found him there, reading.

He looked up.

"Mrs. Reynolds's list," she said.

"Long?"

"Manageable. There's a question about the east wing water supply you should know about." She told him. He listened in the way he listened when the information was going in correctly, without interruption, one hand flat on the open book. When she had finished he said he would speak to the mason himself, and she said she had already approved it, and he was quiet for a moment and then said, good.

She took the chair by the other window. They read in the same room for the rest of the afternoon without further conversation, which was not uncomfortable.

Dinner was quiet. Darcy asked about the road south of Derby. There had been reports of a washed section near Belper, and she told him what she had noticed, which was not much. The conversation was not strained. It was the conversation of two people who had run out of urgent things to say and had not yet identified what came next.

Georgiana had left for a fortnight with the Hursts before the wedding, a visit arranged before any of August's events and not interrupted by them. The house was therefore theirs alone, which was not uncomfortable. It had not been uncomfortable for some time.

After dinner, Elizabeth took her candle to the library rather than the sitting room. This was a choice she had made three or four times now. She had lost count of exactly when it had started, and Darcy had not remarked upon it. The library was the better room in the evenings: larger, cooler, the fire throwing a longer light. She had found, over the months, that she thought better there, and that Darcy did not find her presence in it an intrusion because he was generally there himself.

Tonight he was not. She read for an hour, heard him in the passage once, and then the house was quiet.

In the morning she walked the kitchen garden before breakfast.

The gardeners had been busy in her absence. The beds that had been overgrown in June were cut back to order, and there was a smell of turned earth that was not unpleasant, and the late asters were still growing lavender and white along the south-facing wall. She had planted none of this. She had inherited it, along with the house, along with the household's particular rhythms, along with the opinion of every tradesperson in three counties about Pemberley's new mistress.

She had an opinion on the kitchen garden herself now. It had come on gradually, the way opinions did when you were paying attention without meaning to: the herb beds were poorly positioned relative to the kitchen door; the cutting garden was too far from the house to be convenient; the walled section was wasted on decorative plantings that nobody cut. She had mentioned this to the head gardener, whose name was Birch, in August, not as a directive but as a question - *does it not seem a long way to carry the flowers?* - and Birch had looked at her with the careful expression of a man revising his estimate of someone, and said that it did, and that the previous mistress had preferred it so, and that he himself had always thought it a pity about the herbs.

She had told Darcy about this conversation. He had listened, and the next morning he had gone to speak to Birch himself, and the herb beds were now in the process of being relocated. This had happened in September. She had not asked him to do it, and he had not told her he intended to.

She thought about that, walking along the wall.

The letter from Jane arrived mid-morning, forwarded from Longbourn with a week's delay. Jane wrote as Jane always wrote — with a composure that, if you knew her, told you considerably more than the words themselves. Bingley was well. Netherfield was being got ready for winter. Mrs. Bennet had redirected her energies toward Kitty's situation with an application that Kitty was finding wearing. Lydia had written from

Newcastle with the cheerfulness of someone who had produced a satisfying resolution to a problem that had, technically, been someone else's.

She does not appear to know, Jane wrote, *what it cost. Or if she does, she has decided not to know, which may come to the same thing.*

Elizabeth read this paragraph twice. Then she put the letter in her writing case and went to find her desk.

She had been writing to Jane more frequently since the summer; longer letters, less careful ones, the kind where the sentence you wrote to fill space turned out to be the sentence you meant. This one took twenty minutes and covered three sheets, which was more than she had planned. She described Pemberley in the fall. She described the kitchen garden and Birch, and the herb beds. She described the quality of the light on the drive last evening, which she had not yet described to anyone, and which she found she wanted to put somewhere.

She wrote: *I find I am glad to be back. I notice this the way you notice a change in weather, not dramatically, but as a fact one might as well acknowledge, since it is already the case.*

She had not planned to write that sentence. She looked at it for a moment. Then she continued, and covered the rest of the sheet with a description of Mrs. Reynolds's housekeeping list and the question of Georgiana's sitting room, which were both true and somewhat easier to put in an envelope.

She sealed it before she could revise it into something more measured.

A letter from Georgiana arrived the following day, brief and warm and written in the hand of someone who had been thinking about what to say and had ultimately chosen directness over craft. She was well. The Hursts were the Hursts. She would be home by Thursday and was glad to hear that Elizabeth had returned safely, and she had been thinking, while away, about a piece of music that Elizabeth had asked her about in August, whether she had ever attempted the second movement slowly, as an exercise rather than a performance, and she had tried it, and Elizabeth had been right, and she wanted to show her when she came back.

Elizabeth read this twice for different reasons than she had read Jane's letter.

She thought about the afternoon in August when that conversation had happened; Georgiana at the pianoforte, picking her way through the problem of a passage she had always rushed because it frightened her, and Elizabeth sitting nearby without comment until Georgiana stopped and asked, plainly, whether she thought the tempo was wrong. And Elizabeth had said she was not qualified to judge the tempo but that she had noticed Georgiana always played that part as if she wanted to be through it, and that she wondered whether playing it as if she had all the time in the world might change something. Georgiana had looked at her for a moment. Then she had played it again, slowly, and her face while she played it was entirely different.

Darcy had come in near the end. He had said nothing about what he had seen.

Elizabeth had not thought of herself as someone who knew how to offer that kind of attention. It was not a skill she had identified or cultivated. It had simply been what the moment required, and she had given it, and Georgiana had taken it, and something between them had settled into a different register afterward, less careful, more particular, the way a friendship felt when it no longer needed to explain itself.

She wrote back: *I am glad you tried it. Come home and play it for me properly.*

Darcy found her in the estate office after luncheon.

He came in without ceremony because there was a letter from a tenant at the north end of the home farm, a Mr. Hedley, whose drainage situation they had discussed in July and not resolved before the Lydia crisis took precedence.

He handed her the letter. She read it.

"He's been waiting since July," she said.

"Yes."

"The lower field was already standing water in June. If it isn't addressed before the ground freezes—"

"It won't drain come spring. I know." He looked at the letter she was holding rather than at her. "I want to ride out tomorrow and look at it properly. I should have done it then."

"We left in some haste over Lydia."

"Even so."

She handed the letter back. He did not take it immediately, and she was aware, briefly, of the paper between them, his fingers on one edge and hers on the other, before he folded it and put it in his coat.

"I'll come with you," she said. "If you don't object."

"I was going to ask."

He had not been going to ask. She knew this because he had not asked. But she understood what he meant by it, which was that he would have been glad if she had offered, and she had offered, and the distinction between those two things was smaller than it had been in June.

She went out alone in the late afternoon, when the light was going.

She had no particular destination. She walked across the south lawn to the ha-ha and stood there a moment, looking at the park. The deer were out at the far edge of the wood, four of them, grazing without urgency. The air was cold now and smelled of leaves beginning to go soft on the ground.

She turned and looked back at the house.

In June, she had come here as a traveler. She had stood in roughly this spot, on a different day, in different circumstances, and seen Pemberley the way a visitor sees a thing with the view of someone who knows they are looking in order to form a judgment and then leave. She remembered thinking: this is what was in front of her when he proposed. She had meant it as a point against him, or against herself, or against something. She was no longer entirely certain what.

The house stood in the last of the day's light and looked exactly as it always looked.

She thought about the herb beds. She thought about the letter to Jane, already sealed - *I find I am glad to be back* - and the sentence she had looked at and then let stand. She thought about Georgiana playing the second movement slowly, with all the time in the world. She thought about Mr. Hedley's lower field and the ride planned for tomorrow morning, and about Darcy saying *I was going to ask* when he had not been going to ask, and about the quality of his listening with the flat hand on the open book, the information going in correctly, that she had learned to read without trying to.

None of it was large. None of it announced itself. It had accumulated the way everything real accumulated: gradually, in the margins of other concerns, in the texture of ordinary days.

She stayed until the windows lost the light, then walked back across the cold grass to the door.

Chapter 28: Darcy's Question

She had been reading for the better part of an hour without speaking, and he had stopped pretending to read. Georgiana had excused herself early. A headache, she said, though Georgiana's headaches had a reliable habit of arriving when she was not needed, and since then the library had been quiet in the way it only was when no one felt the need to fill it.

The fire had been built up against the cold that came off the Derbyshire hills after dark, and the candles on the reading table threw a circle of light that made the rest of the room feel very far away.

Elizabeth was on the sofa nearest the fire with a volume she had found that afternoon on the lower shelf. It was one of Darcy's, clearly, because it had his name written inside the cover in the hand he must have had at fourteen, the letters more deliberate than they were now. She had not told him she was reading it.

He had a book open on the arm of the chair that he had not looked at in some time, and the room had the inhabited silence of two people each attending to something, neither requiring the other to account for themselves.

She had noticed this developing over the last weeks. She was not certain when it had begun. At some point, the silences between them had stopped being negotiations and become simply their evenings.

She turned a page. The fire shifted. Outside, the wind moved through the old beeches at the west end of the grounds, and she could hear it faintly through the library's tall windows, a sound like a conversation held too far away to follow.

Darcy leaned back in his chair.

She did not look up even when the silence changed again, slightly, in the way that silence does when someone is no longer occupied and has not yet decided what to do instead. She turned another page, though she had not quite finished the one before.

"May I ask you something?"

Elizabeth looked up then. He was not looking at his book. He was looking at her, with attention she had learned, over months, to read as genuine rather than judicial. Early in the marriage, she had not known the difference.

"You may," she said.

He considered for a moment, not as though he was selecting a question, she thought, but as though he was deciding how to ask the one he already had.

"Before Hunsford," he said. "Before any of it. What did you do with a day you had entirely to yourself?"

She looked at him.

It was not the question she had expected. She had grown reasonably competent at anticipating Darcy's questions. They tended toward the practical or toward the carefully oblique, each one placed like a piece of furniture he was not certain the room would accommodate. This was neither.

"An entirely free day," she repeated.

"One with no obligation to anyone. No calls expected, no letters requiring answer, no sisters to be attended to." He paused. "I am aware such days may have been rare."

"They were not rare," she said. "They were nearly theoretical."

Something crossed his face that was not quite a smile but was adjacent to it. "Then describe a theoretical one."

Elizabeth set the book down on the cushion beside her, keeping her finger in the page out of habit, though she did not intend to return to it immediately.

"I would have walked," she said. "In the morning, while everyone else was still at breakfast. Far enough that Meryton was not visible and I could not hear my mother's window if she opened it to call after me."

"How far was that?"

"It depended on the wind." She considered. "Two miles at a minimum. Sometimes four or five. I had a route through the fields behind Longbourn that came out near a stand of elms that was on Lucas property, though Sir William never objected." She paused. "He was very agreeable about trespass."

"And when you reached the elms?"

"I would sit," she said. "And think about nothing in particular, which is much more difficult than it sounds. Or I would think about everything and let it run until it ran out." She looked at the fire for a moment. "My father's study served a similar purpose on wet days, but only if he was not in it. If he was in it, it was better."

She had not expected to say that. She had said little about her father since the wedding, even to Jane. There was a particular arithmetic to grief she had found, the way certain truths could be handled in daylight and not in conversation, or in conversation and not in letters, and sometimes in no form at all.

Darcy did not respond immediately. He did not, she noticed, redirect toward something more comfortable. He simply received it.

"He would have you in and say nothing?" he asked.

"He would have me in and hand me a book," she said. "Sometimes the same book I had read before, because he had forgotten I'd read it, or perhaps because he hadn't forgotten. It was difficult to tell with my father." She smoothed the cover of the volume beside her. "And then we would both read, and occasionally he would say something, and occasionally I would, and nothing was required of either of us beyond being present in the same room."

She stopped. She had given him more than she intended to, and she did not move to take it back.

"I have a great deal of his books," she said, to put the sentence somewhere. "He left me them specifically. I did not know until Mr. Gardiner managed the estate business and wrote to tell me."

"I know," Darcy said. "Your aunt mentioned it." He paused. "I had the cases brought from Longbourn when they were clearing the study. The ones marked with your name. They are in the east sitting room."

She looked at him.

He said it without ceremony, as though it were a domestic detail he was reporting rather than an act of consideration he expected her to acknowledge. She thought of the east sitting room, where she occasionally sat in the mornings because the light came in well, and the row of familiar spines on the shelf she had assumed were Pemberley's. She had not read any of them yet.

"I did not know they were there," she said.

"I know," he said again, simply.

She returned her gaze to the fire. There was a log that had been burning for some time on one end and not the other, which would make it collapse unevenly in another quarter of an hour. She did not say anything about this.

"After the walking," Darcy said, after a moment, "or the sitting with your father. What else?"

She looked at him again. He was watching her with the expression she had first learned to read at Pemberley, which was not the expression he wore in company. In company, he arranged his face into something contained and slightly remote, which she now understood was not hauteur precisely but something more like the effort of a man who found social noise genuinely fatiguing and had learned, imperfectly, to manage it. At home, in the evenings, he did not bother with the arrangement.

"Lunch," she said. "With whoever was about and willing to be quiet. Jane, usually. Jane has always been the most companionable member of my family on the subject of silence."

"More so than Bingley."

"Bingley," she said, "is constitutionally unable to be quiet for more than six minutes, and at the end of the six minutes he will have said something so genuinely warm that one cannot hold it against him." She paused. "He and Jane will suit each other very well. She will be quiet for both of them and he will be cheerful enough that she will never feel the loss."

"You are not worried for her?"

"I was worried for her," Elizabeth said. "I am not now." She let this rest for a moment in the way it deserved, because it was true and because Darcy understood without her stating his part in it. "After lunch," she continued, "I would read in the afternoon, or walk again if the light held. My mother occasionally required assistance with something in the evening, and I would provide it or not, depending on whether the something was genuine or was a mechanism for keeping all of us within sight."

"Which was it more often?"

"The latter," she said, without rancor. "She is frightened of space, my mother. She has always preferred everyone in the same room, talking at volume, so that the house sounds full. I think silence alarmed her. She associated it with absence."

She had not articulated this before, not even to herself. It arrived now with the mild surprise of a thing that has been true for a long time and has only just been put into language.

"I used to find it exhausting," she said. "All of us in the parlor. The noise. Now I think I understand it better."

"Loss makes different sense than it did."

It was not a question. She looked at him, and he was not looking at his correspondence or at the fire, but at her, steadily, and not as a man waiting for a response he could answer. He was simply there.

"Yes," she said.

The fire shifted again. The uneven log collapsed as she had predicted and sent a brief spray of sparks against the grate, and the light in the room tilted momentarily.

"The mornings," she said, after a moment. "I have not told you about the mornings."

He looked at her. "You said you walked."

"I walked," she said, "but first, before that, there was a window in my room at Longbourn that faced east, and in summer the light came through it very early. Too early, most mornings, for anything useful. I had a curtain that was supposed to prevent this and was entirely decorative in practice." She paused. "I came to think of those half-hours, between the light coming in and it being an hour at which any reasonable activity could begin, as the most genuinely free portion of any day. One was not yet required. One had not yet made any errors. The day had not yet organized itself into its various demands."

She stopped. She was aware she had been talking for some time. This was not, in itself, unusual. She was by nature a person who talked, and she had long since given up apologizing for it. But she was aware that she had been talking about things she did not usually talk about, and that this had happened because Darcy had asked a question that was not about Lydia or Jane or the tenants or what she thought of the Gardiners' last letter. He had asked about her.

And she had answered. At length. Without quite deciding to.

"The half-hour before the day makes its claims," he said.

"Yes."

"I know that hour," he said. He did not elaborate on this, but she believed him.

The fire had settled back to its even burn. The wind in the beeches had quieted. The candles on the reading table had burned lower without either of them noticing enough to replace them, and the circle of light had contracted slightly, which made the room feel smaller in a way that was not uncomfortable.

"And your opinions now," he said. "Are you still recording them?"

"Less wrong and more carefully held," she said. "I kept a journal for a time and then found it too self-serious and gave it up."

"What made it self-serious?"

"I did," she said. "I was very earnest in it. I recorded my opinions on everything as though they would be required later, and when I went back and read them, I found that several of them had been entirely wrong and a great many more had been expressed with a confidence that was not warranted by my actual knowledge." She folded her hands in her lap. "It was a useful exercise, on reflection. One's written opinions are more difficult to revise than spoken ones. It is harder to tell oneself one never believed something when the belief is recorded in one's own handwriting."

"I have done that myself," he said. "The journal." A pause. "I kept one from the age of eleven until about three years ago."

She raised an eyebrow slightly. "What stopped you?"

"I found, as you did, that I was wrong about a number of things I had recorded with confidence." He was quiet for a moment. "The experience of reading it was instructive in a way that did not require repetition."

She studied him. He said it without display, without the kind of self-deprecation that is more posture than genuine, and she thought of what she had come to understand about Darcy over the months of the marriage, that his pride, which she had once taken for the fixed quality of his character, was in fact the surface habit of a man who had not been required by his position or his circumstances to examine himself very often. When he did examine himself, he was not gentle about it. And when he arrived at a conclusion, he did not argue himself out of it for comfort's sake.

"You were wrong about specific things?" she asked.

"A number of them." He looked at the fire. "My opinion of certain people. My understanding of what constituted a satisfactory reason for a decision. My sense of what could be managed without discussion." He paused. "The last category was the most recent."

Elizabeth said nothing. He was not asking for a response, and she did not offer one. The Lydia negotiation and its aftermath had been discussed, accounted for, and put to rest in the terms they had agreed between them. It did not need to be relitigated tonight. The inclusion was honest and she received it as such.

He looked at her with the expression she still did not have a name for, the one that was not the social arrangement, not the judicial attention, not the restraint he wore in public. She had been seeing it more often lately. She had not yet decided what it meant, though she had a growing sense that the decision was less complicated than she was making it.

"Thank you," he said.

Elizabeth looked at him. "For what?"

"For answering." He said it plainly, without inflection that asked her to make something of it.

She picked up the book from the cushion beside her and found her page. "You asked a good question," she said.

She did not look up again for some time. But she was aware, without looking, that he had not returned to his book, and that the silence between them had, once again, become simply an evening.

She goes to bed before he does. He sits a while in the chair she vacated.

Chapter 29: Lady Catherine's Letter

The letter arrived on Tuesday, tucked between a note from Bingley about a disputed boundary fence and an invoice from the Lambton linen draper. Darcy brought it to her himself rather than leaving it with the morning post, which told her, before she had read a word, that he already knew what it contained.

"From Rosings," he said. He set it on the table beside her coffee cup. "Addressed to me. I thought you should read it."

Elizabeth looked at the letter, then at him. He was standing near the window with the look of someone who had already worked through his own response and set it aside.

"Thank you," she said, and picked it up.

Lady Catherine's hand was strong and regular; the letters formed with the confidence of someone who had never doubted that what she wrote would be attended to. The paper was heavy and smelled faintly of the Rosings drawing room. She was probably inventing that.

She read it once, straight through, without expression. Then she set it down beside the coffee cup and looked out the window at the grounds, which were gray and still in the November light.

The letter covered three-quarters of a page. It opened with a reference to Darcy's duty to his family name, moved without transition into a catalogue of Elizabeth's disqualifications: birth, connections, the Lydia matter, the general unsuitability of the entire Bennet establishment, and closed with what Lady Catherine clearly believed to be a decisive stroke: Anne de Bourgh's health was deteriorating. Anne had not complained. Anne had never complained, which was precisely the point. That a woman of Anne's forbearance and family should be set aside in favor of a girl from Hertfordshire who had nothing to recommend her but the good fortune of being available at a moment of Darcy's weakness.

Elizabeth reached the end of the page. She picked up her coffee, which had gone cold, and drank it anyway.

"She mentions Anne's health," she said.

"Yes."

"Is it true?"

"Anne has not been robust since childhood. I have no recent information suggesting any change." He paused. "She is being used as a rhetorical instrument. I do not believe my aunt has asked her permission."

Elizabeth set down the cup. "No. I don't imagine she has."

She sat for a moment longer. Outside, a groom was leading a horse across the yard, and she watched until they disappeared around the corner of the stable block. Then she pushed back her chair, went to the writing desk, and took out paper.

"I would like to reply," she said.

Darcy said nothing. She took this as assent.

She did not draft. She had found, over the past months, that drafting responses to Lady Catherine produced letters that were too careful. It was better to write quickly and revise a single time, before the prose could begin watching itself.

She wrote for perhaps twelve minutes. Then she read it back.

Dear Lady Catherine,

Your letter of the fourteenth has been received and read with attention. I am sorry to hear that Miss de Bourgh's health continues to give cause for concern and hope that the winter months prove kinder to her than recent seasons have been.

I understand you believe this marriage was imprudent. I have not hidden from Darcy that the match was made under circumstances I would not have chosen, nor that the early weeks of our acquaintance were not distinguished by mutual admiration. He is aware of my view, as I am aware of his.

What I would ask you to consider, with the same candor you have extended to us, is whether the outcome you desire - my removal from Pemberley and Darcy's life - is one that Darcy himself would sanction, and whether, if it is not, you intend to continue pressing it. Your influence over him is considerable and founded on genuine affection, and I do not wish to diminish it. I would ask only that you exercise it toward ends he has indicated he wants.

Anne is not a weapon. I suspect she knows this. I hope we may all behave accordingly.

With respect,

Elizabeth Darcy

She read it through once more. The paragraph about Anne had been the question; it would either land correctly or read as impertinence. She decided it was accurate and that accuracy was worth the risk.

She carried the letter to Darcy.

He read it standing up, which took less than a minute. When he reached the end, he was quiet long enough that she began revising the paragraph about Anne in her head, preparing to cut it.

"This is better than anything I would have written," he said.

"I think the paragraph about Anne is the question."

"The paragraph about Anne is exactly right." He looked up. "She will not like it."

"She will not like any of it."

"No," he handed the letter back, "but she cannot object to the manner of it."

"That was the intention."

She folded it, addressed it, and set it on the tray with the outgoing post. It would go on the morning collection. There was nothing further to decide.

She went back to the writing desk and picked up the invoice from the Lambton draper, which was the actual business of the morning. Darcy moved away from the window toward his own desk in the adjacent room. After a moment, she heard the familiar sounds of him working, the rhythm of a person accustomed to long stretches of concentration.

At half past ten, Mrs. Reynolds came in with a question about the linen order, and Elizabeth answered it. At eleven, Georgiana appeared with a book she had been meaning to return, stayed twenty minutes, and left with two more. The fire needed building up, and Elizabeth rang for it. The morning continued.

She did not think again about Lady Catherine's letter, except once, briefly, when the post tray was collected just before noon. A footman lifted it from the hall table with the unhurried efficiency of someone for whom this was simply Tuesday's work. The letter to Rosings went with the rest: unremarkable, tucked among the others.

Elizabeth listened to the front door close then sat down at the writing desk to draft a letter to Jane.

Chapter 30: The Walk

The afternoon had no purpose.

There were no calls expected, no letters requiring an answer before the post went out, no tenant matter Darcy had mentioned at breakfast with the set to his jaw that meant he would be occupied until dinner.

Georgiana had gone to the music room after luncheon and closed the door, which meant she wanted two hours to herself and would emerge improved in temper and unwilling to say why. Elizabeth had stood in the corridor outside the library, considered the book she had been meaning to finish for three days, and decided against it.

She found Darcy in the entrance hall pulling on his gloves.

"I was going out," he said, "to walk."

"I know," she said. "I saw you from the landing."

He looked at her for a moment. "Would you like to come?"

She had already retrieved her pelisse from the chair by the door where she had left it that morning, an organizational habit he had stopped remarking on. She put it on. "Yes."

They went out through the south garden and down toward the long path that followed the river. The afternoon light was bright without warmth, the kind that made distances look deceptive. Elizabeth had learned in her months at Pemberley that the river path was longer than it appeared from the terrace, that the first bend concealed another quarter mile at minimum, and that Darcy walked it at a pace that suggested he was not counting the distance.

She matched it without difficulty. She had always been a walker.

Neither of them spoke. This had stopped being uncomfortable some time ago. She could not have said exactly when, only that there had been a period in the early weeks of the marriage when silence between them was a thing to be managed, and now it was not.

A pair of rooks crossed overhead, making a considerable noise about it. Elizabeth watched them clear the treeline.

"They nest in the elm on the east side of the house," Darcy said. "The one with the split trunk. My steward has been lobbying for its removal for four years."

"On what grounds?"

"Structural risk. The split has widened."

"And you have declined?"

"I have declined. The rooks have the better argument."

She looked at him. "What is the rooks' argument?"

"Occupation," he said. "Prior and continuous. They were there before Saunders was born and will likely be there after he retires. I find it difficult to rule against that kind of tenure."

Elizabeth laughed, not the polite laugh she had once deployed at Rosings when Lady Catherine said something that required a response, but the real one, quick and unguarded, the one that surprised her when it came. Darcy's reasoning was perfectly characteristic: precise, unexpected, with the faint dry edge of a man who had arrived at his position by logic and was not particularly interested in defending it further.

"Saunders must find you very trying," she said.

"He finds me consistent, which he considers the same thing."

They walked on. The path dipped near the water's edge and the grass grew longer there, still green despite the season, and Elizabeth lifted her hem out of habit. The river moved with the unhurried insistence of water that has been at this far longer than anyone watching it.

"I have been thinking," she said, "about the Ashworth estate."

"Have you?"

"You mentioned last week that the drainage problem in the lower fields has been unresolved for two seasons. I wondered whether the issue might be with the original channeling rather than the maintenance of it."

Darcy glanced at her. "That is what I concluded after speaking with Ashworth's agent in August. What made you think of it?"

"Your south field. The one that floods in March. The grade of the ground there reminded me of what you described."

He was quiet in the way that meant he was considering it, not merely waiting for her to finish. She had learned to tell the difference.

"I have been meaning to write to Ashworth's agent with that observation," he said. "I had not yet done so."

"You could do it tomorrow. I can help you draft it if you like."

He looked at her again, this time with an expression she did not immediately catalog. "Yes," he said. "I would like that."

The path curved away from the river briefly, up through a stand of beeches that had mostly dropped their leaves. The ones remaining were the color of old copper, and they moved in the light with a dry, papery sound. Elizabeth's boots were good ones. Darcy had seen to that, without comment, in the first month, and she had accepted without comment, and they had each understood the exchange without requiring it to be named.

"May I ask you something?" she said.

"You may ask me anything."

"That is a very broad offer."

"I have learned," he said, "that declining to answer is always available to me. The offer costs nothing."

She smiled at the path. "A very lawyerly position."

"My father's solicitor was an excellent man. I was fifteen before I understood that not every question required an immediate answer."

"What question were you answering at fifteen that taught you this?"

He paused, and she thought for a moment he would exercise his stated right to decline. Then: "My aunt Catherine asked me, at a dinner with twelve other people present, whether I preferred her daughter Anne to my cousin Fitzwilliam's company. I was fifteen. Anne was seventeen and had not yet decided to be unwell as a general practice. Fitzwilliam was twenty and had just purchased his commission and was the most interesting person in any room he entered."

Elizabeth waited.

"I told her I found the question difficult to answer with fairness to both parties and that I would prefer to consider it further."

"You did not."

"I did."

"At fifteen?"

"I had been well coached in evasion," he said, with perfect seriousness. "It is one of the genuine advantages of a Pemberley education."

She laughed again, and this time it was longer, and she had to look away toward the river to collect herself, because his face when he had said it, entirely composed, only the very corners of his eyes giving any indication that he found himself at all amusing, was the thing that made it so precisely funny. He was not making a joke. He had simply said a true thing in the flattest possible register and waited.

Her father would have liked that, she thought. The thought arrived without warning and did not undo her.

They came out of the beeches onto the bank proper. There was a bench there, weathered to gray, positioned to face a bend in the river where the water slowed over a shelf of flat stone. Elizabeth sat without asking whether they were stopping. Darcy sat beside her, leaving the proper amount of space, which was less than he would have left six months ago.

She noticed.

The river moved. A branch had caught on the stone shelf and the current worked around it patiently.

"You asked whether you could ask me something," Darcy said. "And then asked me something else."

"I did." She had almost forgotten. "What I meant to ask was this: what was Pemberley like when you were a boy. Not the estate. I know the estate tolerably well by now. I mean the house. What it was like to live in it?"

He looked at the river.

"It was large," he said, and she heard in the plainness of it that he was not beginning with the obvious; he was beginning with the thing that had mattered. "I was an only child for eleven years before Georgiana was born. Large houses with single children in them go still in a way smaller ones do not. The rooms are always correct. Nothing is moved. The staff manages everything at a remove from whoever is supposed to be managing them, because it is simpler. You learn the house as a series of correct arrangements."

"And then Georgiana came."

"And then Georgiana came. And she cried for her first eight months in a way that carried through three floors and baffled every correct arrangement entirely." He had not quite a smile but its approach. "She was a very loud infant. My father found it alarming. My mother thought it was evidence of good health and said so at every opportunity."

"And you?"

"I was eleven. I thought she was extraordinary." The smile arrived then, without warning or construction, not the controlled expression he wore at dinner when something pleased him, but one that reached his eyes and was gone before she had finished registering it. "She was the first person I had ever encountered who had no interest whatsoever in whether the arrangements were correct."

Elizabeth looked at him.

She had been seen, she had thought, walking the grounds of Pemberley in the early days of the marriage, seen by the house, by its history, by Mrs. Reynolds's unguarded warmth and what it implied. But that was not the same thing. That was inference.

What Darcy had just given her was not inference. It was a specific child in a specific house, delighted by a specific loud infant, telling her the actual story without dressing it.

"She still has no interest," Elizabeth said.

"None. I have always found it reliable in her."

Neither of them spoke for a time. The branch on the stone shifted in the current and caught again.

"I told her something," Elizabeth said. "Georgiana. In the early weeks. About Wickham."

"I know."

"You know what I told her?"

"I know that she came to me the next day and asked me whether she had been very foolish, and when I said no, she told me that you had said something similar, but that hearing it from you had been different." He looked at the river. "I did not ask what you had said. It did not seem like mine to ask."

Elizabeth considered that. The thought it triggered was not abstract. It was the memory of Georgiana's face at the pianoforte afterward, the easing in her posture that Elizabeth had noticed and said nothing about. All of it arriving now as information about Darcy rather than about Georgiana.

He had known. He had held it without asking. He had waited.

"You have been paying attention," she said.

"I have been paying attention since Hertfordshire." He said it plainly, looking at the river still, in the same register he had used about the rooks and the fifteen-year-old's evasion and Georgiana crying through three floors. Not a declaration arranged for effect. A fact he was reporting accurately. "I was not always paying attention to the right things. But I have been paying attention."

Elizabeth did not answer immediately. The branch pulled free of the stone shelf, and the current took it around the bend.

"I know," she said.

They walked back toward the house. The light had moved while they sat, the afternoon resolving into early evening, the long shadows of the beeches falling across the path at a new angle. Neither of them mentioned the time.

At the edge of the south garden, where the gravel began, Darcy held a low-hanging branch back from the path. She went under it. He followed.

"The letter to Ashworth's agent," he said, as they came up toward the terrace steps. "Tomorrow morning, before the post goes."

"Before the post," she agreed.

They went inside.

Chapter 31: What She Knows

Elizabeth walked the grounds with her hands in her pockets and her hem collecting cold along the bottom seam, and the house fell behind her the way it always did at this hour, without ceremony, without requiring anything.

She had told him this was what she did with a morning entirely her own. He had asked, and she had answered, and she had not thought much of the exchange at the time except to note that he had asked at all.

She thought of it now.

The path curved east along the ridge before it dropped toward the river and she took it at a pace that was not quite purposeful, having nowhere she needed to be for another two hours, and the cold worked at her ears and the back of her neck until both went pleasantly numb. A crow crossed from one stand of oaks to another. The light was coming up behind the clouds, diffuse and gray.

She had been cataloguing; she thought. Not deliberately. She had always found that kind of self-examination more productive when it arrived unbidden, which it now had, and so she let it proceed.

The tenant's note had come first, in her first days at Pemberley. She had found it framed in the estate office, a note of thanks from a family whose situation she had not yet known, and Darcy had come in and found her standing in front of it. She had asked. He had told her, plainly: two bad crop years, no rent taken. A matter he had not mentioned because it had not occurred to him to mention it. It was framed in his office, where no one else would see it. She had thought about that afterward.

She had filed this.

The Bingley arrangement she had understood differently once she saw it executed. Not announced, not confessed again, simply done. He had brought Bingley back to Netherfield with the deliberateness of someone paying a debt they had itemized precisely, and he had done it without asking for acknowledgment, which she suspected was the harder part for him. She had watched his face when Bingley crossed the room to Jane and had seen only that he was watching Jane's face, and she had thought: he is checking the account. He wants to know that it came out right.

She had not told him she had seen that. She had told him, later, that she knew what he had done about Bingley, and he had said nothing, and she had not required him to.

The path reached its lowest point and then leveled. The river was audible before it was visible with a low, indifferent sound, entirely without drama. She followed the path along its bank for a while.

Lady Catherine had come and gone and left nothing behind except the confirmation that Darcy would not be moved on the subject of his wife in front of witnesses. He had not told Elizabeth afterward that he had handled it well, or that he had defended her, or that his aunt was intolerable. He had asked whether she had wanted Fitzwilliam to intervene.

She had said no.

He had said he thought not.

That had been, she considered, a satisfying exchange.

Georgiana's face, the afternoon she had said the thing about Wickham - *I think you were very young, and he was very practiced* - had arranged itself into something Elizabeth still could not entirely name. Not gratitude. Something prior to gratitude. The recognition that she had been given the right sentence for a fact that had been sitting, unnamed, for two years.

Elizabeth stopped walking.

The river ran over its stones without consulting her.

She had known, going into the marriage, that she was making a transaction. She had known the terms and had, on balance, judged them the least-worst available. She had not expected to revise this judgment. She had expected to manage the arrangement with the intelligence and good humor she applied to most unpleasant necessities, and to arrive, eventually, at something that could be described as a reasonable domestic peace. She had thought this would be enough.

She had been wrong about what it would look like.

The river walk had happened on an afternoon when neither of them had anything else to do with the day. No prior obligation, no errand that had brought them outside first. They had simply both been at Pemberley on a Tuesday in September with the afternoon available, and the path had presented itself, and neither of them had proposed turning back.

They had disagreed about something: the management of a disputed boundary, or it might have been a book, she could not now remember which had come first, and she had argued and he had held his position and then conceded one part of it when she pressed him on a specific point, and she had been aware, during all of this, that she was enjoying herself.

He had said, at the bench by the water: *You have a habit of walking when you are thinking something through. I have noticed it since Hertfordshire.*

She had looked at him.

He had not embellished. He had not said it as a compliment. He had said it as a man reporting an accurate observation, which was how he said most things, and she had understood in that moment that he had been watching her the way she watched people, not to catalog their deficiencies, but to understand the logic of them. The architecture.

Since Hertfordshire. Since Netherfield, then since before the entail, before her father's death, before any of this. Since the beginning, when she had been only a woman in a muddy hem who had walked three miles to nurse her sister and had not thought it worth explaining.

He had seen that. He had kept it.

Elizabeth looked at the water, and the word came to her plainly: *met.*

Not rescued. She had not been rescued. She had made a calculation and executed it with her eyes open, and the results had been better than the terms suggested, which was a kind of satisfaction. Not managed, not accommodated, not made comfortable in the way a household makes a guest comfortable by removing all the edges from the furniture. Those were things that had been done, in various degrees, and she had noted them and not confused them with what they were not.

Met. By someone who had looked at her from a distance, and then from a closer distance, and then across a dinner table and a carriage and a disputed boundary and had seen the same person at each remove. Who had asked the right question; what would you do with a morning entirely your own, and received the answer and kept it and not tried to improve upon it.

She turned and walked back toward the house.

The light had come up enough to give the oaks their detail back. The house was visible from the top of the ridge, its windows dark at the upper floors, one light already moving in the kitchen wing. Her hem was wet through, and her hands were cold and she had been out for the better part of an hour.

She went inside through the garden door, which was unlocked because she had left it so, and stood in the passage long enough to pull off her half-boots and carry them rather than mark the floor.

At the window of the small sitting room she paused. The grounds outside held the last of the gray light, the oaks standing in it solidly, the river somewhere beyond them doing what rivers did without regard for conclusions reached on their banks.

She had been falling in love, she thought, for some considerable time.

Elizabeth set her boots down and went to breakfast.

He was already there. He looked up from his correspondence when she came in, and then looked again, at her damp hem, her color, the hour, and reached across and poured her coffee without being asked, and returned to his letter.

She sat down and drank it.

Chapter 32: The Choice

The evening had no occasion.

That was the thing Elizabeth kept returning to, later; there had been nothing to mark it from any other Tuesday in late November: no letter arrived, no visitor announced, no difficulty requiring resolution. Georgiana had retired early with a headache. The rain had been persistent since mid-afternoon and showed no interest in stopping. Darcy had been working at his desk in the library since dinner; Elizabeth had been reading in the chair nearest the fire, and the book was good enough to hold her attention until, for no specific reason, it did not.

She set it down. She looked at the fire. She looked at her husband, who was reading something with the focused quiet she had come to associate with estate correspondence. It was not the tight containment he wore in company, but a genuine, undramatic concentration. He turned a page. He made a brief notation in the margin.

She had been watching him for some time before she understood she was watching him.

He had asked her a question, two months ago. He had not phrased it as a question then. He was not a man who asked for things directly when the asking might be refused, but she had understood it. He wanted to know whether she was still there for the same reasons she was when she had arrived. Whether the arithmetic still held. Whether yes, in her mouth, still meant only what it had meant at Hunsford.

She had not answered him. She had gone to bed, and he had sat in her chair, and neither of them had returned to it.

She considered how she would answer now.

The structure of it was not complicated. It was only honest, which was a different difficulty. She had said, in this very room, on an evening in what felt like another life, that she would not pretend to have feelings she did not possess. The inverse was also true: she would not withhold what she did possess, once she had identified it correctly. That had always been the more reliable version of her integrity, not the refusal to lie, but the refusal to equivocate.

She picked up her book. She put it down again.

Darcy looked up.

"Is the fire too warm?" he asked. He said it without irony; it was simply the nearest explanation for her restlessness.

"No." She paused. "I have been thinking."

"About?"

Elizabeth looked at the fire for a moment. She had a habit, when she was not certain of her words, of locating the right ones by speaking around them first but she found she did not want to do that now. He had said, in Netherfield, that he wanted her to choose. She intended to make it legible.

"When I agreed to marry you," she said, "I told myself it was arithmetic. That I had looked at what was available and selected the answer the sum produced." She did not look at him yet. "I think I was honest about that, at the time. I was not concealing something warmer beneath the practicality. I was simply practical."

Darcy said nothing. She heard him set down his pen.

"I am not being practical now," Elizabeth said. "That is what I have been sitting here working out. The entail is resolved. My mother and sisters are settled. Lydia is... contained. Jane is at Netherfield and outrageously happy." She looked at him then. "There is no arithmetic left. And I am still here."

The fire shifted. A log dropped lower, and the light changed.

Darcy did not speak immediately. He was looking at her with an expression she could not quite name. It was not the unreadable composure he had worn for most of their marriage, but something beneath it, open in a way he rarely permitted in a lighted room.

She thought: I may have miscalculated.

She kept her eyes on his and did not revise.

"I had not," he said finally, "allowed myself to expect this."

"I know." She did know. She had watched him not expect it, for months, with the discipline of a man who has decided that hoping for a thing will not change whether he receives it.

He stood up from the desk, but he did not come toward her immediately. He stood where he was, as if he were being careful about the distance. "You said once that you would not pretend to feelings you did not have."

"I remember."

"This is not pretense."

"No," Elizabeth said. "It is not."

He crossed the room then, not quickly, and sat in the chair across from her, the chair that was, by some domestic drift she had not consciously orchestrated, now simply his chair, the one he occupied when they read together in the evenings. He was close enough that she could see the firelight on the angles of his face.

"I want to say something," he said, "and I would ask you to let me finish it before you find its flaws."

Elizabeth folded her hands in her lap. "I make no promises. But I am listening."

The corner of his mouth moved. Not quite a smile, but the precursor to one. "I have been watching you," he said, "since the first evening at Netherfield. That is not news to either of us. What I did not understand then, and took some considerable time to understand, was what I was actually watching for." He was looking at her steadily. "I thought I wanted a particular kind of woman. Accomplished, well-connected, of appropriate family. I did not think I was watching for someone who would argue with me about a tenant's drainage problem and be demonstrably correct, or who would write a letter to my aunt that accomplished in twelve lines what I could not have managed in forty."

"That letter was not kind," Elizabeth said.

"It was precise. Kindness was not the point." He paused. "I am saying, imperfectly, that you are not what I thought I wanted. You are considerably more than that, and I have understood it for long enough now that it is not a novel discovery. It is simply true."

Elizabeth looked at him. He had said it the way he said everything that mattered: quietly, without ornament, as if the words were worth exactly what they contained and no more. She had spent months learning to trust that quality in him. She trusted it now.

"I have been falling in love with you," she said, "without noticing I had started." She said it plainly, the way she decided to say it. "I notice it now."

The room was very quiet.

Darcy reached across the small distance between the chairs and took her hand - just her hand, nothing more dramatic than that. His grip was careful, as if she might retract the offer, which she had no intention of doing.

"Then we are agreed," he said.

"We are agreed," Elizabeth said.

Outside, the rain continued against the windows. The fire burned down another inch. At some point Darcy moved from his chair to hers, or rather to the arm of it, which was not quite the done thing, but which the hour and the privacy made irrelevant, and Elizabeth did not remark on it, because she did not want to.

She did not retrieve her book. He did not return to his desk.

Chapter 33: Resolution

The Gardiners arrived on a Wednesday, which meant Mrs. Gardiner had time to form an opinion of the glasshouses before dinner and Mr. Gardiner had time to assess the shooting, and both of them arrived at the table in excellent humor. Darcy had arranged both without consulting Elizabeth, who learned of it from her aunt's amusement.

"He asked your uncle three questions about the coverts," Mrs. Gardiner said, while they dressed for dinner, "and listened to the answers. All three of them."

"My husband is not so easily impressed."

"No," her aunt agreed. "Which is why he was."

Elizabeth said nothing to this. She moved a pin.

They were four nights in all, and the Gardiners made themselves easy in the way of people who approve of what they see but are too intelligent to say so directly.

Mr. Gardiner and Darcy rode out together twice. Mrs. Gardiner walked the grounds with Elizabeth each morning, did not complain of the cold, and asked sensible questions about the household and the tenants. She did not ask a single question about the marriage that Elizabeth was not ready to answer. This was, Elizabeth thought, exactly what she had always valued in her aunt and had not been certain she would have now, in these circumstances, with Darcy's name attached to everything.

She had it. She was glad of it in a way that was difficult to put into words, and so she did not try.

On the third morning, Georgiana came down to breakfast already dressed for going out.

Elizabeth noted the gloves first and the careful way Georgiana had them already in her hand rather than waiting to collect them at the door. Then there was the focus of her attention over the toast rack: present but pointed somewhere else. Georgiana had been sleeping well these past months; she had been easier at Pemberley than at any time Elizabeth could measure against. This was different.

"I thought," Georgiana said, addressing the toast rack, "that if you had no other engagement, I might accompany you this morning. On your walk."

Elizabeth reached for the coffee. "I had planned to go into the village."

"Yes." A pause. "I know."

It was a Tuesday market day. The village would have people in it. Georgiana knew this too, which was the whole of the thing being said and not said between them.

"Then you had better eat something more than toast first," Elizabeth said. "The lane past the miller is longer than it looks."

They went without a maid. Elizabeth had stopped requiring one for the village months ago, and making a party of this morning seemed wrong in a way she could not have defended but was certain of. Mrs.

Gardiner, apprised of the plan, said only that she would have the letters ready to post if Elizabeth was going that way. She did not look at Georgiana when she said it. Elizabeth's aunt was a perceptive woman.

The lane was indeed longer than it looked. Georgiana walked beside her with the careful uprightness she had, nothing in her posture that the most exacting observer could criticize, which was itself armor. Elizabeth had come to understand that about her over these months: the excellent posture was not vanity. It was what Georgiana did when she needed to be certain of one thing, at least.

"It is not so different," Elizabeth said, as they came down toward the first cottage, "from the path through the east wood."

"The east wood has no one in it."

"Seldom," Elizabeth allowed.

They came into the market square from the southern end, which brought them past the baker's before the main stalls. Two women Elizabeth recognized from the church turned at their approach, and the moment went as such moments go: the greeting, the names, the polite surprise that Miss Darcy should be among them today. Georgiana answered each thing that was directed at her. Her voice was even. She did not say more than was required, but she did not retreat behind Elizabeth either, which had been Elizabeth's quiet fear for the first half of the lane.

One of the women, Mrs. Prewitt, who managed the church flowers and formed opinions quickly and expressed them at length, asked Georgiana about the piece she had played at the Michaelmas tenant dinner. The tenant dinner had been held at Pemberley; some of the village families had been present, and Mrs. Prewitt had evidently been among them and had been saving the question for two months.

Georgiana looked at her for a moment. Then she said that it was a Clementi sonatina, and that she had chosen it because it was more forgiving of nerves than it sounded.

Mrs. Prewitt laughed. Georgiana looked briefly startled by this. The laugh had been genuine, uncomplicated, and entirely without condescension, and then she said something further about the fingering that made Mrs. Prewitt laugh again and ask whether Miss Darcy might consider playing for the Christmas service at St. Michael's.

"Perhaps," Georgiana said. "I am not yet certain of my plans."

Which was the correct answer, and honest, and she had found it herself.

They collected the letters for Mrs. Gardiner, and a spool of thread Elizabeth had no immediate use for, and they walked back the way they had come. Georgiana did not speak for some time. The lane turned past the mill and the sound of the water came up.

"She was very kind," Georgiana said.

"Mrs. Prewitt is kind to everyone."

"I did not know that."

Elizabeth considered this. "You do now."

They walked the rest of the lane without difficulty. At the kitchen garden gate, Georgiana paused with her hand on the latch, the same gesture Elizabeth had learned to wait out, the moment before a door was opened or a thing was said.

"I should like," Georgiana said, "to play at the Christmas service. If my brother has no objection."

"I believe he will survive the news."

The ghost of something crossed Georgiana's face that was not quite a smile but came close to one. She opened the gate and went in.

Darcy found Elizabeth in the library an hour before dinner.

He had come, she understood, from somewhere on the estate. There was still mud on his boots that he had not yet changed, which meant he had come directly, which meant he had spoken to his sister first. His expression told her nothing she could name, which told her a great deal.

He stood at the window for a moment looking out at the kitchen garden. Then he said, "Georgiana tells me she walked into the village with you this morning."

"She did."

"And that Mrs. Prewitt asked her to play at the Christmas service."

"She mentioned it to her."

He was quiet for a moment longer. The window held the last of the afternoon light. "She has not been into the village since —" He stopped and started differently. "She used to go with our mother when she was very small."

Elizabeth set her book down on the arm of the chair. She did not fill the silence.

"I did not ask you to do this," he said.

"No."

"I did not think —" He stopped again. He turned from the window, and his expression, now that she could see it properly, was not what she had expected. Not gratitude, exactly. Something less manageable than that.

"She asked me," Elizabeth said. "I only kept pace."

He looked at her across the library in the direct way he had, not the careful social appraisal she remembered from Netherfield, not the composed opacity of the early months of their marriage, but the attention that had grown in its place, which no longer troubled itself to pretend it was something other than what it was.

"Yes," he said. "I know."

He went to change his boots. Elizabeth picked up her book again and did not read it.

The Gardiners left on Saturday morning. Mr. Gardiner shook Darcy's hand at the door and said he hoped they would shoot again in the winter. Darcy said he would arrange it. They both meant it, which was the kind of thing that could not be manufactured.

Her aunt embraced her at the carriage and said, close enough that no one else heard it, "You look very well, Lizzy."

"Thank you."

"I mean," her aunt said, drawing back to look at her, "well."

Elizabeth accepted this. She watched the carriage down the drive until it turned and was gone, then went back inside to find Georgiana in the music room running through the Clementi sonatina with more deliberateness than was strictly necessary for a piece she had already mastered.

A letter from Jane arrived that afternoon, fat with the cheerfulness of Netherfield in late fall, Bingley's enthusiasm for improving the south pasture, and the information that Lydia had written from Newcastle to say that Wickham's regiment had been reassigned to the north. Jane relayed this last item with the careful neutrality of someone who understood perfectly well that it was the best possible news and wished to deliver it without appearing to celebrate it.

Elizabeth read the letter twice. Then she wrote Jane a reply, which began with the south pasture and the Clementi sonatina and ended with a sentence about the reassignment that was as carefully neutral as Jane's had been, and they understood each other completely.

Her mother had written separately to say that Kitty had been invited to stay with the Collinses at Hunsford for the winter, and had she, Elizabeth, any influence with her husband regarding an introduction to a cousin - some relation of Colonel Fitzwilliam, Mrs. Bennet believed - who was expected to be at Rosings in the new year? Elizabeth folded this letter and set it aside for the morning, when she would feel more equal to answering it without irony.

Mary's letter came last. It was three pages, closely written, and the first page concerned itself entirely with a charity school she had organized in Meryton with the rector's wife. The second page described the curriculum. The third page asked, with the directness Mary had always had and which Elizabeth had formerly found trying, whether Elizabeth had any recommendations for improving the instruction of girls who had not been given much opportunity to read.

Elizabeth sat with this letter for a longer time than the others.

She had not been kind to Mary. Not unkind, precisely, and nothing she would be ashamed of exactly, but she had looked past Mary for years without looking at her. The girl in this letter had not grown up in spite of her family's inattention. She had grown up while everyone was occupied with other things, quietly, in the borrowed space of a household that had always given her less room than her noisier sisters.

Elizabeth wrote Mary a full reply. She recommended three books and offered to ask Darcy's librarian for a fourth. She also said, without quite planning to, that she was glad to hear about the school, and meant it in a way she had not expected.

Fitzwilliam arrived the following week for a stay of three days, which was the correct length for him; long enough to be genuinely useful company, short enough that nothing was required of anyone. He and Darcy rode out each morning. He and Elizabeth argued pleasantly about a novel she had read and he had not, and he conceded the argument with the good grace of a man who had lost it fairly and did not mind. He and Georgiana played duets on the third evening, and the music room was loud with the disorder of two people who knew each other's timing well enough to go wrong at exactly the same moment and find it funny.

At dinner that same evening, Fitzwilliam asked Georgiana how she found the village these days. The question was easy, conversational, and could have been nothing at all.

Georgiana said she had been in recently, and that she meant to go again before Christmas, as Mrs. Prewitt had asked her to consider playing at the service.

Fitzwilliam looked at his cousin. Darcy offered him nothing.

"Excellent," Fitzwilliam said. He reached for the salt. "The Clementi?"

"I had thought something livelier."

"Even better."

He collected his hat from the hallway the following morning and said to Elizabeth, while Darcy was seeing to the horses, that Pemberley suited her. She thanked him. He said he meant it differently than she was taking it. Not the house, or the grounds, or even the position. Darcy came back, and the subject changed, and no further clarification was offered or required.

The first dinner of December had the whole table: the Bingleys arrived from Netherfield, Fitzwilliam was still there, and Mrs. Bennet had come up from Longbourn for the week on the grounds that she had not seen Pemberley in the fall and did not know when she should have another opportunity before it snowed, a claim so cheerfully self-serving that Elizabeth had received it in the spirit in which it was intended.

Mrs. Bennet at Pemberley was precisely what Elizabeth had always known she would be: louder than the room required, more emphatic than any topic warranted, and genuinely delighted in a way Elizabeth was no longer entirely immune to. She had always loved her mother as one loves something simultaneously exasperating and dear, the way one loves a force of nature that has shaped the whole of one's life and cannot be reasoned with and shows no signs of diminishing.

Jane sat beside Bingley and looked, as she always looked these days, like a person who had received the thing she had wanted without having ceased to deserve it. Bingley, for his part, managed the table with the social ease he had always possessed, talking to Mrs. Bennet with real attention and to Fitzwilliam with real warmth and to Darcy with the shorthand and the gaps of long friendship with the things not said because they were already understood.

The soup had been cleared and the fish brought when Mrs. Bennet, addressing the table at some volume, delivered her opinion of the Robinsons' second daughter, who had made what Mrs. Bennet described as an inexplicable match when there had been a perfectly good alternative not ten miles away.

The Robinsons' second daughter had been known to Elizabeth since childhood. The perfectly good alternative was approximately forty-five and had a habit of clearing his throat at intervals.

Elizabeth looked up.

Darcy was looking at her already.

Neither of them said anything. Jane was occupied with Bingley. Fitzwilliam had found something of great interest in his wineglass. Georgiana, across the table, met Elizabeth's eyes for one brief moment and then pressed her lips together in the way she had when she was being very careful not to express an opinion.

Mrs. Bennet continued.

Elizabeth and Darcy did not look away.

Chapter 34: Coda

The third volume of 'The Monastery of St. Columb' was on the breakfast table when Darcy came down, which meant Elizabeth had been at it since before first light. She was reading the way she read books she was not yet certain about: at speed, with suspicion, not reading so much as consuming, turning pages with a speed that suggested she did not know whether the novel deserved her but intended to find out.

Darcy poured his coffee and sat. He looked at the spine.

"Roche," he said.

"Roche," she agreed, without looking up.

He ate in silence for several minutes. Outside, a thrush had set up somewhere in the kitchen garden and was making its feelings known at considerable length.

Elizabeth turned a page. Then another. Then she closed the book on her thumb and looked at the ceiling in the way she had when something had either delighted or offended her, and she had not yet determined which.

"Well," Darcy said.

"There have been," Elizabeth said, with the careful precision of someone assembling a legal case, "two separate instances of an infant exchanged in secret. In three volumes."

"That is — "

"I am not finished. The hero has been operating under a false name since volume one, which we are apparently only now intended to understand as significant, and the heroine has just discovered that one of her three fathers is not in fact her father at all, though I confess I have lost track of which."

Darcy set down his cup. "Three fathers?"

"She has accrued them over time."

A silence.

"And yet you are on the third volume," he said.

Elizabeth looked at him. "That is precisely my point." She opened the book again. "If it were merely bad, I would have put it down when I picked up the first volume at Michaelmas. There is something underneath the machinery that is worth the machinery. Miss Elmere alone is worth two of the fathers."

"Who is Miss Elmere?"

"A minor character who prefers her heroines in desolate apartments rather than snug chambers. She says it keeps the interest alive." Elizabeth paused on a page. "I find her very sensible."

Darcy looked at her with the expression he had that was not quite amusement and not quite exasperation and had become, over the months, one of her preferred things to produce in him.

"The plotting," he said, "is — "

"Extravagant."

"I was going to say unmoored from any principle of cause and effect."

"That is a longer way of saying extravagant." She turned a page. "But cause and effect is not what Roche is doing. She is not interested in probability. She is interested in whether you can be made to feel something, and she generally can make you, which is not nothing."

"It is not sufficient."

"It is not sufficient for 'you'," Elizabeth said, without heat. "You require that a thing earn its effects through sound construction. I require only that the effects arrive." She looked up at him over the book. "We have had this disagreement before, under different titles."

"We have," he said. "I have not yet been persuaded."

"Nor I." She returned to the page. "Fortunately, we have the whole of Miss Roche's remaining catalog to work through."

Darcy rose to refill his coffee. He paused at the sideboard and said, without turning, "Does the hero recover his name?"

Elizabeth considered this. "He is in the process of recovering it. He has recently been revealed to a room full of witnesses, which has helped."

"And the heroine — "

"Is about to marry him, I think, though I am not certain she knows it yet. There is a veil involved." She turned the final page of the volume and closed it. "I shall need volume four."

"It is in the library."

"I know where it is. I put it there." She rose and looked at him across the table. "The baby-swapping is, I grant you, one time too many."

"Twice too many."

"Once," she said, and went to get volume four.

Darcy was out with the steward by the time she had settled into the window seat. She could see them from where she sat, Darcy in his riding coat, the steward with his ledger, moving along the edge of the south field where the drainage had been a persistent problem since August. Their conversation was too far to hear, but she had learned to read something of its essence from a distance: the steward's pauses, Darcy's typical stillness when he was thinking rather than deciding, the occasional gesture that showed agreement had been reached.

She watched them for a moment and then looked down at volume four.

The letter to Jane was written after luncheon, when the light had moved to the west-facing windows and the house had settled into its afternoon quiet. She wrote it at the small desk in the sitting room rather than in the library. The library was where she worked; this was where she wrote to Jane, which was a distinct thing entirely.

Dear Jane,

The Gardiners have been and gone, and the house is quieter for it, though not unhappily so. Uncle Gardiner and Darcy have made arrangements to shoot more soon and to fish in the spring, which I believe both of them intend more seriously than they have indicated, and Aunt Gardiner has given me her opinion of the glass houses, which is favorable, and of the housekeeper, which is very favorable, and said nothing at all about anything that was not asked of her, which is why I am always glad to see her.

I must tell you about this morning, as I expect it will become the story I tell about this winter when I look back on it. We argued about a novel at breakfast, Darcy and I, which is itself unremarkable; we have made a habit of it since September. The novel in question is 'he Monastery of St. Columb,' by Mrs. Roche, which you may have read, and if you have not, I recommend it on the grounds that it contains two separate infant exchanges and a hero who has been living under a false name for three volumes without significant inconvenience, and these things are either exactly what you want or exactly what you don't, and Darcy is emphatically the latter.

He is not wrong about the plotting. The plotting is, by any fair accounting, a gothic structure held together by sentiment and the goodwill of the reader.

But he requires a novel to have earned its effects through sound construction, and I require only that the effects arrive, and we are at an impasse that I do not think either of us particularly wishes to resolve. He asked, at the end of it, whether the hero recovered his name. I took this as a concession.

He would not.

In other news of Pemberley: Georgiana walked into the village with me last week - her own idea, her own feet, the full length of the lane and back - and spoke to Mrs. Prewitt about the Christmas program at church with more composure than I would have managed at her age under easier circumstances. I will not make more of this than it is, only that she came down to breakfast with her gloves already in her hand, and I understood what that meant, and we went. She has been running through the Clementi sonatina ever since with an attention that suggests she means to be ready.

Fitzwilliam came and went and was, as ever, exactly as useful as he intended to be and no more. He and Darcy rode out every morning. He and I argued about a different novel, which I won, and he admitted it, which is more than some people do.

Your letter about the south pasture reached me on Friday. Give Bingley my warmest opinion of his ambitions for it. Tell him also that Darcy has a view on drainage that he will share if asked, but that he will not offer it unless asked, which I mention only so that Bingley knows to ask.

Thank you for letting me know the regiment has gone north. I will not say more about this, as there is nothing more to say.

Mary's school: I have sent her three books and a fourth recommended by Darcy's librarian, who was very thorough about it. If she needs anything else, she is to write me directly and not go through Mama, who will lose the letter.

It is nearly dark. Darcy is coming in from the south field and will want his tea and will probably tell me something about the drainage that I will be expected to have a view on, and I will have one, because I walked that field myself in October and I know where the problem is, and it is not where the steward thinks it is.

I am well, Jane. I am, I think, what Aunt Gardiner meant when she said well, which is different from merely well, and I am glad to be able to write it to you without any qualification I can think of.

Your Lizzie

She folded the letter and reached for the sealing wax.

Outside, Darcy had dismissed the steward and was standing at the edge of the kitchen garden, working his way along the espalier on the south wall. Not the drainage; that was the other direction. He had dismissed the steward before doing it. He checked on such things with a regularity that she found, obscurely, one of the more endearing things she had learned about him.

She sealed the letter. She did not interrupt him.

The thrush had started up again in the kitchen garden. It was still making its feelings known at considerable. She watched them both from the window until it was too dark to see.

She picked up the wax again and sealed the letter to Jane.

Epilogue

Mrs. Bennet arrived on a Monday, which was two days earlier than she had said she would, and she brought Kitty.

Elizabeth received this news from the housekeeper with the composure she had been developing since her own wedding breakfast and said that of course they were expected and would Mrs. Reynolds please ensure the blue room was prepared and that the small sitting room off the west corridor was available for morning use. The west sitting room was, she had discovered, the correct distance from every room Mrs. Bennet might otherwise colonize.

She was in her seventh month. The stairs to the west corridor were not a problem yet, but she had begun to notice them.

Darcy was in his study when she stopped in the doorway to tell him. He looked up from his correspondence, read her expression with the accuracy she had stopped finding disconcerting around the eighth month of their marriage, and asked: "Kitty as well?"

"Kitty as well."

He set down his pen. "The west sitting room."

"Already arranged."

He nodded and picked the pen back up, which was, Elizabeth had come to understand, his way of expressing that he found her management of such matters entirely satisfactory and had no intention of interfering with it. She went to write to Jane.

Jane's baby was six weeks old and named after their father, which had made Mrs. Bennet cry for three days and then refer to the child, in all subsequent correspondence, as *the dear little Thomas* with a possessive warmth that Bingley appeared to find entirely reasonable. Elizabeth found this characteristic of Bingley, who had no instinct for suspicion where kindness was available as an alternative interpretation. She had told Jane so. Jane had said that she thought it a very fine quality in a husband. Elizabeth had considered this and conceded the point.

She wrote:

The baby's picture in your last letter was so like him that I had to set it down before I could look at it properly. Darcy has put it on the mantelpiece in the library, which he did without comment and in a position of some prominence, which I believe constitutes, for him, an expression of considerable feeling.

She paused, looked at what she had written, and left it.

Mama arrives today. I will write again when she leaves.

Mrs. Bennet did not stay to dinner on the first evening. She had, she said, fatigued herself with the journey and required early rest, and so Elizabeth sat at table with Darcy and Kitty and Georgiana, which was the pleasantest possible arrangement that the visit was likely to produce.

Kitty had changed. Elizabeth had been watching it the way she observed things she had not predicted:, and with some revision of her earlier conclusions. Without Lydia to orbit, Kitty had needed somewhere to put her energy, and Georgiana had proved to be the answer: they wrote to each other, they played duets when Kitty visited, they had opinions about novels and communicated these opinions at some length. Kitty was becoming a person of moderate sense and real warmth, which was more than Elizabeth had thought to hope for two years ago.

At dinner she told a story about a neighbor's pig that had escaped its pen and disrupted a village gathering, and she told it well with timing, and a precise rendering of the neighbor's face, and made Georgiana laugh until Georgiana had to press her napkin to her mouth and apologize to those at the table.

Darcy did not laugh, but he looked at Kitty afterward with an expression Elizabeth recognized: a revision in progress.

"Your sister tells a story well," he said, when they were alone.

"She is improving generally," Elizabeth said. "I intend to take some credit."

"On what grounds?"

"She admires me. It is an excellent foundation for improvement."

Darcy looked at her across the fireplace and said nothing, which was also one of his methods of expressing agreement.

Mrs. Bennet appeared at breakfast the next morning in excellent spirits and said, in rapid succession: that Elizabeth was very large and ought to rest more; that the breakfast room was cold, though it was not; that the baby's room - she had inspected it - lacked sufficient provision against drafts; and that Jane's Thomas was the finest baby in England with the possible exception of the one currently being prepared, who she expected would be equally fine and would she please be sent for the moment anything began.

Darcy listened to all of this from behind his coffee.

Elizabeth said that the baby's room had been examined by the physician and found excellent in every instance, and that she would of course send for Mama when the time came, and that there was more coffee if she would like it.

Mrs. Bennet would like it.

She then asked Darcy whether he thought the entail on Pemberley might be broken in favor of a daughter, if it came to that, and Darcy explained, without impatience, that Pemberley was not entailed and that any child would inherit on equal terms.

Mrs. Bennet received this information as if it confirmed something she had known all along, nodded with great satisfaction, and asked whether there was any prospect of Georgiana's being settled soon because she was a lovely girl and it would be a shame.

Georgiana, who two years ago would have gone pale and looked to her brother, said pleasantly that she was in no particular hurry and had a great many things to occupy her in the meantime.

Mrs. Bennet said that this was very well when one was young, but—

The sentence did not continue in any specific direction. It did not need to.

Elizabeth caught Georgiana's eye. Georgiana's expression contained - and this was the thing Elizabeth had been watching arrive over eighteen months, the development she had not known to expect and now found she cared about considerably - a kind of private humor. It was not fake. It was not relief at being tolerated. Humor: the real kind, that requires a person to feel secure enough to find their circumstances funny.

She had arrived at it herself, by some route Elizabeth could not map, though she suspected it had something to do with the novel Georgiana had been writing in a small notebook she kept in the music room and had shown Elizabeth three chapters of, with a diffidence that had not survived Elizabeth's response. The response had been honest, and specific, and largely favorable, and Georgiana had gone back to the notebook with a concentration that suggested she was treating the thing as serious. Elizabeth thought it was serious. She intended to say so again, at the appropriate moment.

On the third day, Mrs. Bennet went to rest after luncheon, Kitty and Georgiana took themselves to the music room, and Elizabeth walked to the library.

She did this most afternoons. The library at Pemberley was long and faced west and in autumn the light came through at an angle that moved across the shelves as the afternoon progressed, so that sitting by the window with a book was an experience of gradual change without any requirement to notice it. She had discovered this in her first winter at Pemberley and had said nothing about it to anyone, which made it, she recognized, a private satisfaction.

She was reading, or she had been reading; the book was open on her knee and she was mostly watching the light when Darcy came in.

He was carrying a book, which answered the question of why he had come: there was a gap in the shelf nearest the window that she had noticed for several days, and the volume in his hand was the right size to fill it.

He crossed to the shelf, slid the book into place, and stood for a moment looking at the row, the way he sometimes stood looking at the grounds after something had been set to rights.

Then he looked at her, registered that she was not reading, and came to sit in the chair on the other side of the window.

She looked at the book on her knee. The baby shifted, a movement she had grown accustomed to over the past months but which still arrived with a quality she could not have described accurately in any vocabulary available to her: not a word she had found yet, in any of the books in this room.

Outside, the grounds were in the late stages of fall. The color was mostly gone, the trees bare at the edges, the sky a particular pale gray that presaged nothing dramatic. In an hour the light would be gone from the window.

She turned a page she had not read.

"Is she troubling you?"

"He," Elizabeth said, because she had taken a position on this matter some weeks ago and intended to maintain it until the evidence resolved the question. "And no. He is considering his options."

Darcy made a sound that was not quite agreement and not quite argument, which she had catalogued as his response to propositions he found insufficiently supported by evidence but was not prepared to formally contest.

"You have put Jane's picture on the mantelpiece," she said.

"The baby's picture." A pause. "There was room."

"There was not room. You moved the Sèvres clock."

Another pause. "It was a reasonable reallocation."

Elizabeth looked at the window. The light had moved another degree across the shelves. She could hear, distantly, something being played in the music room. Kitty and Georgiana, a piece with some ambition to it, stopping and correcting and beginning again.

This was, she thought, without ceremony or even surprise, what she had not been able to imagine from the chair at Hunsford with the cold fire and Darcy's proposal still in the air. Not the house, not the settlement, not even Darcy himself, who had turned out to be - she kept returning to this word because it kept proving accurate – 'more.' More than her arithmetic. More than the man she had calculated. More than she had known she wanted.

She had not imagined the library. She had not imagined the afternoons in it, or his presence on the other side of the window, or the baby in the small room being made ready upstairs, or Georgiana's notebook, or Kitty's improved timing with a story, or the way her mother, God help them both, had said *Fitzwilliam* at breakfast as if she had always intended to be fond of him.

She had not imagined any of it. She was in it now.

"Darcy," she said.

"Mm."

"Nothing. I was accounting for you."

He looked up from the book in his lap. She had learned to receive that look without deflecting it. It had been there, she now understood, since Hertfordshire, through every misreading and correction and negotiation and crisis, patient as something that knew it had time.

"And?" he said.

"The figures are favorable," Elizabeth said.

He held her gaze a moment longer. Then he looked back at his book.

Outside, the last of the afternoon light moved off the window. In the music room, the piece started again, from the beginning, and this time did not stop.

About Annalise Allen

For everyone who finished Pride and Prejudice and immediately started over.

Annalise Allen is a genre fiction author who has found her truest calling in the world of Jane Austen fan fiction. Drawing on years of storytelling craft, she writes Pride and Prejudice pastiche that respects Austen's sharp social wit while giving readers more of the world they love. Her work speaks directly to those who have never quite left Longbourn or Pemberley behind.

Upcoming Titles:

A Partial Acquaintance – Late Summer 2026

What Prudence Demanded – Fall 2026

Connecting with Annalise:

Website: https://annaliseallen.com/

www.ingramcontent.com/pod-product-compliance
Lightning Source LLC
LaVergne TN
LVHW091026080826
845145LV00002B/364

* 9 7 8 1 9 5 0 8 2 8 3 1 9 *